THE SHADOW PEOPLE

THE SHADOW PEOPLE

JOE CLIFFORD

Copyright © 2021 by Joe Clifford
Cover and jacket design by Mimi Bark

ISBN 978-1-951709-40-2
eISBN: 978-1-951709-65-5
Library of Congress Control Number:
available upon request

First hardcover edition July 2021 by Polis Books, LLC
44 Brookview Lane
Aberdeen, NJ 07747
www.PolisBooks.com

POLIS BOOKS

For all the crazy diamonds...

CHAPTER ONE

The night I learned Jacob Balfour was missing, I'd just gotten a date with Samantha Holahan. We were halfway through a marathon Thursday night class. Three hours of Shakespeare. Brutal way to end the long week and even longer semester, my last at SUNY before transferring to Syracuse in the fall. Not dismissing Shakespeare's obvious place in the pantheon of great literature. He has some terrific lines. *All our yesterdays lighting fools and tomorrows creeping in their petty pace.* Wonderful. But it bored me stiff. Whenever I read class assignments, I had to do so standing up. Soon as I lay in bed, I'd fall asleep.

I needed the lit requirement before Syracuse would take me. Might not have been so bad, but it was Shakespeare's histories. Not his comedies or tragedies, which have all the killer parts and memorable quotes—it was the goddamn histories, *Richard III* and dull crap like that. The only thing that kept me showing up each week: Samantha Holahan.

Sam was so cool. Any other girl tries wearing a little red beret, and I'm screaming fraud. But Sam? The short black pixie cut, the rotating men's vests and ties, the rest of that week's thrift store haul, however haphazardly arranged—it fit; her whole presentation was so relaxed, so spot on, so...cool. Even the name sounded cool. During my shifts at Ledgecrest Convalescent, I

7

couldn't help rolling it around in my head. *Sam Holahan.* The lilt and rhythm of it. Twenty-three years old and I was one degree removed from swapping out last names inside swirling pink hearts. I was in a bad way.

I felt pressure to make a move. All evening I'd been besieged by a growing unease, big clock ticking down, cosmic judgment about to be cast. Blame it on the Bard. It was now or never. Three months of sharing the same space as Sam, and the best I'd mustered was a "hey" in passing. I had no game. Not like I was ugly or socially awkward. I was normal. Which was the problem. I was *too* normal. I looked like every other guy on campus: normal height, normal weight, normal everything. So normal I was in danger of disappearing.

Maybe my gut recognized dire stakes—fourth quarter, Hail Mary, they-need-a-big-play-and-need-it-now desperation— because during break, fifteen minutes where you could grab a Coke and stretch your legs, I surprised myself, primal instincts replacing my usual trepidation. Sam was getting one of those little packages of Oreos from the vending machine. I took off my glasses and stuck them in my pocket. Smoothing my hair, I came up behind her, keeping appropriate distance, and made a joke about taking a picture. Because they use the same chemicals in those cookies as they do in developing film. Stupid. I must've managed not to sound condescending because she laughed. More courtesy chuckle. But she didn't run. In fact, she moved closer. Probably because it was so cold. Despite being on the cusp of summer, the skies had cooled, thunderheads rolling in gray waves of tragic doom and beauty. The campus's open-air veranda invited gales, making the second-floor landing a perpetual wind tunnel.

Students bustled between brownstone and brick, cutting out for the day, heading to get drunk. The tall clock tower loomed large, and the newly mown grass smelled so sweet. On the muddied horizon, a burnt orange ball held on before those thunderheads blotted it gone. Ragweed weighted the air, June bugs chirped in fruit fields, and, for once, Upstate New York didn't feel like the ugliest place on Earth. We'd been in the grip of an early season heat wave. Now the night offered relief, a cloudburst to wash everything clean, start over. Not uncommon for this time of year, heat bubbles punctured by sweeping cold fronts, lightning crashing, thunder rolling. I took comfort in raging elements.

After that, conversation came effortlessly. The more we talked, the more I questioned if Sam was just being nice to me. I'd never lacked confidence, but this total lapse in self-esteem couldn't have come at a worst time. Outside of finals, the semester was over. And my Shakespeare class didn't have a final, only a term paper. Which I'd already written. It was now or never.

Before we headed back in, I made my move.

"What are you doing after class?"

"Nothing," Sam said. "No plans."

"I was thinking of grabbing a drink at Thee Parkside." I hadn't, in fact, been thinking of grabbing a drink. And certainly not at Thee Parkside, which was this hipster Pabst and billiards bar out by Blodgett Mills that I'd been to once. I'd blurted out the first bar that came to mind because I wasn't ready to say goodbye.

I braced for the rejection, certain Sam was running through excuses of the better things she had to do. Instead, she shrugged and said, "Sure, Brandon. Sounds like fun."

I stood there, slackjawed, flummoxed, gobsmacked. Forget her saying yes—I didn't think Sam Holahan knew my name. The moment couldn't have lasted longer than two or three seconds, but moments like that have a way of dragging out indeterminately long.

For the rest of class, I had a tough time paying attention.

Never had I less interest in the primogeniture of fifteenth-century fiefdom. I wasn't sure I'd survive the final bell. I felt my cell buzz in my pocket a few times. Calls, not texts. I couldn't pick up in the middle of class. Who talked on a phone anyway?

When class cut out, I played it cool. One chill head bob, nonchalant, stopping short of a finger point and wink. I pushed through the glass doors, into a swirling night, storm winds exposing the undersides of maple leaves. A fat raindrop plopped on my wrist. Checking my cell, I saw I had several missed calls, all from the same number. I knew it was bad news.

I hit redial.

"Hello, Mrs. Balfour."

"I'm sorry to bother you, Brandon."

I turned around and saw Sam Holahan standing on the top steps, backpack slung over shoulder, one strap, looking around like she was waiting for me to walk her to her car or maybe drive with her to the bar.

"Not at all," I said, ducking around the side of the Old Main Building. Even though I was shielded by shrubbery, I felt exposed by interior lights.

"Have you spoken with Jacob?" she asked.

"Not in a few." I hoped Mrs. Balfour interpreted "few" as days or weeks, and not the months it really was. "Is everything okay?"

"No," she said. "Jacob is missing."

CHAPTER TWO

The drive from Cortland to Utica takes over an hour in good weather, and at that moment conditions were anything but—heavens dumping sheets, rain splatting on the tin roof, brake lights shimmering red waves of gasoline, tractor-trailers riding low gears to avoid the glut of emergency roadside vehicles treating storm casualties on the shoulder. I had a lot of time to think about Jacob, especially the end, how it all came crashing down, the apex of his mental illness coinciding with my decision to leave Utica. The two were not unrelated.

Jacob's deteriorating condition wasn't my fault—he was sick— my leaving for college wasn't bailing, wasn't abandonment— sticking around to watch a man slowly drown wasn't doing service to anyone. After everything I'd survived, I owed myself a future. But long drives on Upstate New York highways in the pouring rain at night have a way of worming regrets into your brain and calling you on your own lies. I'd given up on Jacob, leaving him to contemplate the murky waters of insanity—and people like Mrs. Balfour and Chloe to drag the river after he went off the deep end. There was no positive way to spin it.

Jacob and I met fifteen years ago when we lived down the street from each other at Farewell Commons. The upbeat name does a disservice to the squalid apartment complex that sat in the crumbling shadows of the old insane asylum. When you're a kid, you don't pick up on the universal metaphors life throws your way. Like the giant mental institution serving as a hundred-thousand-ton harbinger for the hell that awaits one of you. The closed hospital seemed to tower ten stories tall when I was a kid, like Batman's Arkham Asylum, minus the heroes to protect you on the darkest nights, leaving only the madmen who want to watch the world burn.

Cultural pride, gallows humor, morbid curiosity, call it whatever you want, but over the years I'd read up a lot on the Utica Psychiatric Center, New York's earliest state-run attempt to treat lunatics. That's what it was originally called, The New York State Lunatic Asylum. Not exactly a great moment in signage. I'd spent this past semester picking out literary clues from centuries-old plays, so perhaps I was overanalyzing. But it's hard not to draw the correlation doing eighty on the 81 because your bipolar best friend may have lost it for good this time.

When I moved in with the Balfours, I was pretty messed up. Doctors suggested medications. A stable living environment fixed most of the damage.

Farewell Commons was like several of the sleazy apartment complexes you find in Utica, places you didn't want to be born, places you got stuck, places you died. Slabs of concrete slapped on undesirable plots, unruly sprouts of urban scruff, uneven acres squeezed between liquor stores and laundromats and passed-out bums face-planted in their own sick. Waves of collapsing chain link rippled through high ragweed grasses, discarded appliances and illegally dumped trash. Overturned shopping carts, an oven, the occasional engine block. Stray boots jutted from fields like abstract art on coffeehouse walls. Unlike my parents and me, the Balfours weren't born there. Their inclusion was a pit stop, a temporary embarrassment. The Balfours landed at Farewell Commons, cast out of their more affluent Hills Hart neighborhood, after Mr. Balfour hanged himself in the family's two-car garage.

For eight-year-old boys, even in the midst of tragedy, the world shines bright. The first afternoon I met Jacob, he was riding his Fuji mountain bike around the cul-de-sac, taking air off the ramp he'd made from a busted bench. It was the end of winter, those glorious early days of spring creeping in.

Could've been the timing, the lack of options—maybe it was because I didn't have a dad either—by that point my father was a shell of a human being. Bitter, drunk, inaccessible. He never got over my mother leaving. He'd sit in that chair for days, gazing at a blank spot on the wall, clutching the bottle like a street preacher and his Bible.

Jacob and I became best friends, inseparable. We liked the same music, sports teams, even looked alike, a pair of skinny mop-tops, so much so that people often mistook us for brothers.

In middle school, we decided to start a band. Neither of us could play an instrument or sing. But we wrote songs on the computer and picked out a name, The Hanging Chads, which we thought was pretty clever for the eighth grade. Jacob designed our band insignia, an intersecting figure eight, friends forever. In industrial arts class he made us rings. I lost mine. He never took his off.

Mrs. Balfour, now tasked with putting the family back together, worked more than one job—nursing, waitressing, selling merch on eBay, anything to keep the family afloat. She was seldom home, Chloe was in daycare, and Jacob and I had free rein. Come summertime, the neighborhood was ours to conquer, unencumbered. Those were my most vivid memories of Jacob: exploring the hidden crevices of St. Agnes Cemetery, down to the muddy banks of the Mohawk River, crawling through condemned buildings and houses half underwater, the untended wild terrain of impoverished Upstate New York.

We didn't stay at the Commons long. Once the life insurance came in, Mrs. Balfour bought a regular house, and we moved across town. You'd think that's when things would've gotten better. That's when they got worse.

It's easy to see now, after the fact, what triggered Jacob's mental problems: his dad killing himself. Even if he didn't talk about it much. This wasn't based on anything the doctors said or his mom relayed; it was common sense. Jacob's issues, which manifested slowly at first, grew worse when we got to high school. Always a skinny kid, he began putting on weight. He broke out in bad acne, which isn't uncommon for that age. But in Jacob's case it was because he'd stopped showering, washing, attending to basic hygiene, greasy skin hidden beneath a mass of unkempt hair.

I found it impossible to talk to Jacob as he grew increasingly obsessed with strange things. Finding single shoes. Car doors slamming. The TV started talking to him. There was a secret code to life, a mathematical equation to unlock. The number twenty-three really freaked him out. God, the devil, demons and angels battling for his soul. Crazy talk. I remember the first time the police were called. Jacob had stripped naked and run out on the lawn, bellowing at the moon, begging the heavens not to forsake him.

His mom brought him to experts. He was hospitalized. When he got out, Jacob started outpatient therapy. Nothing seemed to work. I tried to get through to him. But looking in his eyes, there was no light left, like black holes in the sky. Sometimes he'd glance in your general direction. Even when he responded, he wasn't talking to you. More like he was conversing with an invisible person beyond your shoulder. He began having altercations at school, fighting with everyone, lashing out, screaming if he felt another student was looking at him funny or talking about him. And students *were*. How could they not? You'd see this big fat guy, last year's baseball star, walking down the hall, hair greased like he'd smeared a pound of margarine to his scalp, muttering curses, hitting his own head with his fist. Then one day he swung at a teacher, and that was it; they kicked him out. Jacob finished the second half of his senior year having to be homeschooled, various tutors brought in, basically babysitters. None lasted long. Mrs. Balfour did her best to stay positive, writing off bad behaviors as manic episodes. Who was I to argue? I was a guest.

The last year living with them had been hard, and I know after I left it only got tougher. I loved the Balfours, but it was too much. I had to go lest I be infected as well.

I hadn't planned on attending SUNY, the state university ninety miles southwest in Cortland. When it came time to apply to colleges, I found my options limited. SUNY wasn't a safety school; it was the only one that would accept me. SUNY is nobody's first choice. The long-standing joke about the university: where future gym teachers are bred. I wasn't the greatest student in high school. I'm not blaming anyone for my mediocre grades, least of all the Balfours, who saved my life by taking me in, but when I should've been prepping for college, I was trying to repair Jacob. I'd escaped a bad situation with my parents, and now the brief stability I enjoyed with the Balfours had been threatened too. I knew I was smarter than my grades showed.

After I got my own apartment, I stayed in frequent contact with the Balfours; it's not like I cut them off. I loved the family. We'd have Sunday dinners, spend most of the major holidays together. Over these meals, Mrs. Balfour, Chloe, and I would catch up, laugh; and there was my best friend, poking at his turkey and dumplings, silent, staring intently, as if trying to communicate sage wisdom telepathically to a baked bird.

When his mother called to say he was missing, I wasn't surprised. A part of me dreaded this would happen. Another part had been resigned to the fact. I didn't need to say goodbye; I'd been saying goodbye for the past decade.

I hadn't returned to Utica since Easter a year ago. I had a pocketful of viable excuses. Work. School. Assorted assignments. But I spent this past Thanksgiving watching football and eating leftover pizza alone in my tiny apartment.

I don't mean to make it sound like Jacob was completely certifiable. That's not fair. He had good stretches too. When he was on his meds. He complained these pills dulled his sharpest edges, but when he was taking his medication, he could hold down menial jobs, bagging groceries at the Price Rite, sweeping up at the community center. I remember one summer he worked at a coffee shop in Reine. Unfortunately, Jacob had this annoying, unfathomable tendency to *stop* taking his medication. Especially when things were going well. Which made no sense. But he'd wake one morning and decide he didn't need to take his medication anymore. Never occurred to him that the pills were the only thing keeping him sane.

CHAPTER THREE

When I got to the house, Chloe bounded down the steps, wrapping her arms around my waist. In the year since I'd last seen her, she'd sprung up bean-sprout tall and roller-skate skinny. To me, she'd always be that little girl. But here she was, a full-fledged teenager. Mrs. Balfour beamed a pained smile from the porch, descending to give me a hug, saying how happy she was to see me. Worry seeped between the cracks of reassuring words. I wanted to assuage her concerns—this wasn't the first time Jacob had stayed out. He took off frequently, disappearing to Rotterdam and its many surrounding nature preserves. My mind flashed on that one time he climbed the water tower and spray-painted "repent," hiding on the girders, till the fire department had to be summoned to haul him down. The local authorities were sick of his antics, and we were long past the point of repenting.

We tried to catch up like a regular family. Mrs. Balfour asked me about classes, work, plans for the future. I told her about training to be a medical assistant. I asked Chloe a few questions about school and friends, until she grew bored of the dull adult conversation and returned to her laptop, sitting cross-legged on the couch, out of earshot.

"How long has he been gone this time, Mrs. Balfour?"

"Please, Brandon, Lori."

"Sorry." She'd been insisting for years that I call her by her first name, doubling down efforts after I moved out, but I didn't think I'd ever be able to call Mrs. Balfour anything else. Like calling former professors by their first names, it didn't seem right.

"I'm not sure," she said, sounding embarrassed. "Three days?"

That was unusual. Jacob never stayed away longer than a night here and there.

"I've been taking extra shifts at the hospital. I'm pretty sure I saw him Monday morning." Her exhale oozed shame for not having a more definite timeframe. "Jacob was doing better," she said. "I wasn't worrying as much."

"Did he stop taking his meds again?" The question was obvious but needed to be asked.

"I don't know. There are so many bottles in his room. I can't keep track." She looked at me head on, desperate to have me believe he'd really turned a corner. "He's working construction. In Albany. In charge of people. I know. Hard to believe, right? I'm so proud of him. Remember when he was supposed to go to the Netherlands with his baseball team? Before…his troubles… in high school? How confident he was? The *old* Jacob. He's like that again. He's been saving money, going to his groups." She paused. "He's lost weight. He…" Mrs. Balfour trailed off, interest fixed on the window as she stared into the rainy night, no doubt imagining where her son might be.

I didn't ask about calling the cops because I knew the suggestion would only add to her anxiety. Jacob wasn't a violent person, but you see enough stories on the news about how police handle the mentally ill. Standoffs, beatdowns, wrongful deaths. It would scare any mom. Jacob could be, at times, obdurate. Who knew his current state of mind?

"When did you find out he was missing?"

"His boss called this afternoon. Jacob hasn't been to work all week."

"Have you tried any of his friends?" Jacob must've had other friends. Guys he talked to from his group therapy sessions. I remembered he started playing on computers more. Gaming. The weirder he got, the more into virtual realities he grew. Chatrooms and websites, forums. Maybe he'd met someone there.

"Jacob doesn't have friends."

That didn't make me feel better.

Even though we were several years removed from high school, I tried to recall the names of people in our graduating class, anyone Jacob might still be in touch with. I couldn't come up with anything. At one time, he'd been popular. Not quarterback famous—he played baseball, and was pretty good— but by graduation, Jacob didn't play any sports and had pushed away everyone.

Since I didn't have class tomorrow and wasn't scheduled for a shift, it was decided I'd spend the night, help sort this out in the morning. My old room, Mrs. Balfour said, was how I'd left it.

As worried as I was about Jacob, I had to admit it felt good to be home.

The bright yellow sun fragmented the floral print of the sitting chair, illumining dust mites. For a moment I forgot where I was, walls foreign, ceiling alien. The displacement didn't last long, but such moments can make you feel forever alone, an astronaut floating in space, aimless, like Major Tom or Elton John.

Taking the stairs, I found an empty house. No Mrs. Balfour. No Chloe, who must've already left for school. The clock read a couple minutes before eight. There was no note waiting for me on the kitchen table, which told me Mrs. Balfour hadn't returned from her shift. I wasn't a kid expecting smiley faces in his lunchbox, but no way she wasn't leaving a message.

My stomach rumbled. I'd missed dinner last night. Come to think of it, I hadn't eaten anything since breakfast yesterday. After poking around the cupboards and fridge, I helped myself to orange juice and a slice of toast.

Then I headed up to Jacob's room.

The door was closed. I knocked. Pointless, but I did it anyway.

Not sure what I was expecting to find, but the scene disturbed me nonetheless. Pulled window shades darkened a musty room. Tripping the light, a childhood fantasy greeted me. Posters of Harry Potter and wizards, *Hunger Games*, elves, fairies, and several species of small woodland creatures. There's nothing wrong with a healthy imagination. But Jacob was the same age I was. This wasn't *Game of Thrones* homage. It was more a state of suspended adolescence; a perpetual thirteen-year-old boy who'd retreated into a world of werewolves and warlocks. Comic books, RPG manuals, cereal bowls slurped clean, deserted, only the spoon remaining. The robust tang of body odor clung to the room, saturating dirty linens and bedding, like sweaty workout clothes abandoned in the trunk of a hot automobile. The rest of the Balfours' house was kept clean. Lived in but not reckless. This felt like a separate residence, which, given Jacob's age, made sense, I supposed. Grant autonomy, agency. I could see Mrs. Balfour trying to instill independence, respecting his privacy, perhaps at a doctor's request. Of course, now that Jacob was missing, his mom must've been inside his room, searching for possible clues.

In between purple posters of Valkyries, mermaids and other talking fish, a *Lord of the Rings* character guide tracing fictional lineage, Jacob had tacked up scraps of paper—magazine clippings, chicken-scratched notes, unfurled pocket maps like the kind they sell at gas stations but you don't see much of anymore because of smart phones and GPS. On the maps, which included not just Upstate New York but parts of the Midwest as well, red lines traced routes, reinforced by multiple circles around tiny towns I'd never heard of. Unsettling. Like Russell Crowe's office in *A Beautiful Mind*. Only there was nothing beautiful happening here. The space felt frantic, unfocused, dirty, a desktop with too many browsers open, spreading pop-up viruses.

Something else added to the disquiet. It took a moment to figure out what that was. Books—hundreds of them—stacked under nightstands, piled slipshod on the carpet, teetering, toppling, multiplying across the filthy floor. I was finishing up four years of college, moving on to graduate school. I had nothing against reading. But I read for school. I read for purpose. This was helter-skelter.

I studied the titles. All different subject matter. Architecture. Chess. Quantum mechanics. Stephen Hawking's *A Brief History of Time*. Another one, *In Search of Schrödinger's Cat*. Marquis de Sade and *120 Days of Sodom*. Robert Anton Wilson, *The Illuminatus Trilogy*. A thin cheap paperback called *The Last Days of Christ the Vampire*. No common thread. Jacob wasn't in school. This wasn't for an assignment. He was reading these for fun. Like bottling ships, collecting stamps, naming stars.

Parts added to greater than the whole, and the muddled space belied a stable existence. The Jacob I'd grown up with was more rock-and-roll jock than he was role-playing nerd. Even the band we were going to start was pretty cool. The Hanging Chads. Who gets political at that age? Jacob's birthday was in May. Gemini. I never went in for that astrology garbage. But I knew enough about the pseudoscience to understand that, of all the signs, Gemini was the one associated with duality, the crazy twins. Jacob was textbook, a parody of the zodiac. All I could think…

I shouldn't be here.

Backing away from the lunatic fringe, I saw them.

Pamphlets. Decks of them. Robin's egg blue stitched like church hymnals, the kind you find scattered in pews around Christmastime. I scooped up a few. *Illuminations*. That was the title on each. A homemade magazine, a zine. Skinny, thirty or so pages. Not stitched. Stapled. The tagline: "The Truth Within The Lie." Clickbait in physical form. I fanned through a copy. Every story written by...Jacob Balfour.

I read a few articles, and soon wished I hadn't. Simply put, *Illuminations* was tin foil hat, feces-on-the-walls insane. Ranting and rambling just this side of *InfoWars*. In between construction shifts, Jacob was moonlighting as a conspiracy wingnut.

The subject matter was alarming enough—who really killed JFK; how the moon landing was staged; flat-earth nonsense—the Holy Trinity of cuckoo nesting. The deeper you dug, the more disturbing it got. Weather machines invented by the government, half of whom were alien lizards that had infiltrated the highest level of the EPA—poisoning our fluoride and melting down Japan.

Most alarming, however, was a section dubbed "The Shadow People."

The Shadow People was a sinister race of doppelgängers, plants sent to spy on us from netherworlds and report back. The Shadow People were forever lurking on the peripheral, shape-shifting entities ever-present and eternally vigilant. Few saw them. Only the "enlightened" could process their existence. Then, once you saw them, you couldn't ignore them; they were *everywhere*.

What could you say to that? It was heartbreaking.

Jacob had taken the time to format this nonsense on a computer, attempting to mirror what you'd see in a regular newspaper. Jacob had to do research, outline, prepare. This was an effort to laud, no? A little ambition? The end product reflected a crazy diamond, the head-scratching rationale you find in any internet comment section, replete with sporadic all caps, misspellings, and a dizzying misuse of semicolons.

Instead of pride, I felt besieged by sorrow. Because Jacob *had* seen the project through. He *had* cared enough to try. For what? Did he plan to sell them? Give them away outside the Price Rite? Starbucks? So strangers could laugh at him? How had Mrs. Balfour missed this?

I debated whether to bring a copy to his mom, present irrefutable evidence that her son had, in fact, gone off his medication. I decided it wasn't my place. Truth was, I wanted to forget what I'd seen and get back to my life. Jacob would come home. Of course he would. Where else would he go?

In the end, I left everything as I'd discovered it, a shrine to madness.

CHAPTER FOUR

Mrs. Balfour still hadn't returned from her shift at the hospital. I wrote a note. I said I was there for her and Chloe, and to let me know if there was anything she needed. I wrote that aside from finals, classes were over for the semester; I wasn't moving up to Syracuse for another few weeks and my schedule at Ledgecrest was flexible, having tapered down with my two-week notice, so call anytime, day or night.

Rereading the note, I couldn't escape the cloying tone of it, overarching, needy. I ached to hear this wasn't my fault. Of course I knew it wasn't my fault. Intellectually. But knowing that in your head and feeling it in your heart are two separate things. I thought about crumpling up the letter and giving it another stab, but knew I'd only reword what I'd already written. Because I *did* shoulder guilt. I *did* harbor regret. And why shouldn't I bear responsibility? The Balfours had taken me in during my time of need, and how had I repaid that generosity? I'd used Jacob's escalating mania as an opportunity to skip off to greener pastures. Now Jacob was missing. Worse than that, judging by that stark raving reading material I'd uncovered, he couldn't tell right from wrong anymore. Maybe they'd find him. Talking gibberish to a half-eaten hot dog in a dirty city alley or chasing shadows in a crumbling brick tenement. He might return home. But the Jacob I knew was gone for good.

So I left the note the way I'd written it, earnestness on full display, and did my best to leave behind what I'd seen. I locked up the house, stashing remorse and storing regret, and descended the front steps to find the old man waiting.

I worked at a convalescent home. I dealt with the elderly daily. I could pinpoint ages to within a couple years. It was a source of pride. But this man… Sixty? Seventy? Older? Younger? I couldn't tell. Grizzled, surly, and disassociated, he projected Clint Eastwood talking to a chair. Skin like tanned leather, indicative of residence in the Deep South, slicked white hair and languid, sloe eyes. Or maybe less Eastwood and more Mike Ehrmantraut from *Better Call Saul*. An old-school tough guy with indefatigable stamina. A manufactured Hollywood illusion, I knew. That's what movies do: sell us an unrealistic ideal. Little old men aren't secret badasses getting into fistfights, even ones like this with his sturdy frame and barreled chest. People that age battle osteoporosis; they don't bareknuckle brawl. One slip and they're in danger of breaking a hip. Still, the man at the door wore his hardness like a badge, with a face that looked like it had stories to tell.

"Lori home?" he said. It was less a question and more an accusation, delivered via raspy growl that testified to a two-pack-a-day habit. I, of course, wasn't scared. But it was difficult to feel relaxed, the way he presented himself. Almost like a cop. Except there was no way this man was on that side of the law.

I shook my head.

"You gonna say hi, boy?" He said it meanly too, adding a snicker. And when I didn't answer: "What are you doing here?"

I should've been the one asking that. This wasn't my home, but I had lived here, growing up inside these walls; I'd spent more time at the Balfours' than I had my own childhood home. Yet, I felt the need to defend my presence.

"I'm a family friend," I said.

"That so?" Again, he delivered the line glibly, smugly, like a truculent teenager and not a cranky septuagenarian.

My car—a 2016 Camry—sat parked in the driveway. I pointed. "That's my car." Which was the only car in the driveway. I had no idea how he'd gotten here.

He scratched the white stubble on his chin. You could hear the sandpaper scratch. Then the old man pinched his nose, cleared his throat, and spat a ball of phlegm over the railing into the bushes. Vile. "Tell her Francis stopped by."

I waited for more. Last name? Where he could be found? That was it. No business card. No phone number. Nothing.

The old man skulked off, past my car, into the road where no other car waited, angling down clean streets that wound through a sleepy suburban neighborhood coming to life. I kept watching as he weaved between the rows of mid-size homes with coordinated pastel trims and morning papers nestled in plastic below the individualized mailboxes that spoke to unique personalities.

He never looked back.

*

My mother was committed to the Utica Insane Asylum. That was the story anyway. Rumor, myth, family legend. The logistics failed the sniff test. Utica closed its doors in 1973 after a long history of questionable practices—earlier than my mom would've been admitted, unless she was locked up as a toddler. I didn't know much about my mother's life. She didn't leave until my fifth birthday. I had memories. Fuzzy. Benign, innocuous.

Shopping at the Save-A-Lot, eating grilled cheese at the counter of the old Woolworths diner, watching rain fall from the backseat of a parked car swallowed by a haze of blue smoke, the lingering stench of cigarettes, baking soda, and other burned objects. These were the days when parents still enjoyed that cool Laramie burn in confined spaces around small children. When I thought back to my mother, I saw a ghost, half dressed and disaffected, almost floating, ethereal.

Did it happen? Commitment? To Utica or elsewhere? I had no way of knowing for sure. Everyone I could ask was gone. But the sound of her voice, its timbre and reflection, remained embedded in my hippocampus. When I recollected these conversations, there was no recipient, no one at the opposite side of a table or on the other end of a telephone line. The subject matter was always the same: my mother blaming all her problems on the Utica Insane Asylum. Electroshock therapy, solitary confinement, images etched by pop cinema and literature, Nurse Ratcheds in the Cuckoo Nest. As if my mother would've been a success had it not been for that unfortunate bout of insanity.

After my mother abandoned us, my father was left in charge. In theory. He seldom spoke to me. He never mentioned her. I was forbidden from saying her name. The one time I brought up the subject was met with such a violent response—not against me—I never mentioned her again. My father, despite all his rage, never laid a hand on me. The windows, mirrors, and walls didn't fare so well. Sometimes I wished my father would hit me. I longed for *any* contact, communication, acknowledgment. I lived in the same apartment with that man, my father, for years, and I'm not sure we exchanged more than a dozen words that entire time.

There was no doubt my mother was not well. Even as a young boy I sensed her behavior was not normal for a mom, wife, woman, human. What plagued her? In terms of a medical label,

I couldn't say. I recollected my father once saying she was never satisfied. I wasn't sure if insatiability was a verifiable psychiatric condition or a lyric in a Prince song. Unlike Jacob, who at least had the diagnosis of bipolar, my mom was just…sick.

The night she left sticks in my mind. My father sitting alone in a dingy apartment, drinking an amber liquid that smelled of mothballs and lighter fluid. I remembered seeing red, blood, like he'd hurt himself. Or was I coloring by numbers? Given her history—the staying away, the various men she met at bars—my mother's absence shouldn't have been anything out of the norm. But I knew nothing was ever going to be the same.

By the time I moved out of Farewell Commons with the Balfours, my father had long been evicted. I didn't know where he'd gone, and I hadn't heard from my mother in years. As I got older, I often thought of going to the police. Find out what really happened to them. Then I'd ask why. I had no interest in talking to either. People die in this part of the country all the time and go unclaimed. Take a bus to New York City. Wander out on a cold winter's night. Freeze to death on a bench, fall in the river, heart seizes up in a skid row hotel, needle dangling from a vein. No ID, no one digs too deep.

Sometimes, when the mood struck, I'd put their names— Buck and Lisa Cossey—in a search engine. I thought maybe I'd get a hit on a domestic violence charge, read of a drug arrest. But I never found anything. Not one word. Like they never existed.

I didn't want to be thinking about any of this that morning. I wanted to hop on the highway, get back to Cortland, ensconced in my tiny apartment to start packing up my little world, divorced from this fractured past.

Instead, I found myself driving by the old Utica Insane Asylum.

The now-out-of-business hospital held tours. Unfathomable.

Who would want to tour a mental hospital, especially one they claimed was haunted? Of course they claimed it was haunted. The macabre sells tickets. Psych wards, like so many of life's horrors, have been romanticized. Glorified notions of insanity. Last year, I took an art history class. Everyone loved Van Gogh. Guys, girls, both swooned. I didn't get it. His paintings weren't good. Just a bunch of goopy paint slathered on canvas, compositions marred by inaccuracies. Nothing looked like it was supposed to, tables and chairs lopsided, shelves uneven, floors slanted, perspective skewed. As if drawn by a third grader with attention deficit disorder, palsy whimsying all over the place. Van Gogh was revered for one reason: because he'd gone crazy, that whole cutting off his ear business, the romance of poverty and wretchedness, the suffering artist, unrequited love, *la tristesse durera*. Who cares? I could've been one of those people, entranced by market-driven presentations of madness, if those closest to me hadn't been afflicted.

The stone columns of the Utica Asylum seemed to loom hundreds of feet tall, rendering the large hospital an ancient Greek museum, a structure erected to a forgotten yesteryear, a monument to spectacle, its perverse history proudly stamped. Human torture and confinement. This was part of Utica's lore, the questionable practices implemented since its inception in the 1800s, lobotomies and patients locked in cages.

Like a hypochondriac diving down the rabbit hole of WebMD and rare communicable diseases late at night, I used to like to read up on the hospital. Doing so fascinated me. The single most terrifying detail about Utica—the skin-crawling, Slender Man, someone-is-watching-you type—was this cage dubbed the Utica Crib, aka the Covered Bed. Which was like it sounds: an open-air coffin with bars on the sides, top and bottom, where they'd lock the most incorrigible and insolent.

By the time my mother was supposedly there, they'd nixed the crib, opting for more traditional methods of sedation, tranquilizers, ice picks jabbed in the frontal lobe, frog brains scrambled for science class. For me, the real terror of Utica derived from depths profounder: a subconscious fear I'd end up like her, unhinged and incapable of dictating my own fate. It's also why I left the Balfours the way I did. I wasn't comfortable around people with mental illness.

As I sat in my car, gazing up at the stone monstrosity, reassuring myself I was too strong to ever succumb to being enslaved by my own mind, there was an irrational, twisted part of me that yearned for it, to be lost in the instability of a life *in extremis*, where nothing could ever be your fault, every transgression explained away. *Yeah, sure, he's a screw up, a loser, a terrible person. But it's not his fault. He's sick!*

Turning the engine, I hit the highway and headed home.

What I couldn't know then was that I'd picked up an unseen passenger outside the Utica Insane Asylum that morning, and that my unwanted guest would not leave my side for a long, long time.

CHAPTER FIVE

By the time I pulled into my Cortland apartment complex, dark clouds had rolled in and a steady summer rain fell. I parked in my isolated corner of the covered garage, consumed by a feeling of dread, and climbed out of the damp basement.

Opening the apartment door, I slid my keys across the counter and, without bothering to turn on the lights, sank in my recliner, bogged down by ennui. Fixing my glasses, I glanced around my tiny living room, taking in my meager possessions—a spattering of textbooks, the chest of drawers that contained all my clothes with plenty of space to spare, the few formal documents I needed to prove I, in fact, existed—I didn't want to tackle the project. I couldn't fathom packing up cardboard boxes I wouldn't bother to label, contents so sparse. When my cell buzzed, I was grateful to see Ledgecrest on the caller ID. In that moment, I couldn't bear another minute alone.

The nursing home needed me to cover an afternoon shift. Often, being asked to cover a last-minute shift was a huge inconvenience. Today, I jumped at the chance, eager to exit the darkness that was my own mind.

Ledgecrest sat a few miles down the road, less than a five-minute drive. Even that much solitude was messing with me.

Nothing on the radio except the same overplayed pop songs and AM zealots predicting the apocalypse. A town that had never been my home whizzed by. I ached to be around people, saddled with mindless tasks, sweeping floors and emptying bedpans; anything was better than wrestling with introspection.

I'd changed into my white jacket, stuffing my wallet and lunch into the little locker, when my cell phone vibrated. Mrs. Balfour. My immediate wish, of course, was that Jacob had been found. The police had retrieved him from the water tower again, or discovered him meandering the outskirts of town, whatever, he was okay, and my life could return to normal. Mrs. Balfour put those hopes to bed.

"No word," she reported, before adding, "I'm sorry I couldn't see you off this morning. There was a backup at the hospital. Wreck on the highway."

I assured her it was okay.

"Thank you again for coming so fast. It was sweet of you."

It wasn't sweet of me. It was the least I could do. But I didn't say that, letting my silence act as acceptance of the compliment.

Mrs. Balfour said she was going to the police this morning. I agreed that was a good idea.

Before she hung up, I remembered her mysterious visitor.

"When I was leaving," I said, "an old man stopped by. Said his name was Francis."

The line went dead. I figured the call had dropped. Which often happened within the thick concrete walls of the convalescent home. When I looked at the screen, however, I saw the call still active.

"Mrs. Balfour?"

"I'll let you know as soon as I hear something."

Then she hung up. If she said goodbye, I missed it.

Despite hopes for a distraction, my fill-in shift was hardly the cure for what ailed. The hospital, full of the infirm and unattended, only reminded me that we are born alone, and we damn sure die that way too.

Ledgecrest was small but clean, the staff, doctors, and nurses all pleasant. No Utica cribs. No holes drilled into skulls. The building wasn't crawling with rats. But it was still a place for the unwell, and it's hard to be around that climate and not feel disquiet.

The hospital featured sixteen rooms, eight on each side. Not the sharpest décor, a lot of the furniture donated, which spelled paisley prints and mismatched earth tones from the 1970s, television models several generations behind. But it was affordable, with a waiting list to get in the door; we always had a full house. The clientele experienced frequent turnover. Like working at a wildlife sanctuary, you had to remind yourself not to get too attached. Yet, that wasn't the hardest part about working there.

It was the smell.

Warmed-over pouches of gruel reheated in microwaves, balmy salves and menthol ointments. Disinfectant bleach masked some of it, but nothing could douse what that smell really was: death. You couldn't escape it. It reminded me of that old Lynyrd Skynrd song. Because you *can* sense when the angel of darkness surrounds you. Death arrives with a distinct odor, sour and musky, erosion so overpowering you can taste it. Sinks into your clothes, your skin, your very being. The scent travels beyond BO and sponge-bathed hygiene, mutating fungi in the blood. It's the departure, a crossing over, the liminal moments between worlds. Humans are not designed to last, motors give, tickers stop, our bodies but temporary vessels. Smoke, don't smoke, eat beef by the bucket, go vegan, run, walk, or sit on your butt. In the end, doesn't matter. You, me, that guy over there, we're all going to die. We're born into this world dying. Only a matter of how long we last. And when the end comes, it's never pretty. Some of these people had survived almost a hundred years, and here they were little more than decaying cells and disintegrating tissues, hunks of meat that had to be rotated to avoid clotting and bedsores.

Ledgecrest was a human Goodwill where families dumped parents and other relatives who had lived long past usefulness. They were burdens unloaded. And I hated thinking of it like that, so callous, jaded, and cynical. Maybe a psychiatrist examines a case study like mine, dissects how I grew up, and sees a man with fear of commitment, unwilling to risk getting attached because he's scared of getting hurt. That would make Ledgecrest the perfect job. But I wasn't like that. I did care. Too much. It's human nature to want to comfort the hurt, lost, and lonely. My childhood had been rough; I knew what abandonment felt like. And I refused to let my unstable inception condemn me to a life devoid of compassion or empathy.

Like every shift, I began by reading notes. Orderlies and nurses charted interactions with patients, regardless of how banal or mundane. Many guests grappled with dementia. The slightest discomfort weighed heavier on their psyche, affecting mood. It was important to note who was agitated that day so we could keep them calm, even if that meant lying to them.

Mrs. Simmons had been complaining about the heat because Mrs. Simmons always complained about the heat. If it wasn't the sun, it was the radiator or the blankets, or the seasoning on bland, low-sodium meals. Plain yogurt was too spicy for her. And Mrs. Calloway had been asking what time her son was coming. Which was heartbreaking. Mrs. Calloway's son, Lucas, lived in Seattle, three thousand miles away. He hadn't visited once since I'd worked there.

Then I turned the page and saw Mr. Johnson had had another episode.

Galen Johnson had been at Ledgecrest almost as long as I had. As a healthcare professional, you're not supposed to have favorites. Of course, that is impossible. You spend so much time with these people, getting to know them, their hopes, their dreams, their final wishes. I had a soft spot for Mr. Johnson. Despite being eighty-nine, he retained a razor-sharp wit and keen sense of humor. He always made me laugh. He was also in the early stages of Alzheimer's, and the lines between fantasy and reality had become blurred.

I read his nurse Mary's notes. The shapeshifters were back. This started about six months ago and had been growing worse. Lately, whenever nurses arrived to change Mr. Johnson's linens or empty his urine bottle—the same nurses who'd been caring for him day in and day out—they would be wearing different skins. It wasn't Mary. It was a shapeshifter wearing Mary's skin. It wasn't Dorian or Sandy. It was a shapeshifter masquerading as Dorian or Sandy. Strange as it was, besides that one odd detail, the guy was lucid. Even the shapeshifting was brought up in a matter-of-fact tone, voice never rising above ragged whisper.

I headed down to 5C to talk to Mr. Johnson, whose eyes crinkled with fondness when he saw me. Part of that was because I didn't patronize him, didn't belittle his intelligence by agreeing with the nonsense. I talked to him like a regular human being, and if that included correcting erroneous assumptions, then so be it. This approach was in direct conflict with the nursing home's protocol, which stated, in no uncertain terms, that staff should never challenge patient delusions.

"Hey, Mr. Johnson," I said, stepping in his room. One of the perks residents at Ledgecrest enjoyed: each patient had his or her own room. "How goes it?"

"I've seen better, Brandon."

"How do you know it's really me?" I grinned.

He waved me off. "I know you, Brandon." For whatever reason, thus far I'd proven impervious to doppelgänger accusations.

Lifting his chart off the footboard, I ran down his meds, which included Donepezil, other cholinesterase inhibitors prescribed to delay the inevitable. Same medications and dosages he'd been on for a while. Couldn't blame a spike or chemical imbalance. According to the morning's report, Mr. Johnson had been "hysterical." Which did not sound like him.

I took the plastic chair beside his bed.

"This morning," I started. "Different skin? Imposters?"

"I know what you think. That I'm an old man losing it."

"Hold up. I don't believe anyone is wearing a different skin or trying to trick you. But I don't think you're crazy. I think your brain plays tricks. Happens to the best of us."

I didn't see the benefit of pandering into false narratives, confirming the impossible because it was the path of least resistance. These weren't little kids with imaginary friends. These were grown men and women who had lived long, rich lives. They deserved respect. They deserved dignity.

Mr. Johnson pointed at his tray. "You mind handing me that water?"

I retrieved the paper cup and tried to position the straw to his lips. He wrestled it free with surprising grip for a man that age.

Outside, strong winds scraped long branches against the glass. A powerful sense of déjà vu washed over me. I knew what was going to happen, what he planned to say, what my reaction would be. Like a clock running a little fast. What good was it to see a few seconds into the future? There wasn't enough time to appreciate or reflect or do anything with this information.

Most of his breakfast, dry toast and low-salt oatmeal, remanded untouched. I had half a bagel in my white coat pocket. I'd stopped off at Bleecker Street Deli on my way in, scarfing a mouthful. I was saving the rest of the egg and sea salt melt for a midmorning snack. When I offered, Mr. Johnson snatched the bagel. I remembered giving him this same half bagel, the way he plucked it from my fingers, like in my dreams, reactions trapped in an echo chamber.

"It's okay," Mr. Johnson said, noshing a bite. "I know you don't see it. It all happens at once. Everything. One world stacked atop the other." He pantomimed with his hands, as though laying brick. "Once you see it, you can't unsee it."

I didn't have any disorders. I was normal. Perfectly normal. But in that instant, I feared I'd contracted misophonia. Each time he bit into the salted egg, I could hear the crunch, churn, teeth grinding, tongue repositioning masticated meats and proteins, the sound loud enough to induce madness.

"Are you all right, Brandon?"

"Fine," I said, readjusting the pillows and blankets, swatting away crumbs, hastening my exit. I gave him a big forced fake grin. "I have to start my rounds. You need anything, beep me."

He kept chewing, slurping sounds hitting my gag reflex.

He darted out a bony arm, snaring my wrist, clutching it. I stared at the long, yellow fingernails that needed to be trimmed.

"Do me a favor, boy."

"Sure," I said. At that point, I would've agreed to anything to get out of there.

"Be ready," he said.

"For...?"

"You might not see the Shadow People now."

I felt the blood drain from my face.

"But trust me, boy, you will."

CHAPTER SIX

For the rest of my shift, I didn't avoid Mr. Johnson. I also didn't find too many excuses to spend time on his half of the ward. I kept telling myself it was a coincidence, that term he'd used. Shadow People. No need to make it into more than it was.

On my lunch break, I pulled up a search engine, out of curiosity, relieved to learn neither Jacob nor Mr. Johnson invented the term. It had always been there, folks using it all the time. Conspiracy wingnuts. Shadow People were boogeymen, spooks, ghouls. According to Wikipedia, methamphetamine addicts, up for days, were the main culprits. I didn't see the need to go further than that, comforted the phrase had simply entered *my* consciousness. Happened a lot with words. Take *verisimilitude* for instance. I'd never encountered that word before college. Almost twenty years of living, not once. Then after starting at SUNY, everyone was using it. Professors. Lecturers. Visiting writers. I'd read it in the papers. Hear it on the news, TV, comedians, movie stars, sportscasters, the average Joe on the street, everybody dropping it into casual conversations at the coffee shop. Of course, it had existed before my awareness. It hadn't been real to *me*. After I'd read about the Shadow People in Jacob's lunatic periodical, these creatures had entered my psyche, making the construct tangible, verifiable. Before that, the Shadow People dwelled in the ether, floating around with all the other things I didn't have room for in my brain. Mineral classification. Vichyssoise recipes. Funk bands.

Still, when Mr. Johnson said "Shadow People," my bones went cold. I could feel the base of my spine tingling, silver freezing marrow. No matter how much I tried to convince myself that the expression was random, luck of the draw, I could not do it.

Following my shift, I stopped at Elmer's on the way to my apartment. I seldom drank. Tonight, I could use a beer. If only to steady rattled nerves.

Elmer's was a college bar, this hole in the wall that would've been a sad and pathetic place for alcoholics if not for its proximity to campus. It was closer than Thee Parkside. I seldom went to either. They were *such* college bars. All day, you'd hear students talk about getting wasted, like alcohol was a much-needed remedy to counteract grueling days. I was young but not so young I didn't know life got harder, and that the problems confronting most college students were field days compared to the soul-crushing responsibilities we'd soon be saddled with.

The bar's storefront presented like an old barbershop, too-bright lights hawking all the worst beers for bottom-barrel prices. I may not have drunk beer often, but I still knew Coors Light was watered-down swill. Honestly, once I stepped inside and heard all the forced exuberance of drunk girls getting excited for "Brown Eyed Girl," I almost turned around and headed home. I didn't need a beer that bad.

Then I saw her.

Only one night had passed since I'd asked out Samantha Holahan, but it felt like months, this protracted, drawn-out separation keeping us apart and breaking us in two. By the way she returned my gaze, I could tell she felt it too. Like a couple old friends reconnecting, a chance meeting in a supermarket on Christmas Eve. Our disproportionate reactions left us reeling, embarrassed in the afterglow. Strange, the way life and circumstance can affect our relationships to time.

Sam was with a small group of friends. As usual, she was dressed like the female version of Duckie from that old 1980s movie, argyle vest and scarf, jangle rings, black boots. I waited for her to lip sync "Try a Little Tenderness." Except Elmer's didn't have anything as cool as Otis Redding on the jukebox. And Sam was way cooler than Jon Cryer.

I didn't want to interrupt her night out with friends, and I wasn't in the mood to be around a large group, but when Sam saw me, she peeled off from her crew to catch me before I could escape.

"Hey," she said, taking my hand, like we'd known each other twenty summers. "How's your friend?"

I'd forgotten I told her the truth about going to look for Jacob. Not like I was a liar. But for expediency's sake, in such situations, I was more likely to skip over intimate details and make up a convenient excuse.

"No new news," I said. "Jacob hasn't come home." I tried to locate a clock, as if knowing the exact time would provide a better update.

Sam turned back to her friends, who slouched too cool for school, a flat pitcher between them, probably talking about some lousy, boring movie no one could possibly like. They had those kinds of faces. Pretentious. One of them beckoned for her to return. I waited for her to invite me to join and was already running through the excuses to say no thank you. Even though I wanted to be near Sam, I disliked her friends, who were the type of people I'd spent my life avoiding. It wasn't their fault. I'd endured too many superficial conversations. I knew how this played out. After a few polite questions about what I did, the collective would veer back toward familiar topics, shared backgrounds and experiences that had nothing to do with me, rehashing the night so-and-so did this or that, prompting howling laughter, way more raucous than the memory deserved; and I'd be lost in the shuffle, chuckling and wincing, eyeing the door, plotting the least awkward moment to ghost.

Instead, Sam leaned in close, breath hot on my ear. "I was about to have a cigarette," she said. "Keep me company?"

Cigarette smoke had always made me nauseous. I still hadn't gotten that beer, which I couldn't take outside anyway. But I wasn't passing up a one-on-one with Sam Holahan.

Elmer's gaudy yellow neon splashed fluorescent on the cracked asphalt, exposing a small parking lot in urgent need of repair. Angry tufts of crab grass spat back through fissures, weeds rejected from the underworld. Chewed-up butts littered the ground in between the crumpled packs of Marlboros and single-serving vodkas from the liquor store across the street. Random, discarded garments, a tee shirt, pair of underwear, weighed down by a thousand rainstorms, dried out and affixed to the tarmac.

Sam lit up, affecting a pose I'd seen a hundred times in films, the one where the woman's arm is cocked and wrist flung out, smoke blown in the opposite direction, a flirty smile on painted lips before she said, "I only smoke when I drink."

I didn't care if she was a chain-smoker. In that moment I didn't care if she was a junkie.

"I wondered when you'd ask me out, Brandon," she said. Which was the first real proof that last night's almost-trip to Thee Parkside had, in fact, been a date. Then, as if catching herself—or maybe remembering there were more pressing concerns: "Tell me about your friend."

Without hesitation, I launched into my mom and dad and that whole convoluted mess, how I'd moved in with the Balfours, watching helplessly as Jacob came unglued. I'd never been much of a talker, and I wasn't in the habit of unloading personal problems, but as I talked about how I'd grown up, the way Sam was listening, *really* listening, it made me talk more, confide. The more I talked, the closer she moved, until she was touching my arm, her face full of compassion, drawing me in. Which created this conflict inside me. There I was, talking about this screwed-up history—my mother and father, Jacob, his father's suicide—conversation I wouldn't burden *any*one with, least of all the girl I had such a massive crush on, but it was that kind of night, a soft summer night with soft summer lights, and I could smell the beer and nicotine on her breath, and it wasn't turning me off. I was getting…not aroused. Under the circumstances, that would've been gauche. But I was feeling *something*. And she was feeling it too, evidenced by the flushness to her cheeks, the way our hands started touching, soothing, caressing.

Then the door opened and one of her friends passed along two pints, which we weren't supposed to be drinking outside. I wasn't one for flouting laws or breaking rules. The girl gave a winking nod, and I felt exposed, like Sam had been telling her about me before I walked in. Self-conscious, I needed that beer more than ever. I practically pounded it. And for a guy who didn't drink, one beer that fast messed with your perception.

After that, time seemed to pass quickly. Cars arriving, people leaving, lights streaming, tracing. Then we were back inside, just the two of us, away from her friends, most of whom had bailed, at a back table, talking about life and love and dreams. Intimate. And it wasn't just me opening up and sharing. After I concluded an abridged version of my screwed-up start (I left out the harshest and most harrowing parts), Sam was telling *me* details about *her* life, vulnerable, tender details: about her turbulent childhood; about how her father had had an affair and how she'd gone to live with her mom after the divorce and how it affected her trust in relationships.

Next thing I knew it was last call. Lingering students scattered. Sam and I didn't move. We'd been talking for hours. I knew what I was supposed to do.

I'd never been great in these spots. Picking up girls had never been my thing, but this was my moment. All I had to do was ask if she wanted to come back to my place. That simple. I was trying to find the rights words. That was when Sam leaned over and kissed me. *She* kissed *me*. The first thing that came to mind was that old Echo and the Bunnymen song, "Lips Like Sugar." This one summer long ago, when Jacob and I were planning to start that band, we spent a sweltering July mining old alternative music. Obscure college bands from back in the day of alternative's infancy. Bearing Witness, The Connells, Material Issue. Music made before we knew what music was. We considered it research for the group we'd be. Old school in the modern age. Like what MGMT became. Maybe Foster the People. We thought we were doing homework, research for developing a sound. I didn't know why I was thinking about pulling mp4s and that time to pretend, all the while kissing my dream girl.

I wasn't drunk. I was buzzed. I'd had a couple. Maybe I was drunk. I was in that perfect state of...happy. I'd gone from this crazy, savage day, one of the worst of my life, everything out of sync, time, place, order, and here it had morphed into one of the best nights I could remember. I knew how cheesy I was being. This wasn't a movie where the guy gives up future plans to stay behind in his lousy hometown to see if true love can work. I mean, it wasn't *Garden State*. In a week, I'd be gone. Nothing could get me to stick around Cortland. Not even Sam Holahan.

I didn't ask Sam to come home with me that night, I didn't press as hard as a lot of guys would have, and I went home alone.

I woke to the sounds of activity bustling below, silly smile still plastered on my goofy face. The morning light glided in, birds chirping, breeze lushing. Lips like sugar…

Hopping up to make coffee, I added grounds, poured water, and switched on the maker, back against countertop, fingertips drumming with newfound rhythm. My cell was on the table. I flipped it over to see the time. There were several missed calls from a number I didn't recognize. Normally, I wouldn't call back an unknown number, but today was not normal.

Stepping outside to the walkway, I peered over vacant lots where ripped plastic bags rippled on stumps, pressed against chain link.

When the operator answered "Utica Police Department," I knew the message that waited for me. I stuck around for confirmation anyway.

They'd found Jacob's body.

CHAPTER SEVEN

When I pulled in the Balfours' driveway, the authorities were already there. Three squad cars and another that was unmarked, framed by the well-coifed suburban fauna that was supposed to ward off scenes like this. This was why Mrs. Balfour moved the family to the nicer part of town, away from narrow streets, alleyways, and brown brick, the sneakers draped over telephone lines—to escape the sirens, instability, and madness. Only to see tragedy prove impervious to manicured lawns and vegetable boxes.

Officers streamed in and out of the canary yellow house, their starry sleeves carting cardboard boxes, evidence retrieved, piled high and ready to be cataloged. Like this was a big-city crime scene with a mystery to solve.

Not that there weren't questions. Where had they found Jacob's body? How had he died? Nobody told me anything on the phone except my best friend was dead.

A cop stopped me on the front steps. Lording his diminutive stature above the iron railing, he squared his stance, inquiring about my business there. The whole affair felt over the top, the opening sequence to a bad cop show, and that's what I was thinking about, Hollywood tropes and fabrication, the analytical approach that comes with advanced literature classes, searching out the meaning of everything—why the moors at dawn? Why are the drapes blue? Which might've been why I was slow in answering. The officer took my pensive response as a challenge to his authority. I didn't make a habit of fighting with police, but this cop—Officer Rafferty—wasn't making it easy. Danzig short with a vocabulary maxing out at about a dozen words, most of which revolved around no, he landed a long way from original. I'd met dozens of Raffertys in my life, unimaginative bullies with limited vocational possibilities. It was either this or maybe high school guidance counselor. Talking my way around a man of such stunted intelligence shouldn't have made getting inside a problem, except this entire ordeal had me all messed up, unable to elucidate. I couldn't formulate a coherent thought or get an articulate word out, and without either, he wouldn't let me in, even after I managed to explain the Utica Police Department contacted *me*. The impasse turned into a shouting match, and the commotion brought to the door a detective who cleared up the confusion and waved me inside. Stalking the steps, I glared at Officer Rafferty, which was, admittedly, immature on my part, but I was aggravated. He didn't notice.

Mrs. Balfour sat at the table, a pair of uniformed officers standing at attention by her side, sentinels stationed around the besieged queen. The whole scene was so surreal. On the walls surrounding us were the same see-through cupboards I'd grown up with, housing the same healthy cereals and whole-wheat pastas, the organic cheese crackers snuck into my lunchbox as special treats. There was the landline phone, mustard yellow, cord dangled in curly cued piggy tail, covered in dust because no one called landlines anymore except telemarketers. Same refrigerator, microwave, blender, magnets celebrating cherished family moments. The kitchen and house *looked* the same, but it wasn't. Everything had changed.

No sign of Chloe. Still at school, I figured. I made my way down the hall, squeezing between the photographs of dead people. A cop stepped aside so I could tell Mrs. Balfour how sorry I was and hug her, another guest paying respects in the receiving line. Neither response felt adequate. I searched for the right words, the tools to comfort and console—I didn't suffer an inability to express myself—but I couldn't think of anything fast enough before I was ushered away, whisked into the adjacent dining room, where a woman detective waited.

The detective introduced herself as Rachael Lourey and asked me to take a seat. At the long dark table affixed with gleaming plates no one ever ate off of, glasses from which no one drank, I could see Mrs. Balfour sitting in the next room, shattered.

For as long as I'd lived with the Balfours, the dining room was like this: staged. A tall grandfather cupboard loomed behind, stacked with commemorative plates, teacups, and other fancy stemware. On the walls, the whimsical signage and folksy artwork, old timey sayings about the meaning of community and villages, hand-stitched doilies about the human heart, blond-haired, blue-eyed Jesus keeping watch. Given the circumstances, these details broached absurd. The Balfours were far from rich, but Mrs. Balfour had done her best to decorate the home with elegance. Not coming from money or aristocracy, she lacked the blue blood birthright and intrinsic taste that comes with it. Her attempts at interior decoration felt hokey, cheesy, canned. The sincerity was genuine, and intentions mattered. Sitting there, however, among the framed pictures and crocheted affirmations, embroidered witticisms about what it means to have a home and be a family, I felt like a fraud. Because I had neither. And what I'd been gifted, I'd neglected.

Detective Lourey didn't speak, content to study me with extreme prejudice and judgment. More cops ascended the staircase to my left, up to Jacob's room—while *more* descended toting armfuls—hard drive, computer, assorted boxes—which distracted me, the frenetic energy of movement. I saw peeking out the top of one of the boxes the pale blue stock of Jacob's homemade zine, *Illuminations*. I had the strangest sensation, as if I were watching an overlay, a sheet of tracing paper laid atop the original, resulting in translucent obfuscation. What was the reason for such a thorough investigation?

The detective knocked on the table, calling my attention, as if I'd been the one derelict and causing the delay.

After the perfunctory expression of condolence for my loss— my loss being nothing compared to Mrs. Balfour's—the detective started peppering me with her questions, zero to sixty like that.

"When was the last time you had contact with the victim?"

"Maybe a year?"

"A year?"

"We weren't close."

"I thought you were Jacob's best friend."

"I wouldn't say that. Necessarily."

"Necessarily what? You weren't his friend?"

"No, I was. You said best friend."

"You're objecting to the classification you were close?"

"I'm not *objecting* to anything."

"Is there a reason for the hostility?"

"I'm not being hostile."

"You sound upset."

"I am upset. Sorry if my answers are brusque."

"Brusque?"

"It means—"

"I know what it means. How old are you?"

"Twenty-three. Same as Jacob. What's that got to do with anything?"

"What can you tell me about Minnesota?"

"Its top export commodity is soybeans and corn."

"Do you think this is funny, Mr. Cossey?"

"No. Why would I think it's funny? My best friend is dead. There is nothing funny about this. I'm not laughing. I'm not even smiling. What kind of question is that?"

I could only throw up my hands, the conversation a whirlwind, the scenario a circus, the give-and-take of two people not on the same page, or even in the same book. Water meets oil. Pickles and sponge cake. Pete Davidson and Ariana Grande. Things that didn't belong together. The only information the police had divulged on the telephone was they'd found Jacob's body, information relayed at the behest of Mrs. Balfour. I was there to help. I didn't need prompting—my first move would be to see Mrs. Balfour—although sitting there now, under intense fire, that police phone call was sounding more like a demand than a request, answering questions an on-the-record response to a formal inquisition.

Because of my contorting facial expressions, Lourey eyed me with increasing suspicion. Her questions had me squirming, overthinking and second guessing what I was doing with my hands. Time sped up, playing with perceptions as the exchange circled around again to more questions I couldn't answer, which had me acting guilty, like when you walk out of a pharmacy or super-mart and the shoplifting alarm sounds, and even though you know you didn't do anything wrong, the panic sets in, that sensation you've been caught. I couldn't slow my pulse or get my heart to beat regularly, distress fueling more anguish, a snake eating its own tail. I was answering a detective's questions concerning a death—of course I was acting odd! That wasn't on me. The detective's entire approach—her formality, the severity of tone—left my mind painting pictures without all the facts, rendering a skewed portrait.

"Are you listening to me, Mr. Cossey?"

My mind circled back to the first question she'd asked when I sat down, a word she'd used.

"Wait. You said 'victim.'"

"Excuse me?"

"When we first started talking. You referred to Jacob as the victim. Does that mean foul play was involved?"

"Who says that?"

"What?"

"'Foul play.' You don't sound like a twenty-three-year-old college student."

"I work at a convalescent home. Perhaps I've picked up the lingo, lexicon, World War Two vernacular—what's that matter?"

"Are you always this confrontational?"

"I'm sorry, Detective. I don't feel as though I am being combative. You say 'victim,' it implies malicious intent. Is that what happened?"

My brain ran wild through all the seedy and squirrely sections of town, which defined half of Utica, places that could devour a man like Jacob. An abandoned factory, a welfare hotel, under the bridge, face down in a river. Jacob liked to roam. I recalled the summer he made it to Plotter Kill, the nearby preserve, where a ranger found him perched on a rock, naked, cradling a tree husk, crouched like the pineapple king, barking at the moon.

"What can you tell me about Minnesota?" the detective asked again, ignoring my question.

"What's Minnesota got to do with any of this?"

"That's where Jacob Balfour's body was found."

I waited for the punchline because this *had* to be a joke. Plotter Kill Preserve was forty minutes away; Minnesota was a twenty-hour car ride. Jacob didn't have a car. He didn't have a license, far as I knew. When I lived with them, his mom picked him up and dropped him off everywhere. After I got my license, I was tasked with drop-offs and pickups to and from school. Anytime Jacob disappeared into the night, he did so on foot. The occasional hitched car ride, short bus trip. He kept a rusty old bicycle hidden in the woods. But you can't pedal eleven hundred miles on an interstate in less than a week, and I didn't see anyone, even a lonely trucker, picking up a headcase like Jacob and driving him across state lines, not in his current condition. Or maybe that's exactly what happened. Jacob accepted a ride from the wrong person, a homicidal maniac… I tried shutting off my brain from taking me to such dark places.

I glanced toward the next room, where Mrs. Balfour sat. Her expression remained glazed over, a million miles away.

I braced for what came next, Detective Lourey's response and the horrid details of a gruesome crime. Instead, the detective said, "Thank you for your time, Mr. Cossey." She moved toward the door, showing me out.

"Wait. That's it?"

"That's it," the detective said, slapping closed her little notepad.

"Hold on. You ask me to come all the way up here, grill me—"

"No one grilled you, Mr. Cossey."

"But what…what happened to Jacob?"

"I'm sorry," the detective said. "That's all we're at liberty to divulge right now."

"Please."

Perhaps my sincerity caught her off guard or appealed to the better parts of her humanity, but Detective Lourey paused, wrestling with how much—if any—could be shared. Her posture deflated in resignation. I found the entire display disingenuous.

"The cause of death appears to be a hard blow to his stomach."

"From what, like, a fist? Someone punched him?"

"No. A fall. It looks as though the victim fell down into a quarry."

"Why do you keep calling him a victim?"

"Landed on a hard, sharp object," she continued, ignoring my question. "The fall punctured his stomach, delivering the fatal wound."

None of this made sense. I wanted to check on Mrs. Balfour, who I knew couldn't hear from the other room. Still, I felt compelled to lean in and whisper. "Jacob wasn't well."

"We are aware of his mental condition."

"That's it? He fell...and landed on a rock...in Minnesota?" It sounded even more preposterous when I said it aloud. A rock. A thousand miles away.

"The quarry is filled with rocks," Detective Lourey said. "Many of which are jagged, pointed, sharp. As for why he was at a quarry in Minnesota, that is what I am trying to find out. I was hoping you might know."

Two minutes ago, I'd wanted out of this house. Now, despite the detective's persistent movements to show me the door, I wasn't ready to leave.

"Did he...suffer?" I asked.

"Death wouldn't have been instantaneous. He was bleeding internally. It would've been hard to move. It does appear he tried driving for help."

"Driving? He didn't have a car—"

"He tried driving out of the quarry on a piece of construction equipment. An excavator."

I remembered Mrs. Balfour said Jacob had been working for a construction company. I wouldn't know my way around an excavator.

"He didn't get far," she said.

"This is horrible." I rubbed my eyes, dragging my hands down my face, raking flesh. "How can you have no idea when he died? There's rigor mortis, evidence of trauma." I began ticking off an itemized list on my fingers. I worked with the aged. I knew how death manifested. Any medical examiner worth their salt should be able to pinpoint, or at least approximate, a reasonable time of death based on how the blood had coagulated if nothing else. There was more she wasn't telling me.

"We can't say definitively," Detective Lourey said, gathering her things, signaling the big cop in the next room, "because the body was so badly burned."

I dropped in a seat. The big cop came in but I didn't move. I could see she didn't want to tell me the rest. I wasn't going anywhere until she did.

Detective Lourey halted packing up. "He couldn't get far on the excavator because he'd lost too much blood. He passed out, the engine got too hot, and the turbocharger caught fire. We were lucky to ID the body." Before I could ask, she added, "Dental records. Fingerprints."

This story kept getting worse.

CHAPTER EIGHT

The funeral was held the following Tuesday. A miserable overcast concrete-gray day slabbed with hard black clouds that threatened downpour. But it didn't rain, which would've been a welcome relief, a cleansing to cut through the sloppy humidity. Instead, we suffered the indignity of that in between state. Messy, wet, warm, stuffy. Water dripped from the trees as if the leaves themselves were perspiring, a rainforest in Upstate New York. Not sure it mattered the sky never broke. You still got damp, so much precipitation in the air. My suit felt soaked through, down to the tee. Even though the morning wasn't cold, I couldn't stop shivering.

The details surrounding Jacob's death had been impossible to shake. I had nowhere to turn for clarification. I couldn't grill Mrs. Balfour. My meeting with Detective Lourey had left me with more questions than answers. Leading up to the burial, I replayed our exchange ad nauseum. Nothing made sense. No consistency. Despite the detective's frequent use of the word "victim," Jacob's death had been ruled an accident. Never mind the preposterousness of a man in Jacob's state traveling a thousand miles to hurl himself to the bottom of a pit—this was the official determination, final say, case closed. Then again, aside from my random truck driver serial killer theory, I didn't have a better one to swap in its place. The detective's parting shot, that an unrelated quarry explosion was responsible for the fire, didn't quell confusion or temper suspicions. What was I suspicious of? That someone had abducted and murdered my mentally ill friend? For what? A robbery? Jacob didn't have anything worth stealing. And if you're going to kill a guy, what makes Minnesota so special? Maybe the simplest answer was the right one: Jacob had gone off his meds, and his latest breakdown delivered him somewhere far away and fatal. I didn't believe it. I didn't *not* believe it.

Knowing nothing about construction, I looked up excavators and turbochargers on the web. At least that part of the story panned out. Apparently, turbochargers could be problematic, combustible. Something about turrets, main hydraulic valves, and engines running at high heat, leaks, and debris. There was a magic number of three thousand PSI where hydraulic fluid was concerned. If the air/fuel mixture was off, turbochargers could ignite the flame. Manufacturers were supposed to put in firewalls to combat the problem but accidents still happened.

When I pulled up to St. Paul's, the intimate gathering center for believers and alcoholics on scattered weeknights, AA commandeering the location on faith's off hours, I slogged out of my car, shutting the wet creaking door, and popped my umbrella to join the rest of the guests in the black parade. I longed for rain, a bargain baptism to rinse away this pain. Despite my upbringing, I didn't believe in the supernatural or demons or invisible men in the sky. The evil I felt was grounded in stone-cold reality, the sad truth that fashions a thousand useless gods. Because that's what this was, eons of evolution, humanity crawling from the primordial slime, and the first order of business: find an all-knowing, all-powerful deity who will oversee, protect, keep us safe. Go visit the children's cancer center and tell me about God. Watch a ninety-year-old man suffer the indignity of dying alone, eating baby food, and soiling himself in adult diapers. In life, he could've been a lawyer, a banker, or a business owner. And this is how you go out: drooling like a toothless infant, helpless and unable to control your bowels.

The whole reason we were here today was because Mr. Balfour hanged himself in the family garage, which set in motion a series of disastrous events. Jacob's slow descent to hell began with his father's selfish act and ended with him several states removed, dying in a ditch with a ruptured stomach, charred beyond recognition. No one knew how he got there. And no one would try too hard to figure it out. People like Jacob didn't provide a service. You couldn't get anything from them. Therefore, they were expendable.

Given Jacob's mental health problems, the trouble he caused the community with his unhinged antics, I had expected a sparsely attended affair. But St. Paul's parking lot was overflowing, cars spilling into the backup one at the old community center. A hundred vehicles clogged the lots and side streets, unleashing droves of mourners who descended with the pious reverence reserved for the death of celebrities. Inside the church, every pew was filled. A sellout was hard enough to pull off on Christmas let alone a middle-of-the-week ceremony for the town nutcracker.

I tried to brush aside the cynicism I felt creeping in. That wasn't me. I strove to maintain a positive outlook. Regardless of our inception, we have the power to change lives. Our fate is, ultimately, in our hands. But does that philosophy apply to the sick and suffering, the broken and the damned?

It was touching to see so many people taking time off work to pay their respects. I was happy to have been proven wrong. People *did* care about Jacob. Though I soon realized that wasn't it. These people weren't here for Jacob; they'd come to support Mrs. Balfour. I shouldn't have been surprised. People loved Mrs. Balfour, who gave so much of herself, a friend to everybody, a living saint if ever there was one. They should've chiseled another marble slab, added her likeness to the field of pious and prayerful in the common garden.

The well-attended church ceremony prohibited my speaking in depth with Mrs. Balfour. After I placed my flower arrangement at the altar, I waited my turn in the receiving line, relegated to another local acquaintance uttering empty platitudes about being sorry for her loss, as meaningless as thoughts and prayers in the wake of a national tragedy. I watched the liturgy slumped in a back pew, awash in the organ's drone and children of the corn chorus, feeling alienated and alone.

I'd never been religious or spiritual. When I'd first come to live with the Balfours, I attended weekly services out of respect for Mrs. Balfour, who possessed a devout faith. And because I was eight—at that age you don't get much agency. When I hit my teens, I was able to wriggle out of going most Sundays. Of course, I had to go for Jesus's greatest hits: Christmas, Good Friday, Easter. Birth, death, resurrection. I didn't have anything against Catholicism. At least no more than what I held against the rest of organized religion, whose stranglehold on fear and convention offended erudite sensibilities. I could appreciate the rituals and performance, the rites and tradition, stained glass pictorials and Stations of the Cross.

Today, however, as I observed the priests glide by in their gilded robes, ivory, emerald, and gold, hands held up to heaven, promising salvation and eternal life, I couldn't suppress my ire. I grew angrier and angrier with all these fools around me, caught up in mythology, the vacant promise of hope based on a campfire story.

There was one moment, however, where logic and internal debate gave way to the external and awesome. The sun cracked the sky, and the heavy cloud cover parted. A bright light seared through the glass ceiling, and a golden ray struck the casket with laser-like precision, illuminating the cherry wood. And in that instant, I felt the presence of something bigger. I ached for that conviction to remain, desperate to believe. I wished I had faith in anything.

Then it was gone. The clouds returned to blot out childish beliefs as shadows crawled over the church floor. That sunbeam had been nothing but a confluence of cosmic chance—celestial rotation, rate and time, a solar alignment conspiring to create the illusion of security. And as the light slipped from the crown of the casket, with it went all poetry, leaving only the disillusion of broken promises.

The white wreaths juxtaposed against the colorful bouquets were pretty, though. Shades of cream and titanium, accents of maroon and violet, asleep in beds of fresh green.

The congregation celebrated life with hymns, their ragged, off-key voices joining in unity, masking the tone deafness.

Mrs. Balfour had chosen a younger portrait of Jacob, one from before he was sick—a time I remembered well and lamented often. Blown up and placed on an easel, the photo showcased Jacob at thirteen, fourteen, smiling, displaying the hope and joy he did not possess at twenty-three.

The priest read several passages from the Bible. About life never ending; about how no one is ever really gone; about how we keep their memory alive in our hearts. Comforting. "He's at peace." "He's in a better place." Sounded nice. But this lip service only works if you remind yourself how horrible the deceased's existence was to begin with. You don't say billionaires who die cruising the Mediterranean on their yacht are "in a better place."

Afterwards, we all headed to the cemetery. About a third of the church made the pilgrimage, a good forty, fifty people. Except when I glanced around and took in their faces, these weren't the same people. Which didn't make sense. Guests at the church were familiar. At the cemetery, I didn't know a soul. The weird part was—the part I couldn't explain—they weren't strangers either. For instance, I recognized Mr. Caliandri, who'd given me my first job, rotating milk and stocking shelves at our local market. Except it wasn't Mr. Caliandri. Years pass, people change, but this wasn't the same man. He was a facsimile, a representation, a forgery. I couldn't shake the impression these were stand-ins for the real thing, replacement actors hired. Ridiculous, not true, impossible, but my mind would not let it go.

When I was younger, I used to watch soap operas with Mrs. Balfour. Although, in my memories, I couldn't see her face. I wasn't watching them alone, I knew that. Chloe was too young. Jacob wouldn't have watched soap operas. I recalled another person in the room with me, an older presence, compassionate, kind. Who else could it have been? Maybe I was conflating memories of Ledgecrest, mixing up players. Only the soap opera I remembered watching, *Guiding Light*, had been off the air for years, long before I started at the convalescent home.

The reason I was thinking about soap operas in the first place was this device they employed. When an actor left a role and another took over, a calm voiceover would state, "Now playing the part of Phillip Spaulding is..." And that was that. Didn't matter if the new actor looked nothing like the old one. The viewer accepted this new representation. From now on, this was what the character looked like. And that's how I felt at the cemetery, like I was surrounded by different actors playing familiar parts.

A gloomy pallor hung heavy over the rest of the day; the finality of ashes and dust wasn't going to lighten the mood. And why should it? A disturbed young man had been struck down in the prime of his life. That his fate came at his own hand? The bitterest pill.

Soft breezes lushed through budding cherry blossoms and sodden pollen drenched the fragrant air. I wanted to believe what they say—how the wind is everyone we've ever known. I wanted to believe that the goosebumps on my skin weren't because temperatures plummeted but because I was part of a greater collective. Jacob, my mother, my father—everyone I'd lost was still present in my life, as if I could will them near me by refusing to let them die. If I could keep them on this plane, I could force them to be participants in my world, and a chance to repair remained—patch up, thread needles through hearts and carry on.

I could not, of course, do any of this.

The dead stay buried.

CHAPTER NINE

Afterward, Mrs. Balfour hosted the reception at her house, which further thinned the herd. I never understood the post-burial party, mourners gathering in black to look somber while sampling cheese platters and casseroles. I appreciated the need for community and camaraderie. The world keeps on spinning with or without you. But like so many human rituals centered on ceremony, this one felt odd, awkward, a forced step in the stages of grief, which left me feeling cut off. The alienation rooted deeper than canned green beans, fried wonton shrapnel, or ruminations on Kübler-Ross.

Since the church, I'd felt a strange presence. Like with the wind at the graveyard, I wanted to assign identity to cosmic divinity, thus ruling out all things creepy-crawly, but it didn't feel like that kind of sensation. This felt real, tangible, an actual person—or persons—watching me.

We have an innate sixth sense that tells us when someone is watching us. It's steeped in our bones from caveman days to avoid ending up in the jaws of feral beasts. You can be sitting in a car and feel the driver next lane over doing it. Laundromat, supermarket, gas station. At the Balfour home, eyes circled me, predators waiting to pounce. Which left me whipping my neck around, thinking I'd catch a creeper lurking, letting their lascivious gaze linger too long. But I never did, not once. No one was watching me.

Poking around the buffet table, a smorgasbord of donated dishes, warmed-over fare consisting of various noodle pies laden with sauces out of a can, I found I didn't have much of an appetite.

I entered the dining room, a space seldom used for eating. Mrs. Balfour had set it up as a family museum, with pictures of her and Mr. Balfour, Jacob and Chloe on the sideboard, shelves, and walls. Today, these photographs served as memorial: half the people in these pictures were gone.

Out the window, on the front lawn, I saw them. At first, I didn't recognize the old man talking to Mrs. Balfour, even though I'd seen him a week earlier.

Francis.

He and Mrs. Balfour were by the long row of parked cars, two wheels tilted up on the curb, partly concealed by the hedgerow. I couldn't make out what they were saying but I could tell the conversation was not friendly. Mrs. Balfour was doing most of the talking, restrained expression teetering on explosion, repressing ballistic for the neighbors' sake. Mrs. Balfour stabbed an accusatory finger at the window where I stood. I didn't think she saw me but still felt the need to duck behind the drapes, using the taupe curtain to shield me from view. Observing their interaction, I felt like I was invading privacy, a spy. I'd never known Mrs. Balfour to lose her cool like that. She was furious, animated and gesticulating, arms swinging wild. Her face betrayed murder. She pointed up the road, into the distance where suburbia's safe confines ended and the cold, uncaring city began. Francis dropped his head, turned, and trudged toward that horizon.

The party didn't last long after that, guests dwindling down to single digits until there were none. Chloe snuck off with a friend.

I stuck around to help clean up, even though Mrs. Balfour told me it wasn't necessary. I didn't plan on pressing her about the argument with the old man. She'd looked rattled when she came back in, distraught, face colored crimson.

I wanted to alleviate her pain, not make it worse. Curiosity got the better of me.

"That man you were talking to," I said, stoking conversation. "That's who stopped by when I was leaving the other morning."

Mrs. Balfour carried a casserole dish from the buffet to the kitchen counter, opening a drawer and bringing up the aluminum foil. With focused intent, she wrapped the leftovers into a tin brick, sealing it inside a small rectangular Tupperware container. Busy work for idle hands to keep away devils. How could she stand being in this same house, so familiar yet forever altered? Like an amputee with phantom pain, would she hear Jacob pattering downstairs for a late-night snack? Music bleeding from the basement where our band used to practice? There was nowhere to hide. This home would never let her forget.

"That was Francis," she said. "Gary's father."

I had a hard time reconciling name and relationship right away.

"Jacob's grandfather," she added.

"I didn't know Jacob had a grandfather." I knew he'd had one at some point. I figured he too was dead. "He never talked about him." It wasn't just Jacob. I'd known the Balfour family fifteen years. I'd never heard *any*one mention grandparents, and certainly not this Francis character. I knew Mrs. Balfour's parents had passed when she was young. No one talked about Mr. Balfour, Gary, suicide such a taboo. Through all the years and holidays, monumental occasions and developmental milestones like confirmation and graduation, I'd never heard the name Francis. Not once.

Mrs. Balfour set the caked-on dishes to soak in the hot, soapy sink before wrapping her hands in a dishtowel. I could see she didn't want to talk about the man, her furrowed brow and grimace making it clear. I changed the subject. I asked how she was feeling. An obvious question with an obvious answer. A stupid, pointless, small-talk question. She didn't take the out, though. She came around the counter and sat at the kitchen table, patting the seat beside her. Mrs. Balfour was first and foremost a mother.

"Francis Balfour is a sick man," she said.

"Sick?" I answered, joining her.

"Same as Gary. Same as...Jacob. Unwell. Mentally unstable." She stopped to pluck the perfect works from the gray matter. "People who don't see the world for what it really is." Mrs. Balfour drummed her fingers off the table, glancing around the room, trying to locate nothing at all.

"I shouldn't have brought it up," I said. "You don't have to talk about him if you don't want to—"

"There were instances," she said. "With Francis. His behavior. When Jacob was little." You could see her rolling the words around in her brain as she attempted to explain how the family came to the decision to cut a grandfather out of the picture. Literally. No photographic evidence existed of the man. Not on the walls, not in the dining room memorial, not a single magnet on the refrigerator. Throughout all the random photo albums scattered about the house, under benches, on top of end tables, I never recollected seeing the guy. He was a ghost, a dead man walking. For Mrs. Balfour, the sweetest, kindest, most giving human being I'd ever met, the omission spoke volumes.

"Francis's behavior was counterproductive to raising children," she said. "Severing ties was not an easy decision. We used to be closer. In the end, I decided I couldn't have him around my children."

She looked at me funny when she said that.

"I understand. I know all about toxic people—"

Mrs. Balfour hopped up, returning to Tupperware leftovers. "After what Francis put Gary through as a child, with his outlandish beliefs…I couldn't watch him do that to you kids."

I remembered the unhinged reading material I'd discovered in Jacob's room. "How outlandish are we talking?"

"Paranoia. Secret agencies, puppet strings. Remember *The X-Files*?"

"The TV show?"

"Yes. Like that."

"Lizard people in the government."

She nodded. So it was the same crap Jacob was obsessed with and writing about.

"His influence on the kids, Jacob in particular, wasn't good." She caught herself, pulling up short of assigning all responsibility for the hardships endured. "I'm not blaming Francis for what happened to Jacob. My son had a predisposition. My late husband too. But Francis stoked the flames. I didn't want you kids exposed to it. I asked Francis to stay away." Mrs. Balfour shifted, rehousing salt and pepper shakers, sweeping crumbs into her palm, shaking them loose over the sink, before folding dishrags. "I don't think he even lives in New York anymore. Last I'd heard, Francis had moved west. Arizona. That was…" Mrs. Balfour paused to do the math. "Fifteen years ago?"

Right around the time I moved in.

"You haven't heard from him since?" I said.

"First time I'd heard that man's name in over a decade was when you told me he stopped by. A part of me believed he had passed away, and don't judge me for this, but I wish he had. He's malignant. A tumor. I wanted him cut out of our lives."

Mrs. Balfour, the most tolerant and forgiving person I

knew—she'd keep turning cheeks until she was dizzy. What could Francis have done that was so unforgivable? Suffering paranoid delusions wouldn't elicit this scorn. Or would it?

Mrs. Balfour caught my eye. "This isn't anything you should be worrying about, Brandon. You have your whole future to look forward to." She reached over and patted my hand. "This chapter of your life is over." She attempted a smile. "Don't let any of this define you. You take care of *you*."

I returned a sincere, pained grin, as if it would require all my strength to put this behind me, but, yes, I would do my best to honor my dead friend's memory by rising above. It was all bullshit. Yeah, I'd live my best life. I'd get what I wanted. But I wouldn't be honoring anyone but me. I owed reparations. I just wasn't sure how to make restitution, or whom to pay it to.

CHAPTER TEN

I was up early the next day, sprits brightened, raring to go. With coffee in hand and music playing on my computer—the *Garden State* soundtrack, which, despite the film's shortcomings, is a strong compilation—I was feeling myself again and ready to pack up. It hadn't been long since I'd learned of Jacob's passing, but I was starting to heal. Somehow, soon as I opened my eyes, it all felt…different, lighter. Slept well, peaceful dreams where I was floating, untouched, instead of being chased or chasing after an unattainable goal. So much of this life comes down to how you see the world. Viewpoint, perspective. Sure, I could succumb to maudlin and melancholic moods—I had my moments. But I was also in charge of my future. Take my apartment for instance, which was nothing special. I could've let its tiny size and poor location color my attitude, feel woe is me, boxed in by standard white apartment walls. But it was mine, my space, this time. This life is a gift. Sometimes all you need for the moment to hit you like that is awareness and appreciation of the present. A wave of optimism cascaded over me, the way light fell across frames, how sunshine slanted, so vibrant and creamy I could almost taste it, backed by the syncopated rhythm of a drum machine off iTunes. Possibility. That's what I was experiencing, how wide open my road was, my future undetermined. I could go anywhere, do anything. There were two thousand recent graduates who felt the same way, but I didn't let shared commonality water down the sensation. It felt unique to *me*. This was *my* story.

I felt empowered boxing up pots and pans and glasses I would drink out of in another apartment, in another town, as this next chapter of my life began.

And if I were being totally honest, a date with Sam Holahan that night didn't hurt.

I'd gotten Sam's number at Elmer's, and since then we'd had coffee twice and lunch once. I'd steered clear of talking about Jacob, the topic a complete buzzkill. Since Sam was there the night I got the call, I couldn't avoid the conversation altogether. I also didn't have to make it the focal point.

Nothing had happened on these previous coffee and lunch dates. Meaning we hadn't even kissed again. But something was happening. It was that early stage, the getting-to-know-you backstory.

I loved this part of a relationship, that uneasy, nervous, excited feeling you get in your gut when you are going to see her. I didn't mind not having sex right away. I *wanted* to, of course. If this went anywhere, it would happen. Sooner or later. I was in no hurry to get there. I'd had several girlfriends. Once you add the sex, there's no mystery left; and once it's gone, you can't get it back, and then you find you miss the mystery. I longed for the mystery. I was happy to take it slow with Sam. Maybe it wouldn't go anywhere. Maybe my last week in town ended with dinner tonight and Sam and I going our separate ways. I didn't know her plans, if they included me. I didn't know if she asked these same questions, despite her kissing me that night. Maybe she was a girl who kissed a lot of boys. The only thing I cared about right then: I had a date with a pretty girl I liked tonight. And when you have that, what else could you want?

Then came the knock on the door.

Through the peephole, I recognized Francis, Jacob's estranged grandfather and Balfour family pariah. I'd seen him twice in the span of a few days, with that last appearance still burned on my brain, the way Mrs. Balfour banished the old man. Seeing him at my door created a sense of displacement. Like when you run into an acquaintance from the gym at the grocery store or a professor inside Target.

Standing barefoot on my cool linoleum floor, I opened the door, squinting into the shining sun, wondering why this strange, unwanted old man was here.

Francis didn't exude urgency. Which I found odd. Like that bit from *Seinfeld*. You'd think the aged would be the ones most in a hurry, given the limited time they have left. He was dressed in a loose-fitting button-up as if stepping off the Jersey boardwalk, short sleeves rolled and wrapped around a pack of cigarettes. Like a hood from the 1950s: cuffed dark jeans, penny loafers, Ray Bans, silver hair slicked back—another bowling alley hipster you'd find at Starbucks at two in the afternoon working on a novel they'd never finish. But he owned the look, I had to give him that. However old he was, Francis still carried himself a lot cooler than I'd ever be.

"Saw you the other day, remember?" he said without offering a hand.

"I know who you are."

"And I'm guessing Lori's warned you to stay away from me."

I didn't respond.

That made Francis chuckle. "What did she say about me?" He had a voice like a beat-up pick-up truck caught between gears.

The fierce sun beat on my face, its bright stream incriminating, putting me on the defensive, like the hot light in a precinct.

"She said you were sick." I didn't like being so blunt but I couldn't see much, my good mood interrupted. I wanted the guy gone.

"She might have a point." He nodded past my shoulder. "Mind if we talk inside?"

I did. I was in the middle of packing, riding high on tonight's date with Sam, and whatever Francis had to say, I didn't want to hear. Plus, he was smoking a cigarette, which stank. Smokers don't realize that smell never leaves; it attaches to their person. I also eschewed confrontation.

"Fine. But you can't smoke in here."

"You can't smoke anywhere anymore, boy." He flicked his butt over the rails.

When Francis breezed past, I caught his scent. Not cigarettes so much. More old man aftershave, Old Spice or Brut, one of those cheap colognes nobody under eighty buys anymore. Strangely, the scent evoked a pleasing wave of nostalgia for a time that never existed. Which left me wondering how I had associated the smell emanating off Francis with anything positive. Other than pop culture having its way with me, a cool detective or badass cowboy.

Standing in the middle of my kitchen, which was growing sparser with each passing day—packed boxes, Sharpie-labeled bags—Francis took in the college student décor; I'd never bothered to spruce up the place. I wasn't rolling in money, and I didn't entertain enough women to invest the time. I'd spent more than a few winters riding the ramen train until the next student loan check cleared. All my furniture was discounted, picked up at either Goodwill or off the curb, walls adorned with tacked-up movie posters—discarded ones they gave out at theaters at the end of runs. And since my favorite local cinema recycled decades-old B-flicks, there was a lot of Don Johnson, Virginia Madsen, and Tom Hanks before he was famous.

"Can I get you something to drink?" I didn't want the guy to stay, but Mrs. Balfour had raised me to be polite and respectful of my elders, which, at that moment, was ironic, given how much she disliked the man.

"Got any whiskey?" he said.

"It's ten in the morning."

"Beer?"

"I was thinking more like coffee, but, yeah, I think I have a beer left." I couldn't even remember how the beer had gotten there. Maybe this past Super Bowl when a couple guys from statistics came over to watch the Patriots win. Again.

I retrieved the final overpriced IPA that had been sitting in my fridge, untouched since February.

Francis snatched it from my hand, pulling back to study the label, scowling, as if I'd passed him the Koran in Korean. "Extra hoppy?" It wasn't a question, more a spat-out admonishment. Then he shook his head at me like I was the black sheep son heading back to art school, forever disappointing.

"Why are you here?" I asked. Which lacked tact, but I was starting to see why Mrs. Balfour didn't like him. While Francis hadn't demonstrated any behaviors that would've led me to say he was sick, the man exuded abrasive, rude, uneducated, ignorant, and irksome. Showing up this early without first calling? No email? I didn't care that he didn't know my email address or have my phone number. You don't show up at someone's house, asking for alcohol at ten in the morning.

He set down the can of beer on my kitchen table next to a pair of puzzles I'd been working on, one a sudoku, the other a crossword, avoiding the several coasters.

"You like puzzles," he said. Again, statement not question, and one with an obvious answer since I had two of them two feet away.

"A hobby of mine."

The old man scoffed, picked up his beer. "You were Jacob's friend."

"I knew Jacob, yes."

"I didn't ask if you knew him. I asked if you were his friend."

He hadn't *asked* anything. As I mentioned, I avoided confrontation. I'd get into it if I had to, and then God help you—I had a temper, inherited from dear ol' Dad. Until tripped, however, I treated life like Bruce Banner on a breezy, uneventful day. Stay calm. Don't get heated. Don't get mad.

"Yes," I said, annunciating. "I was Jacob's friend."

"Good."

Francis sat at the table before I offered a seat, a breach of etiquette, whipping something from his back pocket. I didn't flinch. Not like I thought an old man had come to my house to whack me. But Francis treated it like I had flinched, smirking. Which pissed me off. I hadn't flinched. He showed his hands, laying down what he'd come to share, smoothing it out with exaggerated peaceful pats. Jerk.

A copy of *Illuminations*, Jacob's lunatic fringe zine.

"Yeah. I know all about it. So what?" I stopped. "Where did you get that?" I'd seen the police carting out all the copies, evidence cataloged after his death.

"You read it?" he asked, ignoring my question.

Studying Francis, I found his insanity's tell, the tip-off that the man wasn't all there. It was in the eyes. They were screwy, hyper focused. Like he could see deep into the defective parts of your soul. Creeped me out.

I nodded. I knew what he was going to ask next, hoping he wouldn't. Because there was no right answer. Jacob was gone. What did it matter what I thought about his descent into madness?

Outside, a bus pulled past my apartment complex. Through the slated window, I could make out a long advertisement. Dentist. Or maybe music festival. Junk removal? I didn't care. I wanted to be on that bus, headed wherever it was going, shipping far away from this conversation.

"I hadn't spoken with Jacob." The words trailed from my mouth with more remorse than I'd intended.

"Didn't ask if you'd talked to him," Francis said. "I want to know what you think of his magazine."

"It's called a zine. Photocopied and self-published. Magazines have publishers, fact checkers, distributors." I hoped he caught my meaning: gatekeepers ensure quality, merit. This was an arts and crafts project. But Francis's stare only intensified, that penetrating gaze unwavering. "What do you want me to say, man? Yes, Jacob and I used to be friends. Yes, I read his crazy rantings. He wasn't well. It's sad. I feel bad I wasn't a better friend. It's too late to do anything about that now."

"Feeling bad won't do a damn thing, boy. You want to make it up to him, here's your chance." Francis swilled his beer. "Jacob didn't kill himself. He was murdered."

Sam and I had reservations for Delmonico's at seven. Granted, that was nine hours away, but those plans hinged on my getting back in the right headspace. I didn't want to be thinking about any of this. Did I think Jacob committed suicide by throwing himself down a gravel pit before setting himself on fire? No. Probably not. I didn't know. The police said it was an accident, I had to accept that. It was weird, sure, but *Jacob* was weird. If he went off his meds, I wasn't placing any fate outside the realm of possibility. More importantly, I wasn't throwing my hat in the ring with a headcase like Francis. I wanted to focus on Sam. Shower, pack, and take a nap. I regretted opening the door.

Francis opened *Illuminations*, his copy worn and tattered

from having been folded too many times. He poked a finger at the table of contents.

"I said I read it. It didn't make any sense. Not sure what you want me to say. Jacob was delusional when I knew him. He got worse. That—" I gestured in the general direction of the zine "—only proves it."

"Yeah," Francis replied, pedantic and bored. "The world is round. Vaccines don't cause autism. *All* food is genetically modified at this point. Ever see what a banana is supposed to look like?"

"Banana? What—?"

"You're not as smart as you think, boy."

I checked the clock on the microwave, letting my stare linger, hoping Francis would take the hint. He did not. If anything, my pause gave him time to gather his thoughts and present a more unified presentation.

"These writings got my grandson killed."

"Writings? It's a cut-and-paste job from a guy who barely graduated high school." I felt bad being dismissive and speaking ill of my dead friend, but I wasn't going to legitimize ignorance and debate whether windmills caused cancer, not with a geriatric Sherlock Holmes.

"You're right. A lot of my grandson's work stretched the limits of logic. He was also young, still learning how all this worked." Francis stopped. "But just because you're paranoid doesn't mean they aren't out to get you."

"What the hell is that supposed to mean?"

"Something he wrote got him killed."

I opened my palms—*Okay, show me the proof.* His suggestion preposterous, baseless.

"My grandson called me the day before they found his body."

My friend had been missing for as long five days. If true, that meant Francis had spoken with him just before he fell in that quarry...

"Does Mrs. Balfour know this?"

"I told her, yes."

Why didn't Mrs. Balfour mention that part to me? Then again, she had so much on her mind. Why should she devote even a fraction of her effort to more unfounded nonsense?

"Did you tell the police?" I asked.

"That Jacob had called me? Yeah, I told 'em."

"And?"

"And they looked like you're looking at me now. I ain't lying. Jacob stumbled on a secret, if by accident. It got people scared, and they came after him. Jacob caught a bus out of Utica, headed west, told me he was being followed and that he was headed for the border."

"Mexico?"

"Canada. Tried to get across. Border Patrol turned him away. He had too much money and jewelry on him. Nine grand. I asked what was happening. He said he didn't think he should tell me, that it would put me in danger too."

"Money and jewelry? What are you talking about?"

Francis shrugged off my questions, as if they were trivial and insignificant.

"Mrs. Balfour said no one in the family speaks with you."

"I talked to Jacob. He was on the run."

What could I say to that? Riches and gold? A fugitive? I hopped up and opened the door into the blistering sun.

The old man pushed himself to his feet, stopping in front of me, eye to eye. Despite his age, he was pretty imposing. I was almost six feet, a lean one eighty. When Francis brushed past, I saw he had me by at least a couple inches and maybe twenty pounds, a barrel-chested old man whittled from hard bone and forged steel.

I stood at the door waiting for him to leave. Francis crammed the folded copy of *Illuminations* back in his pocket, returning with a scrap of paper, which had a number scrawled on it. He slapped the note in my hand.

"In case you change your mind. I'm staying at the Best Western. Center of town."

I smiled, nodded, thanked him for stopping by, and said to have a nice day. Then I slammed the door. I wasn't changing my mind about anything, and the last person I was seeking out was Francis Balfour.

CHAPTER ELEVEN

After Francis left, I debated calling Mrs. Balfour. The visit was disturbing, alarming. Maybe by speaking with her, I could help quell her concerns. Here was this man, whom she hadn't heard from in years, claiming he'd spoken to her son a couple days before he died. That is, if Francis could be trusted. Who was to say he wasn't full of it and off his rocker?

I decided it wasn't worth the gamble. Any remedy Francis offered would surely come with twice the dose of poison. What was I going to tell her anyway? Nothing about Francis's visit offered remedy. It was pure conjecture on his part. In fact, even *if* true—and I was skeptical—Francis's theory of rogue darts hitting a conspiratorial mark would only further agitate, inducing more questions with no definitive answers. The opposite of what Mrs. Balfour needed. She needed closure, not crackpot diatribes masquerading as hope to prolong the misery.

I returned to the kitchen table to try to solve the puzzles I'd been working on. Solving puzzles had always been a great distraction, a soothing detour that allowed me to get out of my head, turn off the wheels, get my brain to go radio silent by focusing on a singular task. The diversionary tactic had worked ever since I was a boy. It did not help today. Words I should've known eluded me. I prided myself on my ability to solve crosswords, especially earlier-in-the-week puzzles before the weekend presented more of a challenge. After I failed to figure out an easy clue for Cathode Ray—an answer I only got after frustration sent me searching the internet, an amateur move—I decided to call Utica PD.

I asked to speak with Rachael Lourey, the detective I'd met at the Balfours. She wasn't in. I left a message, inquiring whether they'd found any cash or jewelry as Francis claimed.

I went back to wrapping all the knickknacks I'd acquired over the years. I had several of these little tchotchkes—tiny glass dogs, plastic people, imaginary villages. An odd hobby of mine, well, more habit. Anytime I encountered a discarded toy or figurine— small ones that could fit in my pocket—I'd pick it up. Now I had entire shelves of these lost children's toys, miniature villages with tiny cars, buses, and little trains that ran on time. I tried to remember when this hobby first started. I couldn't recall. It was when I was young, I knew that.

In the last year alone, my collection had grown exponentially. Walking to campus produced a veritable treasure trove. A quick panic flashed: what if things went well tonight and I ended up bringing Sam back to my place? She walks in a sees a grown man who keeps dolls?

I swept them all into a trash bag. Entire cities destroyed with the merciless fury of a tsunami. I cinched the trash bag and tossed it into the closet with the rest of the belongings I'd be taking to Syracuse. Then I stomped the bag further, stuffing it deeper among earthly possessions, past the clothes already boxed and the manila envelopes stuffed with old papers—social security card, birth certificate, passport. Closing the closet door felt like an accomplishment.

When I walked back in the kitchen, I saw Jacob's zine *Illuminations* by the front door. It must've fallen out of Francis's back pocket. I picked it up, crumpled it, dropped it on top of the trash receptacle. Then I plucked it back out. I didn't buy into Francis's rogue theories—the police weren't incompetent—but I *wanted* to believe something or someone was responsible. Murder didn't change the end result—dead was dead and Jacob was gone—but having a finger to point and feet to lay the blame meant there would be accountability. Justice.

Smoothing out the crumpled papers, I reread the zine. My impression of it hadn't changed. Nothing registered as more accurate or truer than last time. Total cracker-jack noise. Vast global conspiracies. Radiation fallout from blown Japanese reactors tainting the world's fish supply, mercury and isotopes in your sushi. Everyone in on it. It was heartbreaking to read. Wasted potential aside, these stories highlighted a little boy terrified, scared to breathe the air around him because a nefarious, unseen entity, part of this larger conglomerate, this sinister global machination whose sole function it was to profit at another's expense, was out to destroy him. Food, sky, radio waves. All malicious, all hellbent on his destruction, all invincible. How horrible was Jacob's life? He lived in constant fear, forever battling a relentless, invisible, indefatigable enemy. No wonder he killed himself.

Then I saw it again. The Shadow People. The phrase made my skin crawl and gut ache, a knife stuck and twisted. I wouldn't have read it, except this particular article cited a source. Jessiesgirl81. All I could think of was that cheesy Rick Springfield song from about a hundred years ago. They still played it on classic rock radio, which I seldom listened to.

Maybe because it was a female—the prospect that my friend wasn't so lonely—I forged ahead. The writing was dreadful, random nouns capitalized, half the words in quotes, punctuation be damned. The premise: The Shadow People had descended upon a tiny town in rural western New York called Wroughton. Never heard of it. This Jessiesgirl81 was like Jacob's star witness, insider source, having gone deep undercover to get the scoop. In the introduction, Jacob wrote they met in a chatroom on the Dark Web. It seemed to me announcing they met on illegal sites might not have been the smartest strategy. All these miscues paled in comparison to the basic premise of the piece.

The subject matter might've been the craziest of the bunch. The Shadow People were abducting people in broad daylight, and this Jessie had *seen* it, and I guess she was working with Jacob to…honestly, I didn't know what they hoped to accomplish. They couldn't go to the authorities because they sounded like idiots, but now the entire town of Wroughton was in jeopardy, the Shadow People with a taste for human flesh. It was at that point I couldn't take any more.

I started to crumple the pamphlet back up but stopped. I uncrinkled the zine and left it on the kitchen table. No, I didn't believe it. I also didn't feel right tossing the last remnant of my friend in the garbage. So I'd take it with me, like those castoff toys I rescued from the pavement. I'd resurrect them in my new apartment, sticking it all back on a shelf, preserved and protected, so they'd never die.

CHAPTER TWELVE

Dinner with Sam couldn't have gone better. Delmonico's was one of the nicest restaurants in town. Lots of dark red curtains, deep mahogany tables with gleaming, shiny metal parts, a place that never ran out of piping hot breads and cloth napkins. Well-moisturized waiters offered multiple variations on water, still or sparkling or infused with grapefruit and other citrus essences, before running down a list of the day's specials: fresh fish plucked from the cold waters of the Atlantic; rare succulent meats slow simmered with exotic spices; crisp seasonal vegetables. Conversation came effortlessly, Sam laughing at all my jokes, leaving me to wonder how I'd managed to pull this off.

I'd always been resourceful, and I went on plenty of dates, but I couldn't remember the last time I got the girl I *really* wanted. Desire spells disaster. Anytime you want *any*thing that badly, you're bound to be disappointed. Nothing lives up to expectation. You might get what you want, but never when you want it, or how you want it; there is always a caveat, a fine-print warning label that screams, *Careful what you wish for!* Except this time what I'd wished I'd won. And I'd done so without my A game. All semester I hadn't put my best face forward with Sam. Yet, she must've seen something in me because here we were. Whatever her reason for agreeing to date me—and after two coffees, one lunch, and a dinner, I felt comfortable saying we were dating—I was basking in the afterglow of victory. Of course, when you realize what you have, you must accept what you have to lose.

After dinner, we headed to Soyka's, the hipster dive bar down the street. I'd never been a fan of anything hipster—I loathed the ghetto fabulous vibe Soyka's affected. In one of Cortland's nicer neighborhoods, the bar was trying too hard to come across as "street" or "hood" or whatever other vernacular the it-kids used these days to approximate hard-earned style points without taking any of the hits. These efforts rendered the place inauthentic, a poser trying too hard, like that friend from L.A. who casually drops the name of the B-actor who shared a dry cleaner with his mom. Made me sick. All the guys with ironic mustaches and tiny hats, girls strutting around with sailor dresses, stamped with Ed Hardy tattoos, twirling and strutting, acting cutesy or tough or whatever role they were adopting for the night.

I wasn't drinking, unless a pear cider counts. Sam wanted a rum and Coke. The bar strove to project low rent but their prices were still inflated—beer poured in mason jars and served with an assortment of olives on tiny plates for fifteen bucks. You could get the same drinks at the liquor store next door for half the price.

It was crowded for a weeknight, especially now that the semester was over. This wasn't a university town where students returned home for break—SUNY Cortland was a commuter school just this side of a community college. I didn't think there were enough townies to fill a place like Soyka's on a random Tuesday night.

I was standing at the counter to order us a round, Sam at a back table we'd secured. I looked over the line. Most of the patrons were on the older side, closer to forty than my age. I didn't recognize anyone. Not a shocker. I'd been in this town for several years and, outside of school and the hospital, I didn't know many people.

Springsteen on the jukebox. Springsteen was always on any time I braved one of these townie bars. I didn't know the name of the song—they all sounded alike to me. It was the one about never surrendering. Which killed me. Guy was a billionaire. Easy for him to say. Go back to your mansion and take a bubble bath in your boat-sized tub, check your financial portfolio investments. How that guy kept selling himself as a blue-collar man of the people was one of life's enduring mysteries.

From down the end of the bar, I felt it, the way you can tell whenever someone is staring at you, the uneasy sensation it creates. At first, I couldn't isolate the source of my discomfort. I began to squirm, a bug under the magnifying glass.

When I turned, I saw him.

He caught my eye. I stared right back. Usually when you do that, the other person steps off. Not this guy. He wasn't any bigger than I, wasn't that much older, maybe mid-thirties, with a cop mustache and scruff, but he didn't come across like a cop. I waited for him to break off the stare but he didn't. A stupid show of machismo, I knew. But no guy likes to be the one seen backing down. Uncomfortable as it was, I intensified my gaze, aware of the beads of sweat forming on the back of my neck. Finally, he turned away. My relief didn't last long. His attention fixed on Sam, who had to be wondering what was taking me so long. That's what this was about? Sam. Some jackhole moving in on my date, mad because I was having drinks with a woman like Sam Holahan and he was at the bar alone, probably twice divorced and unemployed. Then I caught *another* guy doing the same. Sam to me, me to Sam. Thankfully, the bartender asked what I was having, which gave me an excuse to bail on the pissing contest with these two clowns as I pretended to be engrossed in getting my order right.

When I got back to Sam, I set down the drinks and, without

seeing if either jerk was still watching, planted one right on Sam's lips. A deep, lustful kiss full of passion, which caught her by surprise. I wasn't much for public displays of affection, but I really laid it on, open mouth, hot and heavy.

After we caught our breath, Sam and I attacked our drinks. Well, she did. I nursed the single cider. She pounded her rum and Coke like a shot.

"What do you say we get out of here?" I nodded over my shoulder. "My place is just up Stuart. Not far. We can walk. A few blocks."

Sam searched the bar, biting her lip. "I have to get up early—"

"Come on," I said, turning up the charm. "One drink?" When she didn't bite, I added, "Dessert? I think I have Oreos." I was alluding to that stupid comment I'd made at the vending machine that first night, but it made her giggle.

"I guess…one drink."

I hadn't been thinking of how to get her in bed. I was enjoying the night, taking it slow. I also wasn't ignoring the signs. She was clearly into me, if that kiss had been any indication.

When we got outside, I extracted a twenty from my wallet, nodding at the liquor store across the street. "You want to grab something to drink? I don't have much in my apartment." I recalled the lone beer Francis drank the other day. I motioned to the alley behind Tremont Street. "I have to get my car."

"I thought you lived nearby."

"I do."

"Your car's fine where it is."

"I'd rather park in my lot." That was true. I didn't explain the other part, how when things weren't where they were supposed to be, it made me restless. Not panicky. More…unsettled. It was hard for me to concentrate when my possessions were in disarray. I appreciated routine and order.

She redirected her attention on the liquor store. "What kind of alcohol?"

"Whatever you want."

I assured her I'd be right back and began walking up the alley behind Delmonico's.

A brisk walk on a cool evening, holding hands with Sam, would've been nice. But I hadn't had much to drink and figured I might as well put my car back where it belonged. There's nothing wrong with liking things the way they are supposed to be. Cohesion, logic, order, routine—these are signs of stability, not neurosis.

In the shadows of the back alley, I turned around and watched Sam crossing the street, heading into the liquor store. Bathed in pink neon, backlit by brighter fluorescents, she cast a long shadow. With each step that shadow warped and twisted until it was rendered unrecognizable.

When I turned back around, that distortion lingered as the ally in front of me seemed to stretch further, walls expanding, a cheap gimmick in a horror flick, a room elongated as the camera pans in fast on its subject but the background remains still, Sheriff Brody after seeing Jaws. I assured myself my mind was playing tricks on me—I wasn't buzzed off a single pear cider I'd barely touched. Yet, with each step, I couldn't shake the feeling that I was walking farther than I'd parked. I felt my pulse quicken and that made me angrier. My own stupid brain was creating the problem, internal conflict conspiring to create illusion and confusion. I had zero patience for idiosyncratic mental quirks, and hated feeling at the mercy of anything other than my own conscious thoughts.

The night turned hot, winds rustling leaves, sweeping them up in tiny, dirty tornados, and scattering debris from out of the big blue bins. A raccoon the size of a small child climbed from the trash, reared on hind legs, hissing. I hastened my pace as the ally stretched ever farther. The narrowed, tunnel vision mimicked being sucked deeper into an MRI tube, a discomforting sensation that sparked an odd, tangential memory of when Jacob and I were kids, horsing around after hours at the construction site beyond our cul-de-sac. They had all these concrete tubes, maybe ten, fifteen feet long, about two feet tall. I didn't know what these concrete tubes were for, but being kids, we were climbing on them, crawling through them, making a game of it. Slithering on my back, I lifted my knee too high in one these tubes and got stuck. I couldn't dislodge my leg, and the more I moved my knee, the most entrapped I became, which left me freaking out, screaming, hysterical. Jacob ran to get his mom. It didn't take long for Mrs. Balfour to come. Three, maybe five minutes. Felt like forever. Mrs. Balfour talked to me, got me to calm down, relax. Once my body wasn't so rigid, she was able to pull me out.

I didn't know why that particular memory hitched itself to my emotions or chose that moment to return. It had been a great night, which only promised to get better. Outside of those creepos macking on my date in the bar, nothing was alarming. Why was I so out of sorts? Someone was watching me.

I felt a presence—I wasn't imagining it—I kept checking over my shoulder. No one there. No silhouettes in windows. No eyes peeping over the fence or out any back door. Yet the faster I tried to walk and outrun this perspicacity, the more I suspected my second sight was dead on, my mind a finely tuned instrument of detection. I saw my Camry, but its distance from me continued to stretch, a trick of the lens. I took off my glasses, rubbed my eyes, trying to remember if I drank more than I thought. But, no, I'd had the one glass of wine at the restaurant and the cider at the bar. Maybe I'd gotten a refill? I remembered the kiss but couldn't remember if I'd ordered another. But even if I did, it was only cider. Why was it taking so long to walk to my car? I felt queasy, nauseated. For a second I thought I was going to throw up, resisting the urge. I didn't go in for masculine stereotypes, and Sam didn't strike me as the type to succumb to them either. But no woman is sleeping with a man who can't handle his cider. I could feel a presence at my back. I spun around, shuttering, flinching, shooing, as if a cluster of spiders had jumped on my neck. I couldn't catch my breath, the dark sky ebbing darker, the top of a coffin lowered, and I was suffocating…

Then it was gone. Like that. As if the problem had been the world's light bulb blowing out, and now a fresh one had been screwed in. All good. Problem solved. I could see again. What had that been about? I didn't feel drunk or buzzed or the slightest bit nauseated anymore. And when I turned around this time, the scene behind me unveiled nothing but wood, brick, and the big blue bins from the steakhouse. A refreshing breeze scuttled, offering safe passage.

Unlock door, slip key in ignition, turn down radio, easy. I pulled up the alley, trying to wrap my head around what that had been about. The best I could surmise: exhaustion at the end of a long week.

When I eased out of the alley in front of the liquor store, I saw Sam talking to one of the guys from the bar, the older cop-looking one with that stupid hipster mustache. Which spiked my blood and sent my heart pounding. I'd barely had the chance to catch my breath from my hellacious walk. Getting out, I slammed the door harder than I intended, loud enough that both spun around to stare at me as I stood quaking in the streetlight, fists clenched.

"Hey, you," Sam said, cool as could be, like nothing was wrong.

What the fuck?

The guy from the bar eyeballed me. A primitive part of me, a part I'm not proud of, went to Sam's side, wrapping an arm around her waist and pulling her close. Lamentable behavior, sure. But I wasn't getting pushed around by a hipster in a vest with a caterpillar on his lip.

"This is T," Sam said to me.

"T?" I repeated, rolling my eyes so far into my skull I saw the alley behind me. What a stupid poser nickname. T. "What?" I said. "Like the drink?"

"Like the initial, man," T replied, all smiles and good sported, looking much younger than I'd pegged him for in the bar. "Short for Anthony." He made like he was offering to shake my hand.

Nice try.

I jammed my hands in my pockets. I wasn't going to be the one to rise above and be the bigger man. This asshole had been fronting on me in the bar, waiting for us to leave, and as soon as we split up for *a second*, he's there, moving in.

"What took so long?" Sam asked me.

"Huh?"

"Getting your car," she said. "You were gone for twenty minutes."

"No, I wasn't."

We all stood there awkwardly. Sam alternated looks between T and me. She must've been able to pick up on my hostility. But she hadn't seen the way this jerk was trying to stare me down in the bar.

Sam grabbed my hand and shook it, calling my attention. "T said there's a party on Dumas."

T smirked. Snaggle-toothed bastard.

"And you want to *go*?"

"Why not?" Sam said, tugging my hand. "It'll be fun."

"No, I'm good," I said. At that, I considered the matter closed.

Sam wasn't going off with another guy to a party. We were on a date.

"What about you, Sam?" he said.

"She's good too," I said.

Sam snatched back her hand, and I knew I'd screwed up.

I couldn't explain to Sam what T was up to, not in the spot we were in, and he knew it.

I tried to fix the situation but managed to screw it up more. "I thought you had to get up early? That's what you told me in the bar."

"I got a second wind," Sam said. Her tone was confrontational, adversarial, like we were enemies.

"Yeah," I said. "Well, I do have to get up early. So…" Which wasn't true, but she was the one who'd issued curfews. *Now* it's party time?

"Thanks for dinner, Brandon," Sam said.

Thanks for dinner? That's it? Not, "Okay, Brandon, let's stick to our original plan, go back to your place, and continue what's been a nice evening." Fine. If that was the way she wanted it.

"I should get some sleep," I said. I didn't want to get some sleep—I wanted to keep hanging out with Sam, but I'd gone too far now. I couldn't backtrack. Sam wasn't my long-term girlfriend. I couldn't say, "Hey, let's head home." I'd gambled that if given the choice between this joker and me, she'd pick me. I lost.

"Come on," T said to her. "You can roll with me."

Roll with me? *Okay, Del Amitri.* What an asshole.

And Sam left. The entire time she was walking away, she kept stealing glances over her shoulder. I didn't know if she was expecting me to put up more of a fight. What was I supposed to do? Challenge the guy to a fistfight? Duel at dawn? Apologize? I folded my arms and stood my ground. She wanted to party, have at it.

I waited in that street awhile, feeling like I'd been gut punched.

I should've just gone to the stupid party. I wasn't thinking straight. It was that alley. It got me all twisted around.

When I got back in my car, I cranked the radio, and that stupid song by Imagine Dragons, "Thunder," came on, which I fucking hated. I smacked the dash so hard, a shiver shot from wrist to elbow. I could feel a crack, cartilage wrenched, ulna stinging with hot needles. It hurt so bad I wondered if I'd fractured the carpel bones. I wiggled my hand. I could still move it.

The physical pain paled next to the hurt I felt inside. I was such a moron. That T had played me. He'd waited for me to slip up to swoop in. All semester I'd angled for a chance with Sam Holahan. I finally get one, and this happens?

Parking my car in the garage, I walked to my complex, up the stairs to my apartment, where I found my door ajar. I'd been in a rush to meet Sam but not so much of a rush I'd forgotten to lock my door. My place was in an okay section of town, but not so okay you went around leaving doors unlocked.

I pushed it open, flicking the lights, looking for…what? I still had that freak-out in the alley on my mind, the fresh sting of humiliation outside the liquor store, my right hand throbbing from where I'd punched the dashboard. I plucked the biggest knife I had from the cutting board, slinking room to room, pushing open doors, checking inside closets and under the bed like the final girl in a slasher flick. Nothing. No one. I didn't see anything missing. What did I have worth stealing?

After exhausting my search like a melodramatic dope, I returned the knife to its home, dropping in a seat at the kitchen table. I was getting as loopy as Jacob. My stare fell to the kitchen table and I realized something *was* missing.

Jacob's zine, *Illuminations.*

Goddamn Francis. Like I wanted that crap in my house in the first place.

I caught my breath. I was getting all worked up. I could feel my temperature rising. Deep breaths. *Stay cool, Brandon.*

I was not racing across town at midnight to a Best Western to wake a crazy old man so I could yell at him. You want your magazine back so bad, Francis? Have at it. Then stay the hell away from me.

CHAPTER THIRTEEN

When I got to Ledgecrest for my shift, Mrs. Talbot, the hospital's director, called me into her office and asked me to close the door. It's never a good sign when the boss asks you to close the door.

Mrs. Talbot told me to have a seat. I tried not to overreact. I was an exemplary employee, always willing to take an additional shift or go the extra mile, doing whatever was asked of me.

"Are you all right?" she asked. "You look tired."

"Trouble sleeping."

My boss didn't say anything after that, which left me looking around her office, a sad sight. These were the aspects of the convalescent industry I tried to ignore—the underfunded touches that highlighted America's healthcare deficiencies, especially where the elderly were concerned, how one's worth, welfare, and well-being hinged on the size of their savings account. Ledgecrest wasn't making bank off the private insurance of the wealthy. This was a small facility, with most of the patients on one form of government assistance or another. Ledgecrest catered to a particular demographic, mostly locals of modest means whose families couldn't take care of them anymore. Administrators like Mrs. Talbot—who wasn't far from retirement herself—were not rich. The woman had been working at the hospital most of her life, paycheck-to-paycheck paltry, small office reflecting that.

Dusty souvenirs sat in dustier corners, keepsakes picked up during yearly sojourns to Lake George or Lake Champlain, Niagara Falls, travel destinations within driving distance. Coffee mugs, heavy on word play, World's Best Grandma and inoffensive eldercare puns, sat between the brood of grandchildren in cutesy picture frames.

"Brandon," she said, calling my attention back to the moment, as if I'd been drifting. "Did you talk with Mr. Johnson the other day?"

"I try to speak with each patient every day." Which was true. I did my best to reach out, take the time to touch base, excluding no one.

I wore this attention to detail as a source of pride. Yet, Mrs. Talbot's face squinched sour, demonstrating she did not share my enthusiasm, as if my selflessness were a display of overzealousness or, worse, ego. Normally, I liked my boss. Mrs. Talbot was older, stuffy, not flexible, but I believed she was a good person and competent supervisor. In that moment, however, I didn't like her and found her managerial acumen lacking. I could feel an admonishment coming on. She was about to chastise me for doing a *good* thing.

Mrs. Talbot tented her fingers, an officious posturing that grated with its pretentiousness. "We feel like you are making it too personal with Mr. Johnson."

We? There was no one else there.

"I was talking with the other nurses," Mrs. Talbot said, clarifying her statement.

"Who?" Mary, Sandy, and Dorian all liked me.

"Mr. Johnson had another episode this morning."

"He had an episode the other day too. That's why I went to speak with him. To make sure he was okay."

"Acknowledged," Mrs. Talbot said, wielding that particular word like a dart. "Today, he had to be sedated. The initial dose did not work. He grew agitated, and we had to administer a higher dose. At his age, a man like Galen Johnson carries greater risks." Mrs. Talbot slowed her diction. Like I was a patient she needed to placate. Like I didn't understand the risk of medications and sedatives. "You know hospital protocol, Brandon. You chose to undermine authority and violate that protocol."

"Who complained?"

"That is not important."

I tried to recall which nurse was on duty that day. I thought it was Mary. But Mary liked me best. I was closer to Mary than I was any other nurse. Mary gave me a card on my last birthday and a pair of jokey socks with lots of puzzles because she knew I liked puzzles.

"Brandon, we've talked about playing favorites—"

"I'm not playing favorites—"

"There is a reason we don't want to challenge patients' delusions. Galen Johnson has dementia. He is old. Pushing back on his delusions can have catastrophic repercussions."

"I am well aware of—"

"Telling him he was wrong challenges his perceptions. Again, against hospital policy. We want to keep patients calm, reassure them, make them feel safe—"

"I tried to connect with him on a deeper human level. Maybe others should be following that lead. We are in a business of compassion, aren't we?"

"Compassion?" Mrs. Talbot inhaled bull-like through her nose. "Do you know his insurance ran out? We keep him here because he has nowhere else to go. Housing a patient who is not paying for a bed, food, shelter. Don't tell me about compassion. He is very ill. He won't last the year—"

94

I stiffened my posture, folding my arms, head high. "I'm sorry, Mrs. Talbot. I don't think I did anything wrong."

Mrs. Talbot reached in her desk, retrieving an envelope. It had the Ledgecrest insignia stamped in red, off kilter, a shoddy job at a quick printer. Unprofessional. That's the problem with this country. No one takes pride in their work.

She placed the envelope on the table and slid it forward.

"What's this?"

She pursed her lips. "We think it's for the best if we conclude your employment."

"Will you stop saying 'we'? There is no 'we.' We are the only ones here, Carol." Normally, I wouldn't address a superior that way. "You're firing me?"

"No."

"Sounds like you are."

Mrs. Talbot's face washed sympathetic. Phony. It was her grandma expression, offering a second helping of chocolate chip pancakes to soothe a hypersensitive child. "You were planning on leaving in another week anyway. We are paying you for your time." Mrs. Talbot grinned. "You aren't losing any money—"

"This isn't about money."

Mrs. Talbot glanced around her tiny office as if searching for a clock, but she knew damn well what time it was.

"Fine." I snagged the envelope and stuffed it in my back pocket. "I'd at least like to say goodbye."

"We don't think that's a good idea."

Not a good idea? I'd cleaned up after these people for the past seven years, since I was a sophomore in high school. Emptied their bedpans, given them sponge baths—I'd been a friend and caretaker—I'd been more of a family to them than their own family had been. Now this woman was going to deny me a last chance to say goodbye? Extract me from their lives without *any* acknowledgment?

Mrs. Talbot stood, ignoring my simple, reasonable request, reaching over the desk for a handshake. "You've been a good employee. If you need a recommendation, don't hesitate to ask."

I stared at her, jaw clenched, teeth grinding over the injustice. I dropped my haunches. There were other hills to die on.

"And best luck at Syracuse," she added.

When I got to the door, I pointed down the hall. "Is it all right if I get my belongings out of the locker?"

"Of course."

I made toward the lockers, stole a quick glance back, then darted down the hall to Mr. Johnson's room.

He was sitting up in bed, looking gaunter and frailer than the last time I'd seen him. An old man, Mr. Johnson wasn't expected to look spry, but today his skin slacked off his skull, melted cheese congealed, and his eyes sank deeper in their sockets. His intense gaze fixed straight ahead, at a spot on the wall. I followed his line of sight but nothing was there.

"Mr. Johnson?"

He turned his head, slow and deliberate. It took a while for his eyes to find me, as if he were searching out fabled lands across murky waters. A smile came to him. It was weak and tired. "Brandon." The way he said my name made my heart break, as though this would be the last time we'd ever speak.

"Hey, Mr. Johnson. I wanted to say goodbye."

"I heard. Some of the nurses were complaining that you were too nice to me." He laughed and coughed at the same time, spitting out gobs of dark yellow phlegm lodged in his trachea. He covered his mouth with part of the bed sheet, wrapping up the mucus and whatever other decay raged inside. Someone needed to change his bedding, but I didn't have time.

I checked down the hall for Mrs. Talbot. I could hear the faraway echo of footsteps.

"I'm off to grad school anyway, Mr. Johnson."

"Since this is your last day. Do me a favor? Call me Galen."

I laughed, and he glanced at me oddly. I had to assure him I wasn't making fun of him. "A friend of mine—the woman who raised me—says the same thing. I don't know why it's so hard for me to use first names."

I waited for Mr. Johnson to laugh too. I was making a joke. But he didn't laugh. Instead, his face washed grave and concerned.

"That's because you're scared to get attached, son."

His words were an obvious observation. Anyone aware of my personal history could've said the same. Hearing them today felt like I'd been run over by a bus.

"It's okay," he said. "People always leave, don't they? That's life. Saying goodbye. You say goodbye to me today. Tomorrow? Who knows? Maybe I say goodbye to everyone else."

"Don't say that, Mr.—Galen."

He waved me off. "I'm not scared of dying. You live long enough, death stops hanging over your head. You accept it as part of life." He looked around his room, at the wires and machines hooked up, lines running to his veins, pumping life-nourishing fluids, prolonging the inevitable.

I heard the footsteps again, closer now. I didn't want to waste what little time I had left. Why does it always seem we are racing against clocks?

I thought I heard "Brandon" from down the hall.

"Come here, boy," he whispered, beckoning me nearer. I leaned my ear next to his mouth. His breath was hot and rank. I could smell the bacteria taking root, the fungus winning territory, staking claim, refusing to abandon its spoils.

"Watch out, boy. The Shadow People are on to you now."

I pulled back, studying his face, waiting for him to snicker at his joke. It had to be a joke. But he didn't laugh, just stared at me with those deep-set old man eyes, like they could see right through my flesh and sinew, past my marrow and beyond organs, to pluck something precious from the furthest reaches of my soul.

A cold hand clasped my arm.

CHAPTER FOURTEEN

When I walked outside the rest home, I saw the boy in blue.

Kid, teen? Young man? Shabby, wiry, he wore a padded blue coat, overkill considering the temperature. He stood across the street, staring at me. I couldn't pin down his age—he couldn't be much younger than I was. Eighteen, maybe. Kids that age don't always have down social graces. He didn't intimidate me. I almost stomped across the street to ask what his problem was, the way he stood there gawking. It was rude. But I didn't. Because I was self-aware enough to understand what was happening. I was pissed—pissed at getting fired, pissed at the personal slight—and I wanted to scream. So here was this poor, dopey kid who had the misfortune of being at the wrong place at the wrong time, this scruffy-faced urchin who looked homeless, burdened with a heavier load than I would ever know. Instead of confronting the boy, I stared him down until he walked on, along the train tracks that ran through the tall grasses and reeds of the trestles, vanishing in the fields of mud and bone.

This wasn't about a homeless kid.

I knew a better place to direct my rage.

When I pulled up in front of the Best Western, aiming to unload on an old man, I accepted my aggression was still misplaced—I wanted to be mad at Mrs. Talbot or my coworkers. But Francis *had* jimmied my lock. He'd broken into *my* apartment. I didn't care if he'd dropped *Illuminations* by mistake. It's called manners. I'd have been happy to return the zine. If he'd have contacted me during normal hours, left a note, come back later. At a time that worked for me. He'd made the mistake of leaving it behind; he could wait to remedy the situation.

For all these reasons, I may've pounded extra hard on the motel door. I wasn't aware how hard until the maid on the landing whiplashed my way. I stopped banging and waved back, hoping to convey a misunderstanding.

The door pulled inward. The old man stood in a pair of tidy whities, squinting, scratching his white beard scruff. Francis didn't look surprised to see me, nor did he appear self-conscious or intimidated by the man whose apartment he'd broken into. His grizzled visage seemed to welcome confrontation. He was lucky I wasn't there with the police.

I smelled liquor emanating off him, the cheap, sour, day-after kind, where inferior sugars and yeast leak out your pores. The odor was stamped in my earliest childhood memories of my birth parents, who never shied away from tying one on, regardless of the day or time.

Francis left the door open and walked to the dresser, which was littered with pant pocket treasures—spare change, cigarettes, matches, keys, crumpled receipts. He inspected a bottle of Jim Beam. It looked empty from where I stood, but apparently there was enough for a gargle and rinse. Like it was mouthwash, Francis poured what was left into his open mouth, swished it around. But he didn't spit anything out, savoring the bargain booze. Then he snatched his Winston's and a pack of matches.

"Close that," he said.

I stepped in and shut the door.

"Deadbolt too."

I locked the door, turned the deadbolt, then slid the chain over the no smoking sign. I mimed, *Good enough?* Then for fun, I pulled back an edge of the drapes, which were drawn, peeking down the landing. I didn't see anyone, not even the maid.

Francis made no move to get dressed, standing bowlegged in his stretched-out undies that barely covered his skinny old man legs. He still hadn't bothered with "hello" or asked what I was doing there, which told me he already knew why I was there. He scowled and bulled toward the sink at the end of the room.

He let the water run, heating it up before splashing his craggy, weathered face. The sink wasn't even in the bathroom, place so small. It was carved into an alcove beside a closet without any doors. In that moment, I felt sorry for the guy. His only son, dead. Only grandson, dead. Remaining family wanted nothing to do with him, and here he was taking a bath in a sink at a Best Western. Why was he still here?

The water kept running, growing hotter, more steam rising until, shrouded in a cloud, Francis began lathering up a bar of soap. Grabbing a razor, he started scraping away the scruff. Like sandpaper rubbed over a walnut. I was surprised he was using a disposable razor instead of a straight blade from the '20s.

It was up to me to get the conversation started.

"I don't appreciate your letting yourself into my apartment."

Francis kept scouring the old white dust off his old white face, silent.

"For one," I began. "It's against law. I could have you arrested." Once it came out of my mouth, I recognized the empty threat. I wasn't calling the police on the guy. Given his age and the fact he was retrieving personal property, I doubted they'd write him a citation. I was angry. And getting *angrier* by the second. Other than telling me to batten the hatches, Francis hadn't said a word.

Hadn't bothered with a feeble excuse or lame justification. Not even an "I'm sorry" as a gesture of goodwill. He leaned on the sink as hot water steamed the mirror. On his back, upper left clavicle, a tattoo of the number twenty-three nested in a crown of thorns. No clue what that faded ink on weathered blue skin signified, other than to serve as a reminder to never get a tattoo.

I found his lack of manners egregious. I didn't bother with a courtesy cough, folding my arms and steadying myself until Francis was good and ready.

He blotted his scraped face dry with a hand towel. Freed from the whiskers, he didn't look any younger. In fact, shaving produced the opposite effect since now you could see all the cracks, crevices, and craters.

Swiping his pants off the back of the toilet, he stepped into each leg before sliding over a tight plain white tee, tucking in the tails. From the high shelf, he pulled down a small suitcase, a beat-up black rolling bag. He started emptying the hotel's drawers—socks, underwear, shirts, dirty laundry. Then sat on the bed, and one by one fitted his loafers.

"Are you going to say anything?" I asked.

"I didn't break into your apartment."

"Right. Someone else picked my lock to steal that stupid zine."

Francis stared me down, conviction unwavering, daring me to call him a liar.

"Are you really telling me it wasn't you? You expect me to believe that?"

"Believe what you want to believe."

"Who else would want that stupid zine?"

"Listen, boy. For *one*, I didn't need it back." Francis unclasped his bag, rifled around the bottom, and pulled out several copies of *Illuminations*, waving them in the air. "Wasn't my only copy." He stuffed the zines back. "And I wouldn't need a refresher on the subject matter since Jacob ran most the topics by me before he wrote 'em."

"His mom told me she hasn't had contact with you in years."

"She hasn't. But I talked to Jacob all the time."

"Bullshit."

"All the time," he repeated, slowing down his diction in case I was hard of hearing or just obtuse. He hopped up, sticking a finger in my face. "Don't call me a liar again."

"I didn't call you a liar."

"Jacob wasn't sick. My grandson could see things other people couldn't. They called him sick—like they call me sick—because it's a convenient way to dismiss us, push our contributions aside, ignore the truth." He shook his head and fired up another cigarette. "We're not sick. We have our eyes open."

I pointed at the door, red streak slashed through a cartoon burning butt. "It says no smoking." Then at his rolling bag. "And since it looks like you are about to check out, I'll tell you, they're going to charge your credit card. Never mind the cancer it's giving you, a cleaning fee is a couple hundred bucks. Cigarette smoke is *very* obvious to people who don't smoke." It wasn't like me to talk this way to my elders—I believed in showing respect. This was the second time I'd done so in the same day. But I didn't like this man, didn't appreciate the wringer he'd put Mrs. Balfour and the family through; he seemed to show no regard for civility or basic decency, so why should I? He was a liar too. I wasn't this repressed, uptight goody-goody, but there are rules for a reason. It's easy to say rules are meant to be broken. It's also lazy. Like cynicism, it's the path of least resistance.

"The hotel can try." Francis swept all his toiletries into the shaving kit, which he then stuffed into the rolling bag, before zipping it shut. "I'm surprised there was anything on that card I gave them." He plucked the lone shirt left on a hanger, the button-up he'd worn to the funeral reception, a faded yellow short-sleeve that had seen too much sun and been washed too many times. Reaching in the pocket, he extracted a wad of money. "I prefer to pay in cash. Those cards have chips in them. Tracks everything you do."

In that get-up, with his silver hair slicked back and the pair of two-toned, beat-up, brown-and-cream shoes, he looked all set to hit the lanes.

I remained rooted to the floor, arms folded, still waiting for Francis to make this right.

On his way to the door, he stopped beside me, letting go the bag to place a hard hand on my shoulder. The gesture made me feel small. He wasn't *that* much bigger, but I felt diminished in his presence, like a little kid in the company of a grown-up.

"Take care of yourself, boy." He said it with such heartfelt authenticity, like he'd known me my whole life.

"That's it?" I said. "Where are you going?"

"Don't worry about it."

"Tell me the truth. If you didn't break into my apartment, Francis, then that means someone else did. My lock was picked. That zine was there, and now it's gone." I tried to match his sincere gaze. "I'm not lying."

"I don't think you're lying. That magazine I got in my bag, *Illuminations*? You think it's a bunch of gibberish. And, sure, a lot of it is far-fetched—everything isn't a plot by Big Pharma. But my grandson wasn't stupid. Jacob touched a nerve."

"How?"

"Wish I knew." Francis shook his head. "But that's why they killed him."

"Why who killed him?"

"That's what I intend to find out."

"What—where are you going? You can't just..." The whole

premise felt absurd. Jacob stumbled upon a secret worth killing to protect?

"You have my number," Francis said. "In case you need to find me. I hope you don't have to. Sorry I got you into this. You were Jacob's only friend."

"I told you we didn't talk—"

"Maybe not. But they've seen me talking to you, which means they'll be keeping an eye on you."

I didn't ask who or what "they" were.

"Don't talk to anyone," he said. "And whatever you do, don't search anything on your computer or cell because they'll be monitoring it."

He picked back up his bag and made for the handle.

Did I want to ever talk to Francis Balfour again? Hell no. Once he walked out the door, I'd be rid of him for good.

I patted my pocket, reassuring myself I still had that number, just in case.

CHAPTER FIFTEEN

Walking out into the bright sunshine of the Best Western parking lot, Ponyboy leaving the cinema, I wanted to forget all that gobbledygook about ghouls, goblins, and medicine men. At my car door, I pulled out all the crap in my pockets and tossed it in the center console so I could sit in comfort. I couldn't shake the sensation, the eyes on me.

Maids on the landings, holding their vacuum cleaners but not vacuuming; maintenance men tinkering with valves on the wall, ratcheting back and forth, going in circles, making no progress. A few spaces down, a family of five piled out of an SUV, but they didn't look like a family, facial features too disparate, a hodgepodge of low-rent character actors poorly cast in roles they had no business playing, thirty-year-olds as high school students, Scarlett Johansson as a person of color.

I knew I was thinking crazy thoughts. I knew I was being irrational. I couldn't rise above or set aside. People were watching me; this awareness, like a hall of mirrors cast back on itself, persisted as I drove away.

Beneath ribbons of wispy white clouds, crooked buildings tremored in the distance, the shape of the world felt warped, like I was viewing my surroundings from inside a goldfish bowl. When I stopped at the Price Chopper for groceries because my apartment was so barren, this sketchiness intensified. Stalking the aisles, mothers and children stopped arguing over which cereals had too much sugar. They studied me, casting judgment. Unlike the boy in blue, I had no recourse this time. Stare back, ignore them, they didn't retreat, stares lingering as I took corners.

I wasn't imagining it. *Of course* they were staring at me. Why shouldn't they? I looked cracked out, eying the supermarket like a D-list celebrity pretending he didn't want to be recognized but secretly relishing the attention, Carrot Top in a coffee shop. I'd always been grounded, persuaded by the soundest logical argument. Common sense wouldn't let me explain this away.

I'd opened a portal. In my brain. One that wasn't grounded in reality or rooted in fact, and thus was unwilling to be persuaded by logic. By entering that arena, I'd granted my subconscious license to explore, run and roam free, and it was taking me places I didn't want to go. It got even worse when I left the Price Chopper.

People waiting at bus stops but not getting on any bus. National Grid workers perched halfway up phone poles, hanging in their harnesses. A priest on the church lawn lights up a butt, takes a drag, watches me as I drive by, but he's not praying for my soul...

I'd see these street corners with a gas station or coffee shop or some other architectural landmark, and it would look *exactly* like *another* street corner I'd seen. At some other time. In some other part of town. And even though I knew—the logical, rational, sane part of me—that what I thought I was witnessing was impossible, my skin still tingled, wriggling with worms squirming beneath the surface, aching to break free for their first taste of light.

No matter how hard I tried to steer the internal conversation elsewhere, my own mind waged internal war. I swear to God I almost checked myself into the ER.

Then I remembered last night. Sam and that asshole outside Soyka's. I might come up short. I might blow this all in the end. But I was not going to lose to *that* guy. My last week in town, I needed to fix the damage. My performance outside the liquor store hadn't been my finest hour. I didn't think I'd done anything *too* egregious. I'd acted strangely, okay, but I could play my way out of that; write it off to being overwhelmed by the move. Maybe Sam would have a different recollection. Or I could convince her she was misremembering, feign surprise at her misinterpretation. I'd been wiped and ready for bed, that's all.

Having a tangible goal, if only for the short term, allowed me to refocus, a mission to remedy some of the pressure I was feeling. I called Sam from the car—it was a reasonable hour. No answer. In fact, it went straight to voicemail after one ring. Like when someone declines the call. I was being too harsh on myself. Maybe she was sleeping in or taking a nap. Then I asked myself *why* she might be sleeping in or taking a nap. *Maybe because she was up all night fucking Anthony.* Then I couldn't get that picture out of my head, the two of them, naked and writhing, him bringing her to climax with skilled precision, orgasm after orgasm, porno sex, a marathon session with a stud. The images in my head traveled beyond pornographic. Soon I had Sam with more than one guy. She'd met a bunch of other jerks at the party and now Anthony and all of them were doing things to her body that had her lost in the throes of passion. She was on her knees, giving, taking, pleasuring them all, and their eyes faced the camera, looking right at me, and she was laughing at me—they were all laughing at me—my ultimate humiliation.

What was wrong with me? I was a good guy. A *nice* guy. Women are always complaining they can't find a nice guy. Well, here I was, a nice guy. Right here, waiting, ready for the taking. But, no, it was assholes like T to whom went the spoils. I felt ready for murder.

I played music to make me calm down. Billie Eilish, The National, Lana Del Rey, older artists like Bonnie Prince Billy and Sun Kil Moon. I opened the window, feeling the sunshine, and refused to look up, accepting no surveillance machines hovered above. I was still me, Brandon Cossey. Normal, regular, good guy Brandon Cossey.

When Sam answered her door, bleary-eyed and alone, such relief washed over me, I wanted to wrap my arms around her, lift her high, spin her around.

"You're alone," I said, perhaps too gleeful.

"Um, yeah." Sam was dressed in a tee shirt and pajama pants, an ensemble she managed to make look chic with her sleep-tousled hair and drowsy gaze. Roused from a deep slumber, she looked tired, out of it, stifling a big, sleepy yawn like the wholesome college student she was.

I beamed a smile and leaned in. Sam's face scrunched up as she pulled away. I didn't take it as rejection. I'd surprised her. I kept smiling. I'm sure I looked like an imbecile. A lot had happened in the past couple hours. Losing my job. Francis. The...people...I encountered. Or rather *how* I'd encountered them, reality observed through one of those old viewfinders you score at garage sales for twenty-five cents, toys from long ago. Click, click, there's the Eifel Tower. Click, click. Now you see a camel, a barn, a donut. How could I explain my morning? The break-in. That stupid zine. Jacob, the paranoia, the dirty, awful thoughts that filled my brain without invitation.

"What are you doing here, Brandon?"

I half laughed, half spat an incredulous sigh that turned into a cough, which I couldn't stop. Sam went to the sink for water while I hunched over, laughing, coughing, trying to maintain my upbeat smile and not break character, breaching hysterical.

"Are you okay?" she asked. "Drink this. Have you slept? You look like you're strung out. Are you...high?"

"Ha! I don't do drugs! I barely drink, you know that."

"Actually," she said, "I don't know much about you at all."

That sobered me up fast. The smile I'd been fighting to maintain, gone. I fought to cultivate a positive attitude. Despite everything, including *her* behavior last night, I'd stepped up, gotten over it, moved on. Then she had to go and say that? I thought I heard rustling inside and peered past her shoulder into the apartment, which was small and collegiate, but like Sam oh so stylish and cool. Obscure indie bands and hip-hop artists pinned to the walls. I'd heard of Daniel Spaleniak and Atmosphere, of course. But they'd be foreign to most. I bet she only listened to vinyl.

"What are you looking for?"

"Nothing," I said. "You sure you're alone?"

"I already told you. No one is here." Sam folded her arms. "Why do you keep asking that? And what business is it of yours?"

What business?

Took me a good ten seconds to come around and respond. "I don't think I'm out of line asking the girl I'm dating—"

"Dating?" Sam now closed the space between us, but not for the right reason. She slapped a hand on the door, which had already begun shutting. "We hung out a couple times."

"Coffee, lunch." I waited before adding, "Dinner." I wanted that one to deliver more of a punch than it did. "We kissed!"

"Once. When we were both pretty drunk."

"I wasn't drunk. And it was twice. Last night."

"No," Sam said, drawing out the word. "*Last night*," she added with great emphasis, "you mauled me. Like an animal."

"I thought it was passionate." I couldn't have said it any sadder.

"Passion? That wasn't passion. That was possessive. You crawling all over me, breathing heavy, shoving your tongue down my throat." She stopped, and I thought for a second she might give me a chance. "And what was that macho bullshit outside the liquor store?"

"That Anthony guy was trying to get with you. In the bar, he was staring me down."

Sam shook her head. "I've known T my whole life."

"And he's probably wanted—"

"T is gay."

"What—I mean—how, what—?"

"How what? He likes boys. What's so hard to understand?"

"But in the bar. He was…eying…you…"

"One, he's gay," Sam continued, leaving me flailing. "Two, he wasn't *in* the bar. T was coming back from the hospital. His mother is sick. Cancer. Stage four. As in not going to make it. T was pretty broken up. He needed a friend last night."

"Why didn't—no one told me. If I'd known—"

"What? You wouldn't have acted like an asshole? I might've gotten around to an explanation, not that I owe you one, but you never gave me a chance before you started acting like a possessive jerk."

"I'm sorry. I didn't…"

"Listen, Brandon. I like you. I mean, I thought you were cute, and all semester I was hoping you'd get around to asking me out or at least working up the nerve to say hi. But after last night, I'm not so sure this is going to work. You're moving away, and I don't have time for—"

I took a step back, recognizing how badly I'd messed up. I needed to spin serious damage control. The way her hand gripped the edge of the door, it was shutting in my face any second. And no amount of pounding was opening it back up.

I didn't want to blow this with Sam. I liked her. I'd misread the situation, confusing the man in the bar with her grieving friend. I wished I could hit rewind, go back twenty-four hours and do the day differently. But you don't get that chance. I played the only card I had.

"Okay," I said, "I'll be honest with you."

Sam waited.

"I told you about my friend Jacob, right?"

"Yes."

"I don't think I explained it right."

I then launched into the uncut version. Same premise, same tragic ending, but this time I fleshed out the origin story, ramping up stakes, punctuated by Jacob's descent into madness. The first time I told Sam the story I didn't want her sympathy or feeling sorry for me. Now I needed it. I didn't lie. Everything I said was the God's honest, one hundred percent gospel truth. I also recognized how hard I was tugging on heartstrings. It wasn't acting. All the emotions and facts were real. When a tear welled, I didn't do anything to suppress it.

When I finished, I said nothing. This was a man throwing himself on the mercy of the court. Didn't get more vulnerable than that.

Took a moment but Sam opened the door and hugged me.

"I'm sorry," I said. "It's no excuse. I'm screwed up right now. The Balfours, my parents." Pause. "Jacob." I didn't mention crazy old man Francis or grappling with bouts of paranoia, since I didn't see how that would help my cause. "I'm not thinking right." I broke free of the embrace, playing stoic, noble. I thumbed over my shoulder, in the vague direction of where my car might be parked. "I understand if it's too much for you. We just met. It's not fair of me to dump all this on you. Jacob was like a brother to me, and now he's dead..." I left it there.

"No, I get it," she said, making it clear I'd struck the right chord. "I have a friend. Kara. Who is…sorta a lost cause. But she's like a sister."

Still, I said nothing.

"You want to come in?"

I did. Very much. I also didn't trust myself to stick a better landing than the one I'd stuck. This was a case of less is more. Walk away now, further ingratiate into good graces, live to fight another day. I hated pity, which was what that wounded, abandoned puppy dog routine I'd played invited.

"No," I said, lachrymose and dripping sincerity. "I should get some rest." Pause. "Spend a little…me time."

"Call me later?" Sam said. "Maybe we can grab a bite, catch a movie."

"Sounds good." I turned to walk away, stopping for one last mea culpa, sheepish over-the-shoulder wave. I smiled, humbled and contrite, having pulled off the impromptu sketch of a good guy going through a rough patch.

When I got to my car, I heaved a heavy sigh of relief. Boy, did I almost botch that big time.

Starting the engine, I would've felt better if a sudden thought hadn't occurred to me: so if that wasn't T in the bar, who was that man inside Soyka's staring me down? How about the other guy? Were they together? Was I wigging out? I wanted to believe that but I couldn't shake what Francis said. I'd seen the zine. I'd asked too many questions.

Was I now a target?

CHAPTER SIXTEEN

Talking one's self down off the ledge is not difficult to do if you have a solid foundation to operate from. I was not Jacob. I was not Francis. I was not any number of the homeless bums I passed as I drove through city center back to my apartment, these lowlifes on cardboard mats, eating the food people left atop trash receptacles, crouching in feces-stained trousers, these alcoholics and drug-addict bums. I wasn't judging. I'd never lacked compassion. I worked in healthcare. I was planning on a career devoted to *helping* others. One doesn't go into nursing with designs on growing wealthy. There's more to life than money. That said, I'd never be one of those people. I *could've* been. My parents abandoned me. I caught a lucky break when Mrs. Balfour took me in. I was grateful, gracious, and humble too. I also knew no matter what, come hell or high water, I had an inner resolve that screamed survivor. I made mistakes. As the Sam debacle last night attested, I wasn't impervious to dropping the ball. But driving off into the distance, looking at how I'd circumvented that disaster, I rode with my head held high, basking, a conquering hero.

I took pride in smooth talking my girlfriend on her porch. Using my wits and wherewithal, I remedied a bad situation. I didn't beat myself up too much over the tactics I'd employed. I hadn't lied. I *had* lost a good friend, and it did bring up a lot of issues from my childhood. Getting laid off from Ledgecrest contributed to my struggles. Losing one's job over doing *the right thing*? Stings. Lesser men would let the stone drag them down. Not me. I was in it to win it. John Lennon was right: there are no problems, only solutions.

Fishing for gum, I instead found Francis's crumpled-up number. Dropping the wad of paper back in the center console, I continued my hunt—I knew I had a pack somewhere—my effort rewarded with a couple sticks of Juicy Fruit. A form of nostalgia. My mom used to love Juicy Fruit.

Before heading home, I stopped off at Starbucks for a latte, drinking it in the parking lot while I checked my email. The drive back to my place was fifteen minutes, maybe twenty depending on traffic.

I hadn't been driving long when I noticed the car in my rearview mirror.

Cortland was a small town, but not so small it didn't get visitors. Despite living there for the past several years, I didn't know every resident. In fact, I knew very few. Not sure why the car in my rearview stuck out, registered on my radar, but I knew it didn't belong; knew whoever was behind the wheel wasn't from here; knew they'd come to do me harm.

When the turn to my apartment came up, I kept going. The car did too. It wasn't on my bumper, maintaining appropriate distance. I took unexpected, sudden turns, and it followed. I took four rights, a big circle. They mirrored every move, leaving no doubt. I passed the Dollar Tree shopping plaza, hooking left at the movie Cineplex, a right by the underpass. Plenty of traffic—cars, trucks, motorcycles—it was easy to blend in.

They never lost sight of me.

I hit the light on Grimes Avenue, stopping on the yellow. I tried to get a good look at the driver. Three cars buffered between us. Couldn't see much. Regular, dark car. I made out at least two faces, maybe a third passenger in the back. I also couldn't stare long. I didn't want to be too conspicuous, let them know I was on to them.

This wasn't me overreacting in a bar, fueled by overstimulation and stress. I'd come down from that jag, thinking levelheaded and clear. These people wanted to hurt me. As certain as I was living and breathing.

When the light changed green, I didn't move, and soon the horns began bleating. The Grimes and Montello intersection was one of the bigger ones in town, attracting congestion. I couldn't blame people for being angry—I was holding them up. Between the horns, I could hear the obscenities directed my way. The whole time, I kept one eye on that car—a blue or black sedan— several lengths back. When the light turned from yellow to red, I floored it, burning rubber and screwing over anyone behind me—including whoever was tailing me.

I took the long way home, hitting the interstate, exiting two towns early, pulling into a gas station. My hands were shaking on the wheel. Filling up, I tried to convince myself paranoia was a bug, contagious. It had burrowed into my brain, inspiring head games, false memories, call it what you want. I'd fallen for it. Even as I told myself this, I could feel my heart pounding inside my chest, a rodent scurrying the walls, frantic and desperate to escape.

Instead of getting back on the road after I was done pumping, I pulled my car into a parking spot and headed inside to get a drink. Less because I was thirsty and more to give me something to do. The cashier rang me up. I grabbed a copy of the newspaper. The guy gave me a funny look. Maybe because I was on the younger side and people didn't read much print these days.

"Crossword puzzle," I said, unsure why I felt the need to explain myself to some high school dropout riddled with acne scars.

Back behind the wheel, I'd started feeling all right, when I saw the kid again, the boy in blue. It was him all right, the same one from the rest home, the scruffy-faced urchin who'd been standing outside after I'd gotten fired. I knew it was the same kid because he had on the same goddamn padded blue coat in summer. He was across the street, traffic zipping past, cars and trucks and tractor-trailers. I wasn't hallucinating him. Then again, how could I be sure? People like Mr. Johnson, Jacob, Francis—each believed his own lies. This is what made delusions so dangerous. To the sufferer, visions seemed real. Except I could prove whether the boy was there. All I had to do was cross the road.

I was on the corner of Second. The way the streets lined up meant to drive to him I had to go all the way down to Leland, make a U, circle back to pull along the opposite side. Or I could save time and run across the street, fifteen, twenty yards, albeit through busy two-way traffic.

I walked to the edge of the gas station lot. He was right there, on the other side, unflinching, brazen.

We remained fixed on one other. With the cars zipping past, my view interrupted, eye contact was hard to maintain. I waited for a break in traffic. Moving van, Prius, pick-up, Prius, and I made a run for it. Cars swerved and laid on their horns, tires skidding. I couldn't keep an eye on the kid, too preoccupied with not ending up a roadkill pancake.

By the time I danced across all four lanes, he was gone.

What was happening to me?

CHAPTER SEVENTEEN

Making my way back to the gas station, I located a proper crosswalk three blocks away. Afternoon thunderclouds rolled in trying to cool off the day, which had remained warm, a recipe for a lightning storm. I felt the first raindrop on my arm. I liked the cloudbursts, the way they'd break the heat, tar fumes rising from the asphalt. I checked the sky, dark clouds roiling, tumbling over one another, darkening the horizon. Comforting. Somehow, time had gotten away from me. I didn't know how—maybe I was gawking at the sky—but it took me twenty minutes to get back to my car. No wonder the gas station attendant stood waiting.

"You can't park here," he said.

"I wasn't. I thought I saw...my friend...across the street."

He gazed out at passing traffic. Beyond the curb, a baseball field unfurled. The scrapyard kind, with an all-dirt infield, a short stack of bleachers on one side. A hard wind swept down. The field was empty. There was no kid.

"You can't leave your car here," he repeated. "I was about to call the cops."

"I'm leaving." I hit my fob to open the door. No beep. Which meant I'd forgotten to lock it, which I never did. I remembered locking it.

"Did you go through my car?"

"Huh?"

"My car is unlocked. I locked it."

"You can't park here."

"And you can't go through people's cars."

"I didn't go through your car, asshole."

I took a step toward him, and he backed up. I wasn't a physical guy, but I also didn't appreciate the invasion of privacy.

Fear gripped me, an unspeakable fear I couldn't explain, like a trio of phantoms was at my back. I spun around. No one there. I stood in the parking lot, on the verge of a fistfight—which I hadn't been in since the third grade with Scott Simard. Cars and trucks from the freeway whipped past. I was hunting specters, tethered to a yo-yo. I'd convinced myself it was going to be okay. And then the car. And then the boy in blue. The gas station attendant. Unlocked doors. A cycle. I was caught in a time loop.

I flashed a stern look at the attendant. "You're lucky I'm in a good mood today, pal." It wasn't posturing. In that moment, I was so wound up, if I threw a punch, I might've killed him.

When I got in the car, I didn't know where to go. I feared going home. My own home. And I hated myself for it, sitting in that Arco parking lot. The attendant ran inside as the skies opened up, the heavens unleashing judgment on me, splashing buckets. On the road, bright strobe after bright strobe, high beams blistering through the murk and misery.

I pulled onto the street, even with the sky pissing rain. The thunderstorm didn't last. Soon, the clouds parted, a golden ray of sunlight streaming through, which only made me feel worse. I kept driving, not watching turns. When I started paying attention, I realized I was several towns away. I pulled into a vacant lot, overcome with exhaustion. I couldn't keep my eyes open. I started passing out for seconds. One or two, not long.

Micro sleeps. I felt I'd been there fifteen minutes battling to stay awake. Then I closed my eyes for another split-second. But this time when I opened them, it was dark.

Through the black night, I heard police sirens, and even though I was far from a fugitive, I woke with a start and fired up the engine, speeding off, a bandit on the run. Me, Brandon Cossey, straight arrow, afraid of the cops. But that was enough to get me back on the road, and you better believe now I was surging awake, flooded with life, a shot of adrenaline straight to the heart. A few minutes into my drive, I understood what had happened. Without enough rest, my body had overridden my poor decision-making, forcing shut down. The lack of sleep explained a lot. Boys in blue and cars following me? No. I'd been exhausted, tripping, hallucinating. None of this was real.

The Shadow People was a silly term invented by sick people. I'd glommed onto it and allowed myself to get sucked in. I needed to make a stand, go on record, refute.

I drove to Ledgecrest to see Mr. Johnson. By now the night was black, black as well ink. No stars in the sky. No light pollution. As if a black hole were behind me sucking it all in, devouring dark matter and solar systems and galaxies, the earth beneath my wheels slipping away. Which was why I could not stop.

Yes, I'd talk to Mr. Johnson. He could help me. With each passing telephone pole and signpost, I accepted how ludicrous this assignment was. Mr. Johnson was grappling with dementia; yet I was certain he held the answers.

Being evening, Mrs. Talbot wouldn't be there. I was confident I could talk any of the nurses into letting me see him. I'd been an employee of the hospital almost seven years. I knew Mary, Dorian, Sandy. We were friends.

The small parking lot was empty, day shift and visiting hours over. I did not see Mary, Dorian, or Sandy's car. Many of these patients didn't get visitors, but during the day vendors and contractors, food service and maintenance workers filled the parking spots with their big vans and trucks, which created the illusion of companionship. The truth was Ledgecrest was already a sleepy, slow nursing home. At ten p.m., it felt like a ghost town.

I still had my key, which Mrs. Talbot had neglected to take back, and which I'd forgotten to return. Turned out I didn't need it. The front door was open.

The lights were low, the soft hum of a radio playing in the other direction. I wasn't doing anything wrong, I told myself. I'd been let go for bogus reasons. I wasn't here to cause trouble, just talk. Still, I felt the need to creep, sneaking like a thief, down the black-and-white checkered hall that smelled of chlorine.

Mr. Johnson's door was closed. I knew I should knock but didn't want to draw attention. Through the little glass window, interior lights off, I could make out his sleeping shape.

Pushing open the door, I guided it with one hand, stopping it from falling with my foot, patient doors spring-loaded and heavy.

"Mr. Johnson," I whispered.

Nothing.

I moved closer.

"Mr. Johnson, it's me, Brandon."

A heavy hand landed on my back and I jumped, startled.

"You shouldn't be here, Brandon," he said.

I did not know this man. He was new. Young, like me. In a weird way, he even looked like me. But…different.

"How do you know my name?"

"You have to go," he said.

"I need to talk to Mr. Johnson."

"If Mrs. Talbot finds out you were here, it'll be my ass."

"Are you my replacement?" No answer. "Please," I implored.

"It'll only take a minute." I started into the room, and when I did, I saw that the bed, which had appeared occupied, was empty, sheets smoothed, pillows propped.

"Where is Mr. Johnson?"

"Gone." He shrugged, devoid of emotion yet colored by aggravation, like he'd told me the outcome of a ball game when I should've known he didn't care much about sports.

"Gone? Where did he go?" Mr. Johnson was ninety, no family. No one to take him on an overnight trip.

"He's *gone*," the new orderly repeated.

And this time I got it.

How had I missed the obvious?

"When?"

"He passed this afternoon, I guess."

"You guess?"

"I didn't start my shift till nine."

"No one thought to tell me?"

"From what I understand, you were fired this morning."

"I wasn't fired. I am leaving for grad school soon. Mrs. Talbot and I both agreed to part ways sooner."

"That's not what I heard," the new guy mumbled.

"Well, you heard wrong." I pointed into the empty room. "I knew Mr. Johnson. Seven years I worked here. Which is a lot longer than you. We were friends. I cared about him."

The new orderly upturned his palms, opening his mouth, but no words came out. What could he say? This wasn't on him.

That was it. Mr. Johnson was gone. Another person who'd been a formative presence in my life wiped away, just like that.

"He was your friend?" the orderly said. This time his voice betrayed genuine feeling.

All I could do was nod.

"Sorry, Brandon. It's hard when we lose the people we care

about." He looked down the hall, lit red from exit signs, the low thrum of machines humming, respirators and heart rate monitors, these tubes and wires that prolonged but could never cure. "But you need to go." He waited. "I won't tell Talbot you were here."

"I don't give a shit."

I stalked out of the hospital, descending into the crisp air.

My phone buzzed in my pocket. Blocked number. I took it anyway.

"This is the police," a man said. "Am I speaking with Brandon Cossey?"

CHAPTER EIGHTEEN

I remained silent.

"Is this Brandon Cossey?" the man asked again, brusque, authoritative.

"Who is this? What's this about?"

"I'm afraid I can only share that information with Brandon Cossey."

"Yeah, sure, this is Brandon. What's going on?"

"Would it be possible for you to come in?"

"Why?"

"Well," he drawled out, "your car was spotted at a scene of interest earlier."

"Scene of interest?"

"You drive a 2016 Toyota Camry, yes?"

"What's this about?"

"Samantha Holahan. She's a friend of yours? She's…missing. Or rather not answering her phone or door. Could be nothing." He chuckled, though it didn't put me at ease. "One of her parents hasn't been able to reach her all day. Probably overreacting. Still, a good idea to talk. A neighbor reported seeing your car. No need to come down to the station. We can meet over a drink, if that makes you feel more comfortable. Keep this informal."

"Actually, no," I lied. "This isn't Brandon. This is his

roommate…Jeff."

"Excuse me?"

"This isn't Brandon. My name is Jeff. Jeff Tietz. I'm Brandon's roommate."

"Why did you say you were Brandon?"

"Because I wanted to know what this was about. Brandon is my good friend, and the police were calling, and since he's not here, I wanted to tell him what this call was about. It's only fair. You can't call, say you're the police, and then not say what it's about."

The cop laughed. "You make it a habit of lying to the police, Jeff?"

"No. Then again, I don't have much interaction with the police." I paused, gave it a hard count. "Neither does Brandon."

He exhaled, exasperated. "Where is he?"

"Working." Once I said it, I realized the mistake I'd made.

"Where's he work?"

"Why? So you can bother him down there?"

"Maybe I'll send a squad car to your apartment, have him wait with you till Brandon gets home."

"Fine. Ledgecrest Convalescent Home. On Kensington Road. That good enough for you?"

"Thank you for your time, Mr. Tietz."

Then the cop hung up. If that even *was* a cop. Sam? Missing? Me, the last person to see her, speak with her?

I pulled up Sam's number. But didn't call right away. I didn't know which looked worse, calling or not. If Sam were indeed missing—and if I didn't have anything to do with her disappearance, which, of course, I didn't—why shouldn't I call? Then again, if I *had* been guilty of a crime, which the cops were hinting at, I'd call under that scenario as well. Any halfway bright criminal would, to throw authorities off the scent.

I didn't need to throw anyone off any scent. I hadn't done anything wrong except think too much. I called. Straight to voicemail. I hung up without leaving a message, before the same circular reasoning brought me back to the beginning. Called again. Left a message. Short, quick, not weird. Just a "Hey, call me when you get a minute."

What was I thinking? I was standing in the Ledgecrest parking lot. Where I'd just invited the police. Why did I give them this address? Maybe they already knew. Maybe that new guy called them. But if that orderly called the cops on me, they wouldn't have asked where I worked. *Maybe. Maybe not. Either way, they know now.*

I hurried to my car, hopped in the bucket, and raced home. When I got to my apartment, I bypassed the complex parking garage and rolled to a stop on a side street, several blocks away, in case anyone had eyes on the place. Head down, hands in pocket, I was just a man out for an evening stroll. Most of the houselights were off. When I encountered any that were on, I made sure to cross the street and stay out of their harkening glow. Best to keep to the shadows.

After I crept into my apartment building, I avoided the main foyer and went up the back steps. I hadn't noticed any patrol cars out front. The cops would be smart enough to send an unmarked vehicle. I couldn't see anyone sitting inside any cars. Hard to be sure. I couldn't spend too much time searching.

With trepidation I opened my apartment door, didn't turn on lights, packing a gym bag with what I could find by the light of my cell.

Outside my window, I heard a car pull to a stop. I tucked away my phone, back against the wall, afraid to breathe. Inching along, I spied out a crack in the blinds. Dark sedan. Like a million cop cars in countless movies and television shows. Like the car that had been following me earlier. Or just a regular car anyone would drive, parked beneath a streetlamp. There were people inside. No doors opened. No heads popped out a window to crane up to my place and get a better look. They were below my window, half a block away. The street, Poplar, had plenty of cars parked along it. This was a residential neighborhood. Gave me a bad feeling, though.

I stole a peek. The interior of the car remained dark. From my distance, I couldn't see much. Maybe they'd already gotten in or out and I'd missed them, whoever they were. Was I really going to stand in a lightless apartment, peeping out the blinds, staring down two stories at a random car?

As I was letting closed the blinds, I saw the flicker of orange flame, like from a lighter, inside the car. Someone smoking a cigarette. And in that brief glow, I caught the silhouette of a man, maybe two of them, perhaps three. It happened fast. Then the interior fell dark again. I didn't imagine it.

Raiding closets, I jammed as many tees and pairs of underwear and socks as I could for an extended trip. At the bathroom sink, I swept up my toothbrush, comb, and deodorant, and then beelined for the door. That car was there for me. I didn't go for new-age bunk but I could *feel* it in my meat and bones. And if Francis was telling the truth about not breaking into my apartment, someone else had. Those guys in the car. Who were they? The police? Why call first and ask to meet if they already knew where I lived? What did this have to do with Jacob? *Illuminations*? Francis? Anything? Nothing? No clue. I wasn't sticking around to find out. In less than twenty-four hours, my whole world had been turned upside down, what I'd been sure of challenged.

My complex had an unmarked side entrance, designed for movers and bigger packages. Heart still in throat, pulse racing like two hours on the treadmill, I took that secret stairwell. Back against the wall, I positioned the car keys in my hand so the blades split my knuckles and kicked open the cellar door. No one waited.

The car I'd seen from my apartment was on the other side of the building, or it had been—I wasn't going looking for it. Slinking with my gym bag, my crawl in the shadows soon turned into a brisk walk, then a full-on sprint.

Jumping behind the wheel, I jammed the key in the ignition, rejoicing there wasn't a gun to the base of my skull—and you better believe I checked the backseat first. A block away, relief surrendered to self-consciousness, then embarrassment. I tried to laugh it off. As ridiculous as these spy games were, the threat felt too real to ignore.

I wanted to be on Cedar, a busier thoroughfare, which ran perpendicular to Poplar Avenue, making it easier to blend in, inconspicuous. Soon as I took the corner, I spied the offending vehicle again. Several blocks up, double-parked, waiting for me. I flooded the engine, jerking a hard left, cutting off oncoming traffic. Avoiding Cedar, I took Rumor Lane, killed the headlights, coasting down the hill, eyes peeled on various mirrors. I was now in a quieter part of town. I let the car roll until I was a several blocks away, in the ravine near the old bus station. A whispering wind brushed branches and swayed tall grassland. I hit the gas and restored the lights, flying out of the basin, blazing beneath tortuous concrete overpasses, taking unexpected turns and circuitous routes, zigzagging quadrants, no rhyme, no reason, leaving no trace. No way anyone could've followed that map.

Nick's Pizza and Subs sat on the edge of town, part of a larger shopping center with architecture rooted in the '70s, rounded font headers redolent of earth tones. The stores were off-brand knockoffs, lesser-known franchises, Mom and Pop markets and eateries, coffee shops. I fished Francis's number out of my center console. Right now, that crazy old man might be my only hope.

I called the number. No idea where the 602 area code was from. What was I going to say? What was he going to do?

The number I dialed reached a dry cleaner, instant voicemail. I tried again, thinking maybe I hit a wrong button. But, no, a dry cleaner. Just like *12 Monkeys*. I was crazy Bruce Willis. Jesus.

I left a nonsensical coded message. "This is Jacob's friend, Brandon. I brought in…a coat…and I lost my ticket, but if a guy named *Francis* stops by to pick it up, that's okay because I won't be able to make it myself as I had *unexpected* guests from out of town drop in," adding that I'd be "at Nick's…getting pizza." I left the name of the plaza. Bonkers. Come morning, some poor lady at Maria's Wash 'n' Dry was going to be mystified. What else could I do? Using a dry cleaning operation as a front for call laundering wasn't outside the realm of possibilities where Francis was concerned.

Where was I supposed to go? The Balfours was the only place I could think of, but if the police *were* looking for me, the Balfours would be next up after my apartment. Some of my old snail mail and bills still went there, the residence listed as an emergency contact, and I wasn't putting Mrs. Balfour and Chloe in jeopardy. I needed a plan, a safe house to hole up in. Until then, reliable Wi-Fi would have to do. Let me poke around and get a handle on what was going down, an accurate picture. Nick's had Wi-Fi.

I ordered a meatball grinder and a Coke, and hunkered by a rear window, with one eye on the road.

I pulled up a search engine on my phone. There was nothing new on Sam. Nothing on Sam, period. No periodical mentioned a missing girl. That should've put my mind at ease. Until I realized it would be days, if not weeks, before such news reached the press. I'd feel better when she called back.

After failing to make a dent in the grinder, I wrapped up the remainder and left a few bills and change on the table. I headed out to my car. I needed sleep, a few hours of rest. Hotels peppered the outskirts in clusters near highway ramps. I also knew most hotels these days required a driver's license, even the scummy ones. There was no warrant out for my arrest, not that I knew of. I was a person of interest, but I wasn't taking the chance. I curled into my backseat. The plaza was too secluded and low rent for a security guard. Last thing I needed was a rent-a-cop in his golf cart, shining a light, asking me for ID.

In between checking for texts or calls that never came, I must've drifted off to sleep, even if it didn't come easily or offer any REM.

The rising sun over the plaza served as an alarm clock. I saw a coffee shop open. Hoisting my gym bag over my shoulder, I headed there, washing up and changing in the bathroom. I ordered my latte and was taking a step back outside when a voice told me to look up, toward the lot. And there they were, sitting in their car, parked beside mine.

I made like I'd forgotten cream, returning to the coffee station, where I fiddled with sugar packets and sticks. Stealing glances out the window, I couldn't get a good look. There were two of them. One I was pretty sure I recognized: the man from the bar that night with Sam, the man I'd mistaken for her friend Anthony, the guy with the mustache. There was another man sitting beside him. It wasn't the boy in the blue coat. This man was older. He could've been that *other* guy from the night at the bar. Which, if true, meant they'd been after me for a while, together, a tag team. They both got out and walked right up to my car. No uniforms, dressed in regular clothes, so not cops or else undercover. They peeked in the windows before scrutinizing the parking lot. The one with the mustache directed a hand across the complex, as if to start canvassing. I didn't know how many other coffee shops or restaurants there were. There was a donut shop and dinette I'd seen open. They started walking in that direction. I ducked out the door, rounding the first corner I saw, which deposited me between two buildings with a narrow passage, big enough to wedge through but not much bigger. Squeezing past putrid trash bags, dodging screeching cats, I emerged in a big back lot, where trucks made deliveries. I was hoping for the cover of tractor-trailers and freight. The dock was dead, lot covered in big puddles. Must've rained last night.

I heard the screeching wheels of a car peel around the corner, gunning my way. I couldn't outrun it. My only option was to go back the way I'd come, but it would just return me to the same place I'd left, where one of them surely waited. I was a trapped rat.

Before I could decide what to do, the car skidded to a stop in front of me.

The passenger side door kicked open.

The last face I expected to see greeted me.

"Get in," Francis said.

He didn't have to ask twice.

CHAPTER NINETEEN

The exertion and stress of the last twenty-four hours knocked me out. Even though I'd managed a couple hours of sleep in the backseat of my car, soon to be towed and property of the county, the respite wasn't enough to compensate for what my body and mind had been through. I wasn't used to questioning whether what I saw before me, with my own two eyes, was there or not.

All I knew: when I came to, we weren't in Cortland anymore.

"Where are we?" I wiped the crust from my eyes.

"Couple hours west."

Francis lit a cigarette. The smell was nauseating. What could I do? It was his car. And the old man had saved my ass.

A couple weeks ago, the last place I figured I'd be was on a road trip with Francis Balfour. A lot had changed in a couple weeks. I had so many questions. He was the only one there to ask.

"Who were those guys? The ones in the car chasing me."

"Not sure it'd make much sense to you." He dragged on his cigarette. "Let's say the type to tie up loose ends."

"How am I a loose end? I don't know anything. I don't know what happened to Jacob. This isn't my fight." Tall highway poles whizzed past as we slipped under a skyway advertising McDonald's. "How'd you know where I was?" I thought back to my phone call to the dry cleaners, wondering if I was playing out a *12 Monkeys* reenactment.

"Same way they found you."

I felt my pockets. "Where's my cell phone?"

"In pieces on the side of the road in Cortland."

"What the hell you do that for?"

"Traceable."

"That's, like, six hundred dollars! And it was off!"

"Doesn't matter. Police can still use it to find you." He glanced over. "Police called you, right?"

"How'd you...?" How did he know that? "Yes, the police called. My girlfriend Sam is missing. She might not be missing, though. Her parents are looking for her. The police wanted me to come in."

"Why didn't you?"

"If she *is* missing, I didn't have anything to do with it!"

"Didn't say you did. But if you're innocent, why not talk to the police?"

"It's...complicated. I'm...seeing things. Cars. People watching me. Not sleeping well. I feel like I'm cracking up."

"You're not cracking up." Francis took another drag before aiming the burning ember at me. In the red haze of the old Buick, he looked positively demonic. "Your eyes are opening. You're seeing the truth."

He didn't say more than that, and I shut up.

I stared out the window, watching barns and farms and old trains whizz by.

Then I must've fallen back asleep. The body is a machine. It has its own automatic hardwire reboot. Mine powered down.

I woke to bright sunshine slathering high wheat fields, buttery, like scrambled eggs fluffed up on light toast. Or maybe I was hungry. My stomach roiled over having been denied proper meals, those few bites of a meatball sub converted to energy by organs and wires, vessels and bone that had to keep the ship going even when the good captain had passed out down below. I let out a satisfying yawn and enjoyed a good stretch. I had to admit I felt safer in this car, driving with this wackadoodle, than I'd felt in a while.

Francis had an arm hanging out the window, so relaxed, cigarette dangling from his lips, Wayfarers on, the world's coolest grandpa. Was this a symptom of his sickness? How he could wax between looking like the spawn of Satan and an extra in a Don Henley video?

"The Egyptians were the first people to see the color blue," he said, as if we were in the middle of a conversation and these weren't the first words I'd heard upon awaking.

"Huh?"

"The Egyptians. Y'know, the Pyramids? The Sphinx?"

"I know who the Egyptians are. I'm getting an advanced college degree. What about them?"

"The color. Blue. Didn't exist until the time of pharaohs and pyramids."

How do you respond to that?

I flashed an okeydokey sign. "Hate to tell you this. Blue is a primary color, meaning it's in damn near everything. The ocean is blue." I pointed out the window, up at the *Simpsons* sky and clouds. "See? Pretty blue—"

"You read a lot?"

"Obviously."

"Ever read *The Odyssey*?"

"Homer? Of course."

"That's the one. Story about a man voyaging across the sea. Spends a lot of time on the ocean. Never uses the word 'blue' when writing about the water. He describes the sea as a 'dark wine.'" He glanced over. "Never blue."

"I'm sorry, Francis. I'm not following. If you are saying the world—the sea, sky, a billion other things on this planet—magically turned blue overnight, I'm not buying it. Sounds like a crackpot theory Jacob would've come up with for his stupid zine."

"Didn't say the world changed colors. Only that the color didn't exist. At least not in recorded history. No mention of that particular color until the Egyptians."

"Sure, whatever, man. What's your point?"

"You're right. The sea and sky, certain flowers, berries have always been blue. The human eye couldn't process the color. Therefore, it didn't exist."

"Great." Thumbs-up. "I'm in a parallel universe. Wonderful."

"There are parallel universes. But not like you're thinking. Several worlds exist simultaneously. All the time, right on top of each other. Some people see the world for what it really is. Some people don't."

"So which one am I seeing?" I knew there was a reason Francis was sharing this anecdote.

Francis flicked his butt out the window. "I think you're seeing the color blue for the first time."

CHAPTER TWENTY

We stopped for lunch in King's Landing, a trucker town off the freeway. How did I end up in this situation? Breaking bread with a geriatric nutcase shaking his fist at chemtrails. Yet, there I was. Because I couldn't go home. The cops wanted me for questioning. I had strange cars following me. People breaking into my apartment. I started wondering if all the crap that went down at Ledgecrest was related.

"Eat up," Francis said.

I'd ordered a burger, even though I had no appetite. I was hungry. But I couldn't stomach the thought of eating. I didn't do well with deviation from the norm. An impromptu road trip to go on the run ran counter to that arrangement.

The restaurant didn't even have a name. Just a burger and sandwich place affixed to the truck stop. Long-haul drivers ducked through the doors, making for the showers in back. The restaurant opened into a novelty shop—useless garbage parents bought to keep kids quiet on cross-country trips. Customers milled about, picking up trinkets, putting them back without buying, periodically glancing in our direction. I didn't know what was real and what I was imagining, if these people, these watchers, were like my color blue.

"What's the plan, Francis?"

"Minnesota."

"I'm not in the mood for a vacation."

He nodded toward the truckers at the filling station. "I'm sure one of those fellas will be happy to give you a ride back home."

Francis stuck a fork in the egg yoke, swirling orange over his toast, which he'd ordered extra burnt. He cut off a hunk of egg and bread, chomping, jaw rotating like a cow chewing cud, slow and deliberate, refusing to respond to a simple question.

I made to go. But where? I was a man without a country.

"Sit down," Francis said.

I acquiesced, as if staying granted Francis a favor, the closest I was getting to saving face. I wasn't taking a Greyhound back to Cortland.

"Before Jacob went missing," Francis said, "he called me. I understood the world he was attempting to infiltrate."

"And what world is that?"

"The same one you are starting to see." Francis paused before adding, "Again." He said it like it should mean something to me. Which, of course, it didn't. "My grandson published several issues of *Illuminations*. He broached subjects the mainstream press is scared to talk about."

"Photocopying is not publishing." I turned to look out the window, eyeing the long road before me. "Everything isn't a conspiracy, Francis."

"Some of it was out there. I'll give you that. Not all of it. You read his piece on Rosemary Kennedy?"

"I perused the zine. Can't say I recall that particular essay."

"Might've been an earlier edition." Francis rained black pepper over his eggs.

"What about Rosemary Kennedy?" I said, taking the bait. "She was mentally handicapped. Like a vegetable, right?"

"Not before her father got ahold of her. Before Joe Kennedy got his mitts on his eldest daughter, she was perfectly intelligent. A little wild maybe. Joe scrambled his own daughter's brain so his sons could be president. Brought her to a back-alley doctor to scrape away her frontal lobe."

"*The* Kennedys? I find that hard to believe."

"Believe what you want. I'm telling you Jacob wasn't afraid to go big-game hunting. You mess with powerful families and their skeletons, people get defensive."

"Are you telling me the—" I leaned over the table to whisper "—*the* Kennedys had something to do with this?"

"Of course not. What do you think? I'm crazy?"

Actually, Francis…

"My point is you poke around enough, throwing darts in the dark, you're bound to hit your mark. Broken clocks, twice a day. Jacob hit a bull's eye."

"About what?"

"If I knew that, I wouldn't be investigating, would I?"

"You'd go to the cops?" Like Francis would trust the police.

"What's your life been like these past couple weeks? Visits from strangers? Tailed by more than that one strange car? Patterns disrupted? Doppelgängers? Frequent episodes of déjà vu?"

"Yes," I said. "Of late, life has been…weird. But that doesn't mean I'm buying into any of this bullshit. There's always a logical explanation—"

"Logical can be illogical."

"That is literally the opposite definition of logical."

Francis ran a finger out the window, up and down, side to side. "This is all one big simulation."

"I've seen *The Matrix*."

"I don't know what that is."

"It's a movie."

"I ain't talking about no movie, boy."

"Frankly? I don't know what you're talking about, Francis."

"Jacob had been doing better," he said, extracting another copy of the latest edition of *Illuminations* while dismissing my input. He dropped it on the countertop, finger tapping. "Wasn't until *this* issue came out that Jacob went off the rails."

"I've known Jacob since we were kids. I loved him like a brother. But he was crazy *way* before playing intrepid journalist. He was never *on* the rails. Not after we were kids, anyway."

"Crazy is a convenient term. A point of view. It's also lazy, predictable, and boring. For some of us, it's a term of endearment."

"Us?"

"You know Jacob's official diagnosis?"

"Delusional?"

"My grandson was schizophrenic." Francis pulled out an orange prescription bottle, placed it on the table. I couldn't read the label. Something long that started with a T. He snatched it back before I could sound it out and use my context clues. "One of many. I'm on a cocktail. Some will tell you schizophrenia isn't hereditary. But my father had it. So did my son, Gary. So did Jacob. It's a term, a classification, a word medical coders need to file claims in the appropriate insurance file. I prefer to look at schizophrenia another way."

"How's that?"

"A gift."

I was a positive guy. Like Monty Python, I liked to look on the bright side of life. But what do you say to a man who claims a brain disease is a blessing?

Francis crooked a finger at me. "It allows you to see what's really there, what others are blind to. The same things you've been seeing of late."

"I'm not schizophrenic. I'm...normal."

"Normal." Francis spat the word. "Another convenient term of the dull and conventional. But it doesn't matter what doctors or the medical community call it. Some see. Some don't."

"Okay, Rasputin. Schizophrenia allows you to see. Great. You're an oracle." I nodded at his tucked-away pill bottle. "If it's such a blessing, why do you take your medication?"

Francis looked me dead on. "Sometimes I don't."

The waitress came to refill our coffee, asking if we wanted anything else. *Yeah, I thought, out of here, right now.* Francis asked for the check.

"I wouldn't expect you to understand," he said after the waitress left. "Most close that door at a young age. It's why kids only see monsters when they're little. Why dogs howl at nothing at all. Then everything returns to status quo. But they are still there. All the time."

"The Shadow People."

"Call them whatever you want."

"Great. Wonderful." I checked out the window. "I have bigger problems than imaginary friends. My girlfriend is missing."

"I doubt it."

"The cops called and said she was. And when I called her, she didn't pick up."

"She didn't pick up because they waited for the moment they knew she wouldn't."

My eyes widened.

"I don't know who is involved. But I promise they've been watching you. Which means they're watching her. They were trying to lure you. Did the call you receive come from the police department?"

I thought back. "The number was blocked."

"Since when do police call from a blocked number?"

The idea that Sam wasn't really missing filled me with joy. It also pissed me off since I had no way of verifying that.

"It'd be nice if I could call her. But you destroyed my cell."

"That was for your own good."

Out the window, I watched tractor-trailers, buses, and automobiles rambling on.

"I'm finding out who killed my grandson." He landed a bony finger on the baby blue pamphlet. "To do that, I have to find which of these theories rattled cages, what drove him to Minnesota— what was so terrifying it was worth killing for."

I dragged the zine over with one finger. I hated giving credence. Except...my life *had* been shaken up as soon as I laid eyes on that zine. I wanted to believe Francis was right about Sam. But that didn't fix everything, did it? Someone had still called, masquerading as the police, trying to come at me. And that was the *best*-case scenario. I flashed back to that day at the Balfours, Mrs. Balfour crestfallen, and the police taking...evidence? Why confiscate Jacob's belongings? What if they weren't really cops? Or weren't good cops? That's the danger of entertaining the possibility of a conspiracy: once you crack open that door and start questioning what's real, the answer is sweeping. None of it. All of it. Everywhere in between.

I spun the periodical around. Domestic plots. International spy games. The pharmaceutical industry's ploy to get the masses hooked on synthetic opiates. A new spin on the Hillary Clinton pizza sex cult, this one involving prominent Albany politicians with added human trafficking. It was all looney tunes. But Francis was right about one thing: Jacob had been going big-game hunting. I started thinking, *What if...?* This sex ring, for instance, what if it *were* real? Well, people would kill to keep that secret, wouldn't they? I felt gullible for thinking that. Because the next header I saw was about...the Shadow People.

I'd seen the article before. "Bodysnatching." Much of it was a screen grab of a chatroom exchange between Jacob, going by the handle RAW, and his "inside source," Jessiesgirl81. Half the piece was redacted with thick black bars, as if this were a top-secret government file. A hot take. Jessie had witnessed the Shadow People snatching bodies…

I slapped the zine shut.

"Jesus effing Christ," I said, "I am *not* playing pretend. I'm a grown-ass adult. I have a life."

"Jacob left a trail. I'm going to follow that trail." He nodded out the window. "Last place he called me is up the road. Twenty miles. Said he was being followed."

"By whom?"

"That's what I'm going to find out." Francis pulled his wallet and dropped a twenty and a ten, covering my portion as well. I didn't get the chance to thank him before he hopped up and bulled for the exit.

He'd almost reached the door when I called out.

"Hold on, Francis. I'm coming."

CHAPTER TWENTY-ONE

The freeway west out of state was a long straight shot. Transportation vehicles of all sizes kicked up pebbles and coughed exhaust. Produce freighters, trucks lugging loads, banged-up, battered cars mixed in with this year's newest models, the pipeline of commerce. Food had to be delivered, comfort shipped in. There was a lot of ground to cover. That was what I thought about as I watched these truckers barrel along, how this was the start of a journey, a commitment; anyone making the trek was in it for the long haul.

At the start of this trip, I felt like I did most mornings when I woke and hadn't yet put on my glasses, the outline of everything and everybody wobbly, the world out of focus, a radio station that needed finer tuning. Now, tooling along the freeway with Francis in his big ol' Buick, the outlook shone clearer. I was tuned in.

We continued on Interstate 80, not talking much. Turned out Francis wasn't much of a talker unless he had a point to make. With all that blue Rosemary Kennedy nonsense, he'd been a veritable chatterbox. Now? Not so much. Tight-lipped and stoic, this current incarnation closer resembled a two-dimensional character chosen by a casting director who sought to fill the part of "grizzled old man of few words," a vehicle to deliver sage advice in between making casually racist remarks you excuse because he's from a different era, saltiness downright endearing in its earthiness.

More than once I questioned why I was even in the car with the man. I didn't know him. Nor did I share his enthusiasm for the cause. I couldn't accept a fantastic scenario where a person would murder, for all intents and purposes, a shut-in. I also had to admit that particular element—Jacob's reclusive status—piqued curiosity. Jacob *never* left Utica or its immediate environs. What drew him out here?

While the details of his death were bizarre, there had to be a simpler explanation. Detective Lourey never returned my call regarding the money and diamonds, or whatever those jewels were. *If* those jewels were. I didn't have a cell anymore to follow up. Despite expressing hunger for the truth, Francis did not display any urgency. Like taking a Sunday drive, he steered his gigantic boat of an automobile one-handed, wrist draped over the wheel, Winston burning in his fingers, cracked tall boy sitting in his lap because Francis didn't concern himself with silly laws about open containers or the dangers of driving drunk. Although I doubted a single beer made a dent in such a seasoned drinker.

He'd said twenty miles but we'd traveled a lot longer than that. We'd had to exit the freeway and backtrack up winding, twisty trails that delivered us deeper into the cuts. The questions were mounting, Francis's relationship to the Balfours topping the list. Mrs. Balfour claimed he'd been cut off, estranged from the family. Francis made it sound like he and Jacob were best buds. Someone was lying.

Despite my interest in probing backstory and getting a better handle on the man, initiating conversation was tough. My attempts were met with clipped, terse responses. Which left me a lot of downtime. No music on the radio—Francis preferred talking heads. Anytime I suggested music—I didn't care what, put on Lawrence Welk or Glenn Miller—he only said no. He also didn't like the volume too high, leaving dialogue a whisper, rendering whatever program we were listening to background filler, more white noise than news program. Sometimes a word or phrase would cut through but never loud enough to allow me to follow a narrative. It was all I could do to identify a topic or subject matter. Programs changed. One was a car show, another religious, political. Then a catchall, its host fielding calls covering an assortment of topics, from UFOs to WMDs. I wished I had the call-in number. Maybe *he* could answer these questions plaguing me. Not that I would've been able to hear the response.

Francis pulled off well before I saw any city, a farming village in the middle of nowhere, a rural Western New York town called Wroughton.

CHAPTER TWENTY-TWO

"Why are we stopping here?" There was nothing but old, small, spread-out houses with sagging roofs and collapsed wooden fences, mangy dogs looking extra hungry.

Francis kicked opened his door, spat, and called me along with his greased white head.

He'd parked far away in the dirt lot, by the high weeds and reeds, still a good fifty yards removed from a shack stuck in the shadows of the sun. We started walking toward it, the nearest building on the immediate horizon, stepping around the occasional shredded tire or empty Coke can, plastic rings and candy wrappers. When we got to the loose gravel, the ground covered with old losing scratch-offs and bottle caps, I realized we were at a bus station, one of these anonymous stops along America's great wasteland. I saw a syringe, a needle, like the kind used for insulin or drugs, right there on the ground, for any kid to find and pick up.

Up close the structure resembled a photo-processing hut you see in pictures, a service rendered obsolete in the digital age. Bigger, but not by much. Nothing about the peeling mustard exterior screamed transportation hub, save for the wood-stamped sign. A small rectangular block dangled from a nail above the door: Wroughton Depot.

No buses waited in port, no other cars in the lot. I didn't see a soul killing time till the next ticket out of this dump. I couldn't imagine who'd catch a bus at this station anyway. To get here, you'd need a car. And if you had a car, why would you need a bus? The high country sun told me it was two or three o'clock in the afternoon. It bothered me not having my phone. I didn't know if Mrs. Balfour was trying to call me back. I had no way of knowing if Sam was reaching out, able to clear up this mess.

"Why are we at a cornfield bus stop?"

Francis didn't answer, instead lighting a smoke. He took a drag, strode forward, stirring up dust, a cowboy arriving for an overdue showdown. I found the adoptive posture strangely confrontational. I figured the guy must've really hated bus stations.

Without discarding the cigarette, he pushed through the front door. No one waited to greet us. An overhead fan whirred, pushing tepid air. Three empty folding chairs perched against a map of the United States, Dr. Seuss's nightmare, circuitous routes to all the places you'll never go. Next to the map, an actual payphone on the wall.

What I thought were running times turned out to be an empty chart. There were rows for departures and arrivals, just no dates or times filled in. Took me a moment, but I did find an actual schedule. Several feet away. A single sheet of yellow notebook paper, thumbtacked askew, handwritten. The bus route didn't go through Wroughton daily. Twice a week. Tuesdays and Fridays. Eleven a.m. going east, two thirty p.m. west.

Even though the depot was abandoned, the doors had been unlocked. We didn't break in, and we weren't trespassing. *Some*one had to have opened up. Décor sparse, chunks of flooring ruptured, dusty allergens clogging the air. Could've used a bum sleeping on a bench with a newspaper blanket to add local color.

I heard the flush of a toilet from deep behind a thick wall. A few seconds later, a large man—stocky and scowling, with a slab of concrete gut, forty or so—emerged from a side door I hadn't noticed, the interior painted the same shade of filthy hospital green. He wore an unbuttoned grey bus shirt. The nametag read Gustavo, a funny name for this part of the country. It also made me think of that goofy old Paul Simon song, *Hop on the bus, Gus…* I remembered hearing it play often on my parents' tiny radio in the kitchen.

Gus glanced our way, moving toward a door that would deliver him behind a plexiglass wall with a mouth hole. Which struck me as hilarious, given the traffic this place invited, the self-imposed exile.

"If you're looking to catch the bus," he said, hand on handle, "you're late."

The man hadn't finished the sentence before Francis was on top of him. Under normal circumstances, I'm not giving a man Francis's age the upper hand against a guy that size. But you would've thought their ages were reversed the way Francis grabbed the back of the guy's neck, pinching it hard, making him squeal until Gus took a knee.

"Francis!"

"What the—?" the man eeked.

"What are you doing?" I hollered. But Francis wasn't paying attention to me.

"You hung up the phone on me," Francis said. "Made me drive all this way."

"Jesus. You're that crazy old guy who called about that kid—" The man twisted and writhed beneath Francis's grip. Understanding this was the result of a previous encounter made Francis's violent introduction less random but no more sane.

"We're going to skip hello," Francis said. "Get to the part where you help me."

I wanted to pull Francis off but I didn't want in the middle. Francis was foaming at the mouth, gnashing teeth, his well-toned forearm a rope of vein and sinew. Would've been like trying to take away food from a feral dog.

Francis removed the cigarette from his mouth, pinching it like he was considering which patch of Gus's exposed skin to use for an ashtray. For a second I really thought he was going to extinguish the lit smoke on the guy's arm.

"I told you on the phone," Gus whined. "I don't know anything."

Francis dropped the cigarette to the tiled linoleum, quashing the burning ember with his heel. Then he nodded at the office behind the plexiglass. "Let's double check, eh?"

The big man held up his hands. Francis let go of the back of his neck, allowing him to stand, the threat of violence implicit. The man opened the door and Francis followed inside. I debated whether to stay, since this was now shaping up to be, at the very least, an assault and battery.

I peeked through the open door, where, against a far wall, Gus hunched over the bottom drawer of a cabinet. I could hear the poor bastard mouth breathing from here. Gus extracted a shoebox full of tapes, the old-school VHS kind, which no one used anymore, Wroughton Depot slow to enter the twenty-first century.

What I thought was an old computer, a first-generation model from a time when the internet was in its infancy, turned out to be a small video monitor. Gus inserted the tape and the picture fuzzed to life. The footage was from a couple weeks ago, date and time stamped in the lower box.

"Fast forward to two p.m.," Francis said.

The man fiddled with big red knobs, dialing in the frequency, making the picture dance, and soon the screen was filled with the large shape of my dead friend.

The image, black, white, and grainy, proved unsettling. The man in the picture no longer existed. Jacob was a memory on a monitor, the real version six feet under, and that grim reality produced indescribable sorrow.

I walked over, and the three of us huddled around the screen, studying the scene, watching the action develop in real time, which, like Gus maintained, didn't show much. Jacob waited at the tiny depot, disappearing from the frame as he went outside to smoke, cigarette and lighter in hand. I wasn't sure what Francis hoped to glean from the footage.

Then things turned strange.

In the video, Jacob began to fidget, whiplashing over his shoulder, spooked, like someone had crept up behind him. He ran inside, craning his neck toward his assailant. But no one was there.

"Who's behind him?" I asked.

Gus shrugged. "I told your grandpa when he called. I didn't see nothing. No one catches the bus here anymore. This depot won't be open next year. This town used to have mills, jobs, reasons to stay. Families have been leaving by the truckload."

"Stop the tape." Francis pointed at the screen, where Jacob, again, could be seen at the window, shuffling uneasily. I saw it too. We all did. A brief flash. A shadow…

"Who's that?" Francis said.

"I'm sorry," Gus said. "I don't remember seeing anyone."

"You see now?"

"I'm sorry, sir—"

"Hit play."

On screen, Jacob jolted, making a straight shot through the

lobby, brisk walk, slow jog, side door to back, to the waiting bus, one would presume, given the proximity to the departure time.

"Was the bus early that day?"

"No." Gus shook his head. "Never is. Late a lot."

"This day?"

"Best I can remember? Late."

"Who else got on the bus?" Francis asked.

"Like I told you on the phone. No one got on the bus that day."

"My grandson did." Francis turned and pointed to the payphone on the wall. "He called me from that phone." Francis pointed at the monitor. "That's him, walking toward the bus."

"I didn't see anything—"

Francis turned out the window. "Where's the next stop?"

"On the bus you think your grandson caught?"

"No, the bus the goddamn president caught." Francis's eyes squinted nasty mean. "Yes. My grandson."

The man fumbled with a map. With shaky fingers, he traced the bus route. "Up here, the routes aren't regular. Each week is different."

"I don't give a shit."

Gus hurried his research. "Maybe Mount Pioneer. Forty miles northwest?"

"You don't sound too sure."

"Depends on if anyone purchased tickets or needed to get off."

Francis seemed to consider this, weighing the truthfulness of the statement, or maybe deciding whether shutting Gus's head in the door would yield a more favorable answer.

"Where is the next *guaranteed* stop?"

"That would be Jamestown." Gus swallowed. "Maybe."

"Maybe?" Francis said.

"There's nothing around here," Gus said. "Gas stations and pawn shops. Wroughton is nothing but pawn shops. I told you this region's dried up. No one comes here." Gus shrugged. "I'm sorry, sir. I don't know what to tell you."

In the car, I didn't say anything. I wasn't sure *what* to say. Francis fired up another cigarette, dialing in another murmuring talk show. But he didn't shift into drive or make any attempt to pull out. Over a crest, the highway whisked by, cars and trucks traversing the plains, splitting rows of corn stalks, damp mulchy scent ragweeding the air. I wished he'd get this thing in gear. I didn't want to come across scared—I wasn't—but nothing stopped Gus from calling the police.

"You were a little hard on the guy in there," I said. "Wouldn't you agree?"

Francis glanced over, disdain painted on his face. "No. I wouldn't *agree*, boy."

"He said he didn't see anything."

"You saw that shadow crossing, didn't you? In the video?" He didn't need me to validate. There was the shadow of something.

"Yeah," I said. "I mean, it looked like a person."

"Because it was a person," he snapped. "A person following Jacob." Francis kept his eyes locked ahead on the mulberry bushes and thorns.

"Where next?"

Francis shook his head. Now I realized why he hadn't already sped off. He didn't know where to go.

I tried to gather everything I'd learned about my friend's disappearance. Which wasn't much. Jacob last called from this depot, before ending up several states over, a pile of ash in a quarry ditch.

Except we *did* have other details of his journey, didn't we?

"Jacob tried to cross into Canada?" I said.

"Dearborn. Near Detroit." Francis turned to me. "If we couldn't get a bus station employee to help, I'm not sure the US Border Patrol is taking up the cause."

But that wasn't what I was thinking.

"Right," I said. "Canada denied entry. Didn't they cite a large sum of cash and jewelry?"

"Jacob cleared out his bank account. He'd been working."

"But the jewelry… Where'd he get it from?"

"How the hell should I know?"

"You said he had almost nine grand in cash. How'd he save that much?"

"Your point?"

"I don't know what Jacob could or couldn't save. I don't know where he'd get his hands on that much jewelry." I looked back at the bus depot. Enough time had passed that I was confident the police weren't en route. "But I'm thinking about something Gus said."

"He didn't say anything. Except this is a shit town."

"Economically depressed."

"Okay, college boy. Would you like to discuss systemic racism next?"

"He said there was nothing here but gas stations and pawn shops."

Francis waited for me to connect the dots.

"Not many places you can unload jewelry without drawing suspicion." I eyed up the road, over hill and dale, into town. "But pawn shops might be a good place to start."

CHAPTER TWENTY-THREE

Downtown Wroughton resembled a post-apocalyptic horror film. Most of the buildings were whitewashed and boarded up, with for lease signs in the windows, many of which were smashed. Even though it was a pleasant day by Northeastern standards, few people roamed the streets. On the cusp of June, the day was mild, pleasant. Late afternoon, the temps were still cool enough that you could walk without sweating. There was also an undeniable melancholy and drudgery hanging over the town, a collective mood of oppression and hopelessness.

Gus hadn't been overselling the squalor of downtown, which consisted of a single main street where all the shops, eateries, and businesses were located, including a disproportionate number of pawn shops. The short stretch had three. Mother necessitating invention, two looked to be newer additions. These pawn shop storefronts were colored brighter, painted shinier.

I slapped Francis on the shoulder, directing him to follow me across the road to the oldest looking operation, called Ace's. The cold stares of huddled strangers greeted us. This wasn't a town that attracted tourists. I didn't know if Jacob had stolen the jewelry, but my gut said if he had, an old-school broker would be more willing to bend rules and deal on the shadier side of the street.

Electric guitars hung in the window, alongside other musical equipment—Casio keys, a snare drum, a horn. Made sense. Rock and roll was a one-way ticket to regret. You start out with big aspirations and end up selling your gear to pay rent. I was grateful Jacob and I gave up on the dream before rock and roll could break our hearts.

Unlike pawn shops in the city, you didn't need to be buzzed past a metal grate to get inside. A little bell dinged above the door, announcing our arrival.

"I help you boys?" The man behind the counter had a country-mean expression with an alcohol-pickled face. Zeroing in on us had been easy. There was no one else inside. Although hearing anyone call Francis "boy" felt out of place.

"Maybe," I said. "I'm wondering if my...brother...was in here."

"Am I supposed to know who your brother is?"

I chuckled. No one else did.

"He took our mom's jewelry," I said. "I think he may've brought it here."

"Any transactions are confidential—"

"I understand—"

"If you think your 'brother' brought in merchandise that didn't belong to him," the man replied with a bored, aggravated cadence, "that's theft. You'll have to go to the police."

"I don't want to get him in trouble."

"I'm sure." The man at the counter scratched his beard, smiling a big, fake smile. "Of course, we don't ever *knowingly* accept stolen merchandise." He pointed out the window. "Fill out a report at the police station. Soon as you have the proper forms, I'll be more than happy to show the police our new inventory list. Then it'll be up to you if you want to press charges. If we have the jewelry in question, that is." He waited, glancing at the clock, the workday almost over. "Of course, if you don't wish to cause your…brother…any more trouble, you might want to fuck off."

I waited for Francis to go after this guy like he did Gustavo at the bus station—not that I wanted to see that. I was surprised when Francis, without a word, turned and left.

When we got outside, I glanced over.

"You can't push around a man in a pawn shop," he said. "They keep shotguns under the counter."

"We should try the other shops."

"What makes you think they'll be any more accommodating?"

"Jacob had to unload the jewelry somewhere. How else did he get that much cash?"

As we discussed this, I felt the eyes around us. Strangers, we stood out.

Francis followed me into the next two pawn shops, and, as he predicted, no one cared, each proprietor as hostile as the next.

Following our last attempt, I saw a café and suggested taking a load off, talk, regroup, get a bite, some coffee, since it appeared it might be a while before we slept. Without a better option, Francis followed me inside. We sat at a scarred, wobbly table in the corner, nicknames and initials carved in the soft wood. I dumped half a pound of sugar in my coffee, hoping to mask the burnt taste of an old pot.

"How do you even know about pawn shops?" Francis asked. "Can't imagine Lori needing to take out a loan on her fancy dishes. Or did she have a secret habit I didn't know about?"

"Mrs. Balfour," I said, taking offense at his slight, "was a wonderful caretaker."

"I'm sure."

"I didn't always live with her."

"I know—"

"And my parents weren't as well off. They drank. They used drugs." I took a sip of the sewage, setting down the mug, tapping out. "Our TV was often on loan, let's put it that way. A lot of weeks what we had in the refrigerator came down to whether we had a refrigerator."

"You remember your childhood that well?"

"Yes. And no." It was hard to explain. I had these stories. Like the pawn shop, the drinking, drugging, but they weren't memories. Not like the ones formed after I went to live with the Balfours. My life was split in two, before and after. The after was clear, normal recollection. Christmases and church and playing with Jacob, visuals getting crisper as time marched toward the present. The before? A television show or movie preview, a highlight reel. I had a list of factoids to repeat but not ones that had been experienced firsthand.

And then it happened again. Until that moment, I'd been having a good day. A regular day. A "back to me" day. The paranoid unease that had plagued me of late had been relegated to aberration. Now I felt its creepy, crawly return even before I saw the boy in blue out the window.

I jumped up from my seat, knocking over the chair, racing into the street. Striding off the sidewalk, I slipped between parked pickups, a tight fit. My knee got caught on a bumper, which forced me to slow a second, crouch, clutch, wriggle free. When I righted myself, I popped out, darting into the street without looking, stepping in front of a gas-guzzling SUV. Instincts took over. Already in motion, I kept going, even though returning to the sidewalk was closer. I didn't have the luxury of calculating odds and checking my math. My legs kept pumping, which was the right move, inertia giving me a half step before the car would've hit me. I fell to my knees, half guitar hero stage slide, half collapse from relief. It all happened so fast. The driver never hit their brakes—they didn't even have a chance to lay on the horn.

By the time I glanced up from the ground, the driver was

around the bend, turning a corner. A few passersby had stopped, rubbernecking and whispering. The entire scene lasted a matter of seconds but drew out longer, my heart caught in my throat, brain unable to process.

I got to my feet, swatting the dust off my pants, squinting into the blazing orange ball sinking in the summer sky.

"What is wrong with you, boy?" Francis shouted from the coffee shop entryway.

I focused my gaze in the opposite direction. Of course the boy in blue was gone.

"You got a death wish?"

"I thought I saw someone."

"Who?"

"This guy, this kid…he's been following me. In Cortland. Utica once. I think…"

"You think?"

"Forget it."

"You almost ate Cadillac grill, boy. This close." Francis smidged his fingers. "Almost gave me a heart attack."

When I looked in Francis's eyes, I would've sworn he was getting choked up. Why? He didn't know me, didn't seem to like me. Then again, watching someone almost getting run over would shake up anyone.

"You were in my father's shop?" she said.

We both turned. The girl was skinny to the point of gaunt, dressed in a loose dirty tee and dirtier jeans, skin an unhealthy shade of pale.

"Ace's," she added.

It took me a moment to realize she was talking about the pawn shop.

"Yes," I said. "We were looking for jewelry that…my brother… took—"

"I can't get you the jewelry back."

"We don't want it back."

Biting her lower lip, the girl surveyed the scene. That's what I saw her as—girl, not woman—even if she was around my age; she seemed fragile, a flower without sun and in danger of wilting.

"Jacob? He your brother?" She alternated between Francis and me.

I nodded. She knew his name. This was a good sign.

The girl turned toward the direction of the pawn shop, which had now closed for the day. "I can't be here." She pulled a chewed-on pencil from her front pocket and scribbled on a scrap of paper from her back. "Meet me here in half an hour."

Francis and I watched her rush past, swirling dust, before turning down a dirt path, going the same direction the boy in blue had gone. At least Francis had seen her, so there was no debating whether she was real.

I looked down at the scrap of paper she'd handed me. An address.

At last, we had a lead.

Francis and I drove his big ol' Buick to the address, a rural residence without a neighborhood, defined by trees, canopies, and bramble. We parked down the road. I made to get out but Francis grabbed me by the arm.

The old faded blue house crowned a hill. Beat up, vacant, smashed windows with a rusted car on cinderblocks in the weeds. It looked abandoned.

"What are we supposed to do?" I asked him.

"Sit tight."

We sat tight while Francis cased the place from his driver's seat. Looking for what, I had no idea.

Soon, the sun had set. Francis and I sat in his old Buick

on the side of this old country road in front of an old beat-up house without lights. This didn't feel like much of a lead. No clue where to go next. I still had all my problems waiting for me back in Cortland. I still didn't know if the police—or whoever was pretending to be the police—were looking for me. The night plummeted country cold.

Francis smoked his cigarettes, ignoring me, eying the house.

"This was a waste," I said.

He didn't respond.

"I guess we should get a hotel room—"

"Shut up, boy. Give me time to think. Someone's inside that house."

"What do you mean?" He saw the same house I did, swallowed in woodland and shrub, incorrigible wilderness. No lights. No electricity. Silent.

With the lit end of his cigarette, Francis pointed toward the backfield. "Someone went in."

"The girl? Let's go talk to her."

"Wasn't no girl," he said.

I squinted, removed my glasses, cleaned and put them back on. Through the settling gloom, I had a hard time seeing the edges of the decrepit house.

Flicking the cigarette stub, Francis climbed out of the car, leaning back in. "You coming, boy? Or you too scared?"

CHAPTER TWENTY-FOUR

Granted, my eyesight had never been good. I was both farsighted and nearsighted, which left a sweet spot of about ten to twenty feet. But I had no idea how Francis knew people were inside that house. Creeping closer, I conceded he was right. I made out the dim blue cadaver lights in the windows, the tint blending with dusk and gloam. Had they been on the entire time?

I was following Francis's lead with no idea what he was going to do. This wasn't a house where you walked up and rang the bell. I now knew there were several people inside and could hear muffled chatter. I couldn't wrap my head around when they arrived. The place appeared condemned fifteen minutes ago. Now I heard voices, low music, murmurs emanating from the cracks in the bowed planks as if the house itself were groaning.

Eyes adapting, I could see the house better even if my opinion of it didn't improve. On the blind side, mountains of trash bags were stacked to the windows, rat-torn holes spilling contents, paper cartons of milk and empty jars of spaghetti sauce. Did garbage men not travel this far into the sticks? The shingled house, dingy baby blue pockmarked with black rot, perched at an angle. Whole place could use a new paint job. Or at least a good power wash. This house was evil. I could feel it. Bad people did bad things inside there. The strangest part was the field beside the house, which was littered with old, junky cars and parts, an automotive graveyard. Not that all were that old. Or that junky. A few looked like they could still run. Some had shells but no engine, others engines but no shell. A handful were in decent shape. Old muscle, meathead cars. At the end, a couple appeared downright drivable, with shiny paint and gleaming chrome. Not high-end, luxury models, but starting from the back of the lot, traveling to the front, you got the sense you were on an assembly line. None of this had been visible from where we were parked. A frenetic energy emanated off the house. As if during the day it had been asleep. Come nighttime, the demons had awakened.

I tugged Francis by the sleeve.

He stopped bulling forward long enough to look at me.

"What are you going to do? Knock?" I gestured around the western backwoods where lawless hillbillies were birthed with a shotgun in their hands and an outstanding warrant on their head. "I don't think it's that kind of house."

"You can wait in the car if you're scared."

"Stop saying that. I'm not scared." I lowered my voice. "I'm also not stupid." There was only one reason people went into houses like this: drugs. This was a drug house, and people who did drugs weren't going to throw open their doors and invite us in.

"I ain't scared of a bunch of junkies," he said. "That girl gave us this address for a reason."

What could I do? I couldn't leave an old guy like Francis alone. A requisite amount of fear keeps us safe. Maybe I *was* overreacting. He didn't seem worried—at all.

When Francis got to the front door, he didn't bother knocking, turning the handle and striding right in.

Low discordant music bled deep within the bowels, rising past rows of rooms with their doors closed. Candlelight illuminated sporadically, flickering flames dancing shadows. We didn't bother with a light switch.

Voices grumbled as we entered a common area, which I deduced to be a kitchen. Less from furnishings and more because of layout. There was no refrigerator. There was part of a stove, with unhooked, unattached, bent pipes dangling from the ceiling in proximity of an exhaust. The peeling paint exposed punctured sheetrock, naked floorboards and studs. Water dripped methodically, plinking in a pan, as far-off storms rumbled in distant black hills.

Dark lumps lay in the corners. Bodies. Not dead, sleeping, evidenced by their sluggish reptile movements. Legs stretched, arms reached, hands pawed, guttural voices groaning, groveling without words, validating my deduction we'd entered a drug den. People, men, women—boys, girls?—as sickly and gaunt as the girl outside the coffee shop populated the cracked linoleum, sleepy snakes on cold rock. Aroused from a state of suspended animation, they stirred, hissed. I spotted several rubber tourniquets, syringes beside burnt spoons and mutilated cigarettes, the wretched slowly coming to life.

"Who the fuck are you?"

At the sound of the voice, I took a step back. Not Francis, who wasn't intimidated by the shirtless guy with the Van Dyke facial hair and bugged-out eyes.

The man presented himself in a back-room doorframe, arms and fingers dug into the molding above. Shirtless, slathered in colorless tats, sinewed and roped without a percentage of extra body fat, the man let go, planting all his weight on both feet. Not that he was big or tall or sturdy. If anything, he was on the smaller side. Still, the floor shook with the disruption as he emerged from the darkness.

"You ain't the cops," the man said, stepping closer. He didn't sound relieved. Stating fact.

"No," Francis said. "We're not the police."

"And you ain't buying. So I'll repeat: why the fuck you here?"

"We're looking for a girl," I said.

He pointed past my shoulder. "Try the donut shop." As my eyes better adjusted to the dearth of light, I caught flesh in the bedroom behind him. A woman's bare leg. He turned and pulled shut the door, stepping to Francis. "You got a smoke?"

For a second I thought Francis was going to tell him to buy his own. I didn't see Francis sharing hard-earned spoils, not with a man of this ilk. I was mistaken. Francis slid out one of his Winstons. Maybe they were the same, Francis and this lowlife, members of the same congregation of the downtrodden. The man didn't say thank you, simply plucked it from the pack. He fired up with a lighter he whipped from his back pocket, face cast craven in the column of flame.

The room brightened, a high moon splashing clear white light across the filthy floor, uneven surfaces rivered with abrasions, a fault line disrupted. The addicts continued to rouse, listless. Their lethargy stood in stark contrast to the half-naked guy in front of us who seemed antsy, agitated, and wired.

"I don't know who you're looking for," Van Dyke said. "But she ain't here."

"We met her at the café."

"I don't care where you met her."

"She gave us this address," I added.

That little bit of information seemed to give him pause. But it didn't last long.

"I don't know what to tell you." He looked back toward his room. "But I was deep up in some guts. I'd like to get back up there—"

"She might've known my grandson," Francis said.

"Listen, Pops. Maybe she did. Maybe she didn't."

Francis's hand clenched and I feared we were going to have another bus depot situation. I didn't expect Francis to get the better of this one. Serpentine, wiry, and underfed to the point of feral, this man looked psychotic. The shaky tattoos meant he'd been in prison. I'd seen that on a TV show once.

I stepped between them. "We're trying to find out what happened to my friend, okay? We met this girl in town. Her father owns one of the pawn shops."

"Lenna Ann," he said, relaxing. "She ain't here."

"You have any idea why she'd give us this address?"

"Because she's a bleeding heart?" The man paused, then nodded. He waited a bit, as if weighing what to say next. "Your friend. His name was Jacob, right?"

"How'd you—?"

The man gestured out the window into the night. "Sold him a car a couple weeks back."

"A car?"

"Yeah. A fucking car."

"How much?" I asked.

"A grand. I don't remember. What do you care? He wanted to buy one. I had one to sell. Your girl, Lenna Ann, brought him by."

"Why here?" I meant why would Jacob come out to a house like this in the first place? Why would he be in this town, period? If he needed a car, countless dealerships operate in Utica. Instead, he catches a bus to this hell house on the hill.

"Because he needed a car, and I had one to sell." He said it like I was the dumbest bastard on the planet. Which was hysterical given I'd just completed a bachelor's and I doubted this tool had his GED.

"You sure it was Jacob?" I asked, feeling stupid once the words come out. He'd already said Jacob's name.

The guy turned into his room. A shrill female voice shrieked, and we heard him tell her to "shut the fuck up."

A moment later he returned with a sheet of paper, passing it along. It was a scan of Jacob's driver's license and the bill of sale for a 1990 Chevy Camaro.

"I'm not selling shit without getting it in writing, y'know?" Then turning to Francis: "Hey, Pops. Got another smoke?"

Francis passed him the whole pack. "Keep it."

The gesture ingratiated Francis into the man's good graces.

"I don't know what else I can tell you, except Lenna Ann comes around, says this guy needs to buy a car. I tell him the price. He gives me the cash. I copy the license so I don't get popped on some bullshit charge. Then he leaves."

"You give him the keys?" Francis asked.

"How you think he got out of here?"

"The spare too?"

The man waited a moment, face twisting, before breaking into a grin. He headed into the other room, returning with a keychain fob, the kind you'd expect to find on a newer model, not whatever piece of crap this guy was peddling. Then again, judging from that side lot, maybe Jacob drove off with an updated version.

"The LoJack?" Francis said.

I had a hard time believing a guy like this was going through the effort of installing an anti-theft device.

Francis extracted his cash wad. My eyes darted around the room. Francis's remained locked on his target. He peeled off two bills, holding them up. "For the fob and the LoJack."

The man must've expected the question. He clapped a sheet of paper in Francis's palm, taking the money in exchange.

Francis examined the paper, satisfied key and documentation matched. Then he slapped my arm. "Let's go."

I wanted to argue, stay longer, find out more. A LoJack wasn't going to do us any good. Jacob was dead, the car impounded. Before I could protest, Francis was already out the door. And no way was I staying in that house by myself.

Into the cool evening air, Francis kept walking at a brisk pace. I ran to catch up.

"Why are we leaving?"

"First you didn't want to go in. Now you don't want to leave? You wanna play paddy cakes with that tweaker?"

"What was he on?"

"Methamphetamine. Crank. Gack. Ice. Whatever they call it back here. Didn't you see the way his jaw was wobbling back and forth? That's speed."

"Sorry," I said, not at all sorry. "I'm not an expert on illicit narcotics."

"Thought you said your folks used."

"They were messed up most of the time, that's all I know."

"Those kids on the floor? They were on downers. Heroin, benzos. That excited boy we spoke to? He was on uppers."

"What difference does it make?"

"A junkie will steal from you," Francis said. "A speed freak will steal from you and then help you look for it."

When we got to the car, he unlocked the door but didn't get in right away, leaning over the roof, gazing around the dark country night. "There's nothing for us here. Jacob didn't take a bus to Michigan or Minnesota. He drove."

"What now?"

"Get in," he said. "We still got miles to go."

CHAPTER TWENTY-FIVE

We stopped for the night outside Erie, Pennsylvania, a Motel 6 in the sticks next to a Flying J. It was late, we were tired. There was nowhere you wanted to stay in Wroughton, and by time we crossed state lines, Francis said he was too tired to go on. I offered to drive but he said no one dives his car but him.

Even though this entire trip was his stupid idea, I still had to pony up my half of the forty-three dollars and sixty-four cents. "A couple hours of sleep," Francis said. "Then we get an early start."

"What do you expect to find in Minnesota?"

"That's where they found his body." That was all Francis had to say on the matter as we entered our room on the second floor, a glorified closet that stank of fast food pasta sauces and, I'm sure to Francis's delight, cigarettes, despite the multiple no smoking signs. Francis locked himself in the bathroom. I said I was going for a walk. He didn't respond.

I had a lot to think about. Namely, what was I doing?

I was on a road trip in an old Buick with a crazy old man. Moments can hit you like that. For a man who valued logic and reason, I had to accept I hadn't been using much of either.

At the convenience mart, I bought a protein bar and a Red

Bull. I considered purchasing a burner phone. Call Sam or Mrs. Balfour. Clear up this mess. Problem was, I didn't know Sam's number—it was in my cell. And while Mrs. Balfour's number was implanted, I wasn't adding to her nightmare. I could get out of this mess on my own.

Walking back to the motel room, I started to see how, like Francis, I was guilty of a playing into a false narrative, one I'd created to explain encroaching malaise, triggered by Francis, Jacob, and that stupid zine.

But what proof did I have of a crime? Nothing tangible. Jacob either succumbed to a fatal psychotic episode or, if I wanted to be critical of police findings, my friend robbed the wrong person. How did he end up in Minnesota? Jacob was crazy. The real question was how did I end up in Erie, Pennsylvania?

The police called while I was having a bad day, claiming Sam was missing, and I freaked out. But what did that mean? Missing. Her parents hadn't heard from her for a few hours so they called the police? That didn't make any sense. Sam was a college student living on her own with plenty of independence. There wasn't enough time to be reported missing. It was a ruse, a con, a trap. By whom? Probably whomever Jacob stole that jewelry from. *Or...*

This could all be explained if I thought about it without emotion, logically—if I didn't let my mind get away from me. And it all came back to Francis. The guy was a harbinger, a conduit of doom, his world defined by oddity and subversion, the belief in an all-powerful conspiracy bringing order to a chaotic world. And that's the problem with conspiracies and its theorists: the comfort afforded by believing someone or something, however nefarious, is in charge. Francis *needed* this to be real. I'd opened the door a crack, allowed the possibility that Jacob and Francis weren't total liars. That's all a lie needs to grow: possibility. Then it can flourish like an invasive weed in an untended field. That's how he'd sucked me in.

There was one common denominator in all of this: Francis. What had happened—what did I know for certain? Nothing. I hadn't been sleeping, was stressed about work and my move to Syracuse, all of which plays with perception. A seed got planted, I got spooked. Wrong place, right time. Or maybe the other way around. My mind took me to a dark cell, imprisoning me, holding hostage rationale and intelligent deduction, the tools I needed to escape. The trap was laid. My friend Jacob, out of his mind, mentally ill, had killed himself, and he'd left behind this crazy little book. That book was alarming, and my natural empathy rendered me susceptible. Francis had filled out the rest of the storyline, using my grief to manipulate me. Or I should say, I *let* him take advantage of me. I allowed him to suck me up into this crusade, rendering me Sancho Panza to join his punch-drunk Don Quixote storming windmills.

I felt so stupid, gullible. I bought into his version of events. Who's to say Francis hadn't been the one calling me in the first place, masquerading as the police? He knew about Sam. I'd mentioned her. The car tailing me? I never got a look at the driver. I put another man in the passenger seat because that was the narrative. Francis had wanted me on this trip from day one. He was a lonely old man. The rest of the bizarre circumstances, taken out of context and on their own? Not all that bizarre. A boy in a blue coat? It could've been different kids. The homeless are pervasive. Jerks in a bar macking on my girl? Sam was gorgeous. Why wouldn't guys be checking her out? I'd taken a bunch of random, innocuous instances and crammed them together, trying to force cohesion, inventing a reality that flat-out wasn't true. I'd played into the cloak-and-dagger plans of a lunatic who admitted not taking his meds. Plan? There was no plan. One minute the guy was beating up on a bus station employee. The next he was walking into a drug house making it rain for useless scraps of paper. I was the one assigning weight, importance to these events. When I thought about it like that, I couldn't stop laughing. I almost ran out of breath, I was doubled over so hard with laughter.

I started formulating my escape plan. Of course I wasn't being held hostage. Francis was in good shape for a man his age. I was in the prime years, the best shape of my life. I wasn't worried about eluding his grasp. The real pain in the ass was getting home. I wondered if I should catch a ride to a bus or train station, airport. Each option invited its own headache. I wasn't up for a long Greyhound ride with a bunch of bums and alcoholics, passing through two-bit towns like Wroughton. I also couldn't justify splurging on an Uber or shelling out whatever it cost for a last-minute flight. The key to budgeting money is sticking to that budget. Missteps weren't a license to break into my savings.

A few belongings remained inside the motel. Nothing so precious that it couldn't be replaced. But my possessions belonged to me, and I determined Francis had already stolen enough from me—in particular my time, which I could've been spending with Sam. Plus, I'd left my glasses in the room. Your eyes need to breathe too. I had another pair back home. Replacements didn't come cheap.

I glanced around the complex, this colorful plaza off the interstate, with plenty of McDonald's and other fast food restaurants, bright reds and yellows, vibrant greens vying for fleeting business—meaning we weren't in a desert wasteland— and suddenly my plan got a lot clearer. I'd wait till Francis was asleep, if he wasn't already, grab my things, head down to the lobby or the Denny's next door. Look for a friendly face that might direct my return to civilization. Along the way, I'd also be sure to pick up a burner. It's impossible to do anything in the modern age without a cell phone. Another reason to distrust a luddite like Francis. I'd call authorities and clear up this entire mess from the road.

Ascending the well to the second floor, I had a change of heart. I didn't *owe* Francis anything. I didn't like him. But the man was unstable. I didn't want him to wake in the middle of the night, see me gone, and have his mind race to illogical conclusions. The guy needed to be in a hospital. But with no family—at least not one who wanted anything to do with him—he'd have to check himself in, and I didn't see that happening.

I couldn't slink out like a coward. I had to say goodbye like a man.

The door being ajar didn't register as anything alarming. Francis smoked cigarettes. Despite the numerous warnings from both the hotel and surgeon general.

"Francis," I called, pushing open the door. "I have to tell you..."

The lights in the room were on. Francis was nowhere to be found.

He went to grab a bite, I told myself. But the door... And there was his key card. The room felt disrupted. I grabbed my glasses from the table.

Even though the door to the bathroom was open and I could see no one was inside, I called Francis's name again before entering. I saw the blood, a bright streak of crimson smeared along the edge of the sink. All the toiletries had been swept to the floor and the towel rack hung by a screw. Did Francis fall, hit his head, and stumble outside? Or worse?

From the landing of the tiny Motel 6 room, I surveyed the parking lot and adjacent facilities. Truckers pulled in, fueling up with snacks and diesel, queued at the exits to get back on the road, an endless parade of taxis. I could catch a ride with any of them, get out of here, leave behind these strange days. I also didn't want to read later how a psychotic seventy-year-old man wandered off with a head wound and, bereaved over the death of his grandson, was found dead in a ditch, clipped by a car in the middle of the night.

Peering over the railing, I didn't see anyone along the lower landing. Maybe Francis had gone for chips or a soda. We hadn't crossed paths. The truck stop was sizable. There were other places, other gas stations to go in the complex. They had a Sbarro's, a Subway, a Starbucks. More unimpressive hotels and gas stations sat across the access road. What reason did Francis have to go there? What reason did Francis have to do half the crap he did?

Leave, Brandon. Get out of here. Not your problem.

Hoping I was mistaken, I returned to the bathroom, running a finger along the edge of the sink. I didn't know what I was hoping for. Leftover ketchup? Wishful thinking. I wiped my finger on a towel. The amount wasn't unsubstantial. Francis hadn't cut himself shaving. The blood ran along the porcelain in a sleek zigzag. It could've been a design. If places like Motel 6 put much thought into stylistic elements. The car keys had been left on the dresser. I grabbed them in case. If these days had taught me anything it was that this trip didn't adhere to predictable. I ran to the door, one hand wanting to slam and deadbolt it, the other taking charge, doing the right thing.

Taking stairs two at a time, I kept my eyes peeled, scouting, listening, ears pinned.

Francis's Buick sat in the same spot. No one inside it. I didn't expect anyone to be. I crept around the side of the building. There were few cars. One RV took up several spots. I went over to investigate. Lights off. No sound within.

I returned to the motel and walked the length of the building, past the vending machines and ice buckets, planning on circling around, canvassing my way back to the room. Maybe Francis *had* hit his head and staggered off, delirious? I didn't know if I should call the police, keep looking, or follow through on intentions to split.

Then beyond the far end of the parking lot, where chain link met tall grass, the length of a football field separating it from the highway, rustling, scurrying caught my eye. A glint of moonlight. A branch in the breeze. No, this was more.

When I heard the scream, I took off in a sprint, covering ground faster than I expected, a surge of adrenaline pumped into my veins. In that blackened space in the distance, I saw them. Shapes, outlines, but human. Two men. I also identified a third figure they were attempting to stuff…into a trunk?

Running as fast as I could, ground shaking beneath my steps, head jostling glasses and vision, blurring the situation. Loud traffic from the interstate perforated the night. Stale winds smacked my face. Over my heavy footsteps and breath, I heard wailing, certain that the voice belonged to Francis. We were far behind the motel; no one was coming to our rescue. It was up to me.

You can't think in moments like that, events unfolding too quickly, pulse pounding, vision compromised. On the freeway overpass, a steady stream of nighttime traffic streaked red and white. No time to think. No gods to lean on. After that last scream, I didn't know if Francis was alive. Maybe that screech had been a death knell as the butcher knife split his ribcage. Whoever could do that would have no problem stuffing me in a trunk too.

The rear of the property was neglected, filled with junkyard trash, garbage swept off the road from trucker drift. Random harder objects, pallet boards and lengths of plumbing pipe.

Which gave me hope of a weapon more substantial than wood, more lethal than stone. Slipping through a breach in the chain link, I felt lucky when my foot kicked the metal pole. Short but sturdy. Still fifteen, twenty yards to go, I started my battle cry, waving the rod, hoping to frighten them off before I had to use it.

Then all at once: the trunk slammed, a lump fell, or maybe it was the other way around; taillights spirited away across the windswept field, back toward the interstate. Like that night in the alley with Sam, the faster I ran, the more I fell behind. I was a good runner, jogging at least four days a week—I did track in high school—but I couldn't catch up, the scene stretching longer and longer. By now the car had peeled onto the highway. I couldn't understand how they'd gotten across the field so fast. My perspective warped, I watched the taillights disappear, another indistinguishable red dot blurred among countless automobiles.

The lump on the ground writhed. I reached for Francis. In the high country moonlight, I could see the knot on his head, the gash on his forehead crusted with blood.

The blues and reds from the parking lot hit our backs, followed by the bullhorn demand to drop any weapons and put hands where they could be seen.

I complied without hesitation.

Francis fired up a cigarette.

CHAPTER TWENTY-SIX

Back in the main parking lot, a crowd had gathered. We weren't at a high-class hotel. Plenty of nights ended like this at the Flying J, with squad cars and a pair of perps corralled in the back of a cruiser. Drugs, whoring, fistfights. But it wasn't often you saw a pair like Francis and me. I'd been called a straight arrow more times than I cared to admit. And Francis? How do you describe a man like that? Lips clamped around a cigarette, despite repeated orders by the cop to put it out, as he bled from a hole in his head and refused to answer questions or accept medical attention.

The officer who got the call must've been nearby to arrive so fast. That didn't mean he was qualified to handle the situation. He wasn't much older than I was.

He stared at me, little pad poised, waiting for a reasonable explanation. Where should I start? What *had* I seen? Random robbery? Jewelry barons? The…Shadow People? Once that car took off for the freeway, someone needed to supply eyewitness testimony, all evidence gone, and Francis was useless. The field where I found Francis was torn and trampled, a muddy mess, leaving no discernable tire tracks. It was my word, and the longer I tried to answer his questions, the more I had to accept I wasn't the most reliable eyewitness. I'd seen…something. There was movement, yes, officer, and other people, for sure. Were they *with* or *near* Francis? I'd been running, eyeglasses jostling, adrenaline pumping, heart rate flooding. Yes, they were definitely with Francis and not far away changing a tire on the side of the freeway. I'm sure, I said, very confident, pretty sure, a definite maybe.

"I'm nearsighted," I said to the officer, before adding, "and farsighted."

He stopped logging my statement, standing there, dumbfounded, while I rambled on, still doing my best to connect myriad loose threads.

A car? Yes, it was a car. Was it closer to where I found Francis? Or the highway? One of those answers verified causality. The other was wasting their time. And I struggled to give an accurate, infallible answer.

"I…um…"

"You say you heard a scream?" the officer said.

"Yes, I heard a scream. I saw…a shadow."

"A…shadow?"

My answers left me talking in circles. A car sped onto the highway. Francis had a head wound. Cause and effect? Two separate scenes, separated by space?

"Someone attacked the guy," I said pointing at Francis, who sat sullen, goose egg knotted on his head.

The way the officer looked at me after that left me unnerved. And, yeah, I got it. There was only *one* person with Francis when the police arrived: me. I wanted to scream, *Well, it wasn't me!* Of course it wasn't me. Francis knew that—that was the *one* thing he'd verified before lockjawing his Winston. I knew I hadn't hit the guy. But between those two absolutes was a bridge too wide to span. I realized what the officer was thinking: something perverted. An old man and a guy my age, late night, roadside motel? What was more likely: an aborted abduction? Or a lovers' spat? I wanted to clear up that misperception.

"He's a family friend," I said, desperate to get his mind out of the gutter, adding, "I thought he might be in danger." Of course, that only added to the confusion.

I'd painted myself into a corner. I couldn't launch into crazy theories of lizard people secretly running the government or any of the other conspiratorial crap Francis and Jacob's stupid zine spelled out. I *maybe* could mention my latest theory about the jewelry, how if Jacob stole gems someone might be out for revenge. The pawn shop. That drug house. A private, connected importer. What did I *really* know? Not much. Plus, I didn't want to get anyone in trouble. What if Francis was connected to this jewelry business? I didn't have any proof of a heist in the first place, and I didn't want to make a bad situation worse with opined conjecture.

The officer stuck Francis and I to cool in the back of the cruiser but didn't shut the door—we weren't under arrest, mild consolation. He went to scope out the motel, skipping our room in favor of the neighboring truck stop and gas stations, the scene a circus, absurd. Mom, Dad, Junior, and Baby Sis huddled by their doors, arms wrapped around one another, parental lectures about never finding yourself in a mess like those two down there. The fried waitresses and haggard truckers, the stoned cashiers, clerks, and other assorted weirdoes you find after midnight at a roadside rest stop in the middle of nowhere. They gathered and peered, peeped and whispered.

Soon, the officer was joined by another man, whom I assumed was the proprietor of the complex by the way he carried himself, the brazen swagger of franchise responsibility, and then they were both gesticulating, at the motel, the road, the muddy field, offering speculative versions of reality.

"You give him your ID?" Francis said. His voice surprised me. He'd been quiet for so long.

"No. Just my first name."

He peered around me, at the cop, a good fifty off in the distance.

"You have the keys?"

"To the Buick. Yes. Why?" I knew why. We hadn't had to supply our driver's licenses at the motel. Late at night, no one asked for the plate number or model of the car we'd be parking overnight. If we left now, we were never here.

Francis patted the bulge of cash in his pocket. We had everything we needed. "Let's go," he said.

I wish I could say saner parts of my brain took over, the reasonable, prudent components Brandon Cossey comprised, the characteristics of a guy who didn't jaywalk, who played by the rules. We hadn't done anything wrong—we'd been the victims. But I didn't want to stick around and take chances others would see it the same way. More questions, deeper examinations, which *would* require last names and photographic verification, information that might then be fed into more efficient computers with broader databases, where my name could pop up as being a person of interest back in Cortland.

So I didn't say a word. Just hopped up, followed Francis, didn't look back. Through the dark lot, around the side of the motel, and into the car. I was surprised by how calm I remained, how few nerves protested, and how little anyone seemed to notice.

It didn't take more than thirty, forty seconds to be in the Buick. No one called after us. No police gave pursuit. We hit the freeway, heading west, the whole surreal episode fading fast in the rearview. I checked the mirrors, anticipating their being filled with lights from the advancing fleet. Nothing. Five, ten, twenty minutes. After half an hour, I stopped worrying.

CHAPTER TWENTY-SEVEN

I had a lot of questions for the old man. At the same time, I relished the silence.

It must've been after we crossed state lines before I said a word.

"Who were those guys?" As soon as I asked the question, I understood why I'd waited so long.

I didn't want to hear Francis's answer.

Nothing he said would satisfy, satiate concerns, or make me feel any safer. Like whenever Francis spoke, I'd have to sift through the wreckage of language and decipher: What was fantasy? Outright fabrication? Pure insanity? Which would leave me searching for that nugget, the cornerstone of fractured logic I could begin constructing a fragment of truth from. This process of extraction and reconstruction was exhausting.

Francis slid out another cigarette, scanning ahead, as if looking for an exit. We were headed to Minnesota, which meant I-90—which we were already on—all the way. What did I know? About Francis? Tonight? His plans? Any of this?

"Francis, who were those men?"

"Who do you think?"

"If you say the Shadow People, I swear to God I'm jumping out of this car."

"Call them whatever you want. They don't want us finding out what happened to Jacob."

"I'm not stupid," I said. "If Jacob's body was found with expensive jewelry, he probably stole it."

"My grandson wasn't a thief."

What was I supposed to do with that? Problem was, I couldn't outright call him a liar. I'd seen the men. I witnessed the blood, dealt with the police. Unless I were willing to postulate Francis staged this too. Preposterous. But any more so than the rest of this madness or his ludicrous theories? I had no choice but to take his words at face value. At least the part about people wanting to protect secrets. I wasn't sure which scenario was more terrifying: Francis being wrong or Francis being right.

As little as two hours ago, I'd managed to convince myself I'd invented a non-existent danger, a little boy playing overdramatic, inserting himself into a world of fabricated intrigue in order to make himself feel important. Who was I? Brandon Cossey, college student slash orphan, twenty-three, a nobody. And that was the *best*-case scenario. I felt better believing I was invisible, innocuous, unworthy of being hunted. The alternative meant threats had stepped out of the shadows, entering a world of certainty and retribution.

"You don't remember me, do you?" Francis said.

The question caught me off guard. My response, the obvious one, given Francis's physical proximity: "What are you talking about? I've been driving with you for two days. Of course I remember you."

"No," he said, drawing on his Winston. "Before."

A disturbing presence sank in its claws, like someone—something—was at the doorstep of my deep subconscious, about to knock—an old acquaintance I might not be anxious to see again.

I glanced over, hit by a wave of déjà vu, remembering the way that cherry tip glowed hot, vivid in the dim light of the cab, trips taken when I was small…

Still, that better part of me, the one so desperate to stay tethered to the tangible and real, rebelled and fought back. "When you came to my apartment last week?" I said, my voice on the precipice of breaking. "Man, what are you talking about? Of course I rem—"

"When you were little. When Lori brought you home from the hospital."

"What hospital? I was never in any hospital." That part was true. I'd never broken a bone, never had an appendix out, no tonsillectomy. Not even a trip to the ER with a spiking fever. I was a bastion of good health. One of my superpowers: a remarkable immune system.

"Shady Acres."

"What about it?" I'd been to the mental hospital often. Visiting Jacob. When I pictured Jacob in there now, however, he was younger than when I recalled visiting him. In these new memories he was five, six. In reality, Jacob wasn't hospitalized until at least a decade later. Was I conflating memories of my mother, a woman I never visited in a psych ward, projecting family legend? Was my brain cracking under the pressure, unable to tell the difference between fact and fantasy? I'd never been to the Utica Insane Asylum.

The long, dark highway was deserted with the witching hour. I didn't know what town or state we were even in, and I didn't care.

"Pull over," I said. "That's it. I'm getting out. I'll hitch a ride. I'm sick of this shit. I'm serious! Pull over!"

"Shady Acres was the mental hospital where you and Jacob met." His eyes on the road, hands on the wheel, burning butt between his fingers, white hair slicked back, so cavalier, so calm. "When you were a patient."

The human mind is a funny thing. They say you only use ten percent of your brain. We've all heard it. Having studied biology and the human nervous system, I also knew it was a myth. We use way more than ten percent. How much more? I didn't have an exact number. It wasn't a full one hundred, I knew that. There were empty pockets, dead zones, areas cut off, inaccessible. We have these rooms in our minds, like the locked-up ones at secretive houses with the plastic draped over furniture so no one can sit down. What's behind that door? What's in the attic? Where's that noise coming from? We don't have access. No map. No key. No clue. But sometimes we don't need any direction or passcode to get in. A word, phrase, or sentence will unlock the door.

I'd never been a mental patient. I had zero recollection of having been hospitalized. Psychiatric treatment? For what? I was, and had always been, rock solid, a testament to normalcy. I worked. I studied. I paid my taxes and didn't break rules or laws. Whatever successes I enjoyed were the result of embracing convention, not flouting it. Only now I couldn't escape the institutional green walls. I *saw* the orderlies, doctors, and nurses, the little pills in tiny medicine cups. I *heard* the unhinged shrieks of the unwell, clanging spoons off the bars, rebelling against their jailers. I *felt* the creepy-crawly on my skin when I couldn't sleep late at night. I stopped envisioning Jacob in hospital gowns, catching my own reflection in toaster ovens and rain-slicked windows. I was the young patient. Five years old sounded right. Around the time my mother left.

"You're lying," I said, my voice hollow and insecure.

"How do you think you came to live with the Balfours?"

"We lived in the same neighborhood."

"And what? Lori invited you for dinner one day and you never went home?"

"How would you know—?"

"I was living there."

"Bullshit. Lori hates you."

"I was living there. After my son…" Francis flicked his spent butt out the window. "Don't worry about my place in all this, boy. Ask yourself: how would Lori gain custody of a child that wasn't hers? Your parents gave you away to a stranger?"

"My parents were a mess," I said. "My mother…left. She had problems. Alcohol, drugs, pills. Lori—Mrs. Balfour took me in." Cold air filled the cab. "My father wasn't a bad man. He tried to save her. I remember driving around with him, going down to the rough parts of town, and there she'd be, on a street corner, selling herself for ten bucks. It was awful to watch what it did to him."

"And you're sure that's the way it happened?"

"That's the dumbest question. Of course that's the way it happened! I was there!"

The roadside zipped by. No stars, no spotlight on the signposts up ahead. I was having a hard time swallowing.

"I was around in those days," he said. "Whether or not you want to believe it. You were a patient, boy. At Shady Acres." He paused. "You ever look for your parents? White pages?"

"It's not 1950 anymore. No one uses a phonebook."

"Online. The interwebs. You try to get in touch?"

"No. Why should I? They didn't want me. I didn't want them. Mrs. Balfour took good care of me. The Balfours were my family—*are* my family. They love *me*." I wanted to break his old man heart.

"Your parents are dead."

"No shit."

"They died when you were little. Your father killed your mother, before he turned the gun on himself."

I looked at Francis. Nothing had changed in his visage.

"Maybe it's hard to find the story," he said. "I don't know how this stuff gets archived. But I remember when it happened. It was big local news."

Like I'd never put my parents' names in a search engine. Over the years, I'd scoured the internet for them plenty. I didn't remember much of my first few years, but I knew my own parents' names—Buck and Lisa—and I sure as hell knew mine too—and it was my real name; I had all the documentation. I knew the town I was born and lived in. I knew the year they let me go. The internet has *all* this. Databases and newspaper articles, and I'd found nothing. Growing irate, I was about to tell Francis to go to hell.

"Maybe your version isn't that far off," he said. "Maybe your old man did catch your mom messin' around. I don't know anything about that. But you got the ending wrong. No one is handing a five-year-old to a neighbor lady. Lori worked at the hospital. She got to know you. She felt sorry for you, developed a fondness. You were going to be released to social services, foster care. She took you in."

"And nobody ever told me this?" The balls on this guy.

"Maybe they did. Maybe they tried. Maybe, boy," and here he paused, bitingly, "maybe you aren't as sane as you think you are. Maybe you are as crazy as the rest of us."

CHAPTER TWENTY-EIGHT

Francis was out of his skull. Of course I'd searched my history. There was nothing there. I started beating myself up for not looking *harder*. But this was how my brain turned on me, warped by the Francis Factor, which is what I'd started calling the effect of conversing with the old man. You'd start out regular and certain, and by the time you were done talking to him, you were wondering when the color blue was invented.

When Francis said that bit about the hospital, my head began leaking, like a thin layer of ice had been cracked, exposing what lurked beneath; and now these brackish waters burbled up from the fissures, spreading across the gray of a frozen lake. The human brain is like that. Super susceptible to the power of suggestion. We reconstruct fractured timelines, slot in events to fill in cohesion and order. We *need* linear chains.

For as long as I could remember, the story went like this: I met Jacob at Farewell Commons. My mother left. My father drank. I went to live with the Balfours. That was the order, the causality, the triggering event and eventual outcome. Only, as we sped along the freeway and conversation turned dry, that sequence got muddled, mixed up; and I had to admit how ludicrous that scenario, *my* scenario, sounded. Francis was right

186

about one thing: kids don't just go live with a neighbor. Children aren't thrift store garments plucked from bargain bins. There's a process to gain custody. Mrs. Balfour must've filed paperwork, talked to a state agency. When did my parents sign over rights? Transfer of parental rights, custody, emancipation—these things take time.

I struggled to find the indignation to argue. I was livid. I wanted to fight with the old man, take these frustrations out on him. But no spark existed. The energy source I needed to fuel the rage, injustice, wasn't there. You can't fake self-righteousness.

Highway, late at night, tumultuous experience, I felt my brain powering down, going into saver mode. This wasn't the time. *Conserve strength, Brandon*, I heard a voice say. I'd always possessed a great ability to shut out distractions. Another superpower. Tunnel vision. If I didn't want to think about it, I didn't think about it. Out of sight, out of mind, and out the window it went. *Redirect and focus on the task at hand.* Screw the Francis Factor and his nuttiness. Take your meds, old man.

Then a more alarming thought struck back: *whose voice is this I'm hearing?*

Because it sure as hell wasn't mine.

Not long afterward, Francis said we were stopping for the night. Another pit stop at another roadside chain—we still hadn't slept. The most surprising part about Francis: for a man so unhinged—he'd admitted going off his medications, meaning he had the schizophrenia present, unencumbered—he wasn't totally reckless. He adhered to an order, routine, as if somewhere along the way, he'd made peace with his beast—he had no problem implementing and sticking to a plan. *He* was in charge. It was as though, in exchange for letting it, the Beast, live, Francis demanded a hierarchy. The Beast could stay. The Beast would play a role. But like any well-functioning organization, a chain of command must be followed. *Francis* was the boss. If Francis and the Beast were to coexist, the latter had to know its place.

I didn't know how long we'd been driving, but if I had to guess, judging by the color of night, the particular hue of bruised, I'd say midnight, a couple hours after the incident at the Flying J Truck Stop. A reasonable time to pull over.

I was shocked when we checked into the hotel and saw the time in the lobby. Three a.m. Meaning five hours had passed. I didn't *remember* being in the car that long. Hour, two tops. What had I been doing all that time?

When we got to the room, I told Francis I was taking a walk. He shrugged, unconcerned by the time of night or where I might be going. Wasn't long ago I was done with this adventure. I didn't know what happened in that windswept motel field, and Francis hadn't instilled confidence one way or the other, but I couldn't leave. A greater power commanded me to stay. Or maybe it was lack of faith in my own abilities. A dirty trick by Francis, implanting memories, instilling self-doubt.

I justified my reversal and decision to stay, assuring myself this was the prudent response. I didn't have anywhere *to* go, or how to get there from a truck stop motel, several states over, at this godforsaken hour. I couldn't leave a sick old man alone. Francis was a determined, gruff old-timer. He'd find his way with or without me. The truth was, in that moment, I couldn't be alone.

Checking in, I'd seen a computer in the lobby. I returned there, pushing open the door and making for the desktop PC.

The clerk, balding, covered in skin tags, and too young to have such loose skin, popped his head out. "What are you doing?"

"I was going to use the computer."

He scratched his head. "Do you know what time it is? Lobby's closed, man."

"We checked in fifteen minutes ago."

"You can check in—"

"But you can never leave?"

He didn't laugh, not getting the Eagles reference and what I thought was solid B-material.

"What's the big deal?"

"It's four a.m.," he said.

Glancing at the clock, I saw he wasn't lying. Another hour lost.

"Make it quick," he said, before scurrying behind the walls, seeking solace with the other mole people.

I shook the mouse. Took ages before a soft haze began crackling, bringing the dust-covered monitor to life.

Fingers poised on keys, I pulled up a browser and sat there, not typing anything. As soon as I did, my world would forever change. Right now, I was Schrödinger's Orphan. Until I put my parents' names in that engine, both realities were true: the one I'd always known, Brandon Cossey, regular guy who'd overcome a hard start to make something of himself…and Brandon Cossey, former mental patient whose father had brutally murdered his mother; a young man whose grip on reality hung by the most tenuous of threads. And I wanted it to stay that way, keeping both possibilities open. I didn't want to lie to myself in the long run. In the interim, however, I embraced the option—keep lying to myself, defrauding, being a fake, if only for the sake of self-preservation and convenience. I could coast a long way on plausible deniability.

The moment I acknowledged the truth, whatever I discovered, I would be altered forever.

My fingers went to work. Mom and Dad. The year I turned five. The name of the town and alleged crime. I typed in the information, pulling back enough to read.

And, of course, there was nothing.

I closed the tab, shut off the monitor, and left, unsure how relieved I should be. Nothing had changed. But nothing would be the same.

I didn't return to my room right away. There was a lot next door, which was filled with dirt and sections of concrete tubing, Bobcat construction machines. In a couple hours, men would trudge out in their jackhammering hardhats, doing whatever men like that did. I couldn't imagine such a life. I had nothing against manual labor, getting my hands dirty with elbow grease for a weekend project. But nine to five, for fifty years? Sounded like prison to me.

Turning back toward the lobby, I regretted missed opportunities. Even if I didn't want to trace my crooked family tree, I could've sent an email to Sam or Mrs. Balfour, perhaps made a video call, but it was the middle of the night. That wasn't why I left so fast. I didn't want to be anywhere near an information portal. I didn't *want* to poke, prod, dig deeper. I kept thinking about what Francis said, about how I'd come to be sheltered. My violent origins, which, if true, meant I had that sickness in me. *If* it were true. And I'd just proven it wasn't. How had I let Francis plant that seed? How had he been able to make me walk to a computer and type in that bullshit? Yet I'd done it, allowing images to wedge themselves in my head, taking firm root, growing like a fungus or stubborn mold. I saw how easy that had been. You read about quack psychiatrists implanting false memories and can't imagine anyone being that susceptible. And those are trained professionals. An admitted schizophrenic off his medications had managed the trick with me.

I felt torn in two, an abused kid who creates alterative personalities to shield himself from factual horrors, saddles himself with dissociative identity disorder to protect a fragile psyche.

Yes, indeed, there existed two Brandon Cosseys.

That first Brandon had been gone so long, replaced so well, I'd forgotten he even existed.

Now I could feel his wanting to come back and be relevant again. He was knocking at my door.

I didn't want him anywhere near me.

CHAPTER TWENTY-NINE

The following morning, we were back on the road, fueled up, which included caffeine, gasoline, and an assortment of unhealthy snacks procured from the Food Mart. Francis lit a smoke. The window was unrolled but the acrid chemicals drifted over.

"Do you gotta smoke?" I was trying to eat a cinnamon bun that came from cellophane, already an unappetizing undertaking.

"Yeah," he said. "It's a habit."

Shades of green whizzed by, all the colors from art class on a palette, emerald, olive, parakeet, and sage, one blending into the next, sometimes seamless, other times jarring, punctuated by brief flashes of chartreuse.

I'd made peace with last night, accepting any "revelation" adhered to the Francis Factor. Whenever the old man spoke, you had to divide by four. Maybe he had been around when I younger. Something about him did feel familiar. As such, I wanted to know more about my childhood, more about when Mrs. Balfour brought me home, the particulars I'd missed. But it would come at a price.

That image I had of an old man, my grandfather, driving me through town in a convertible, offset against postcard summer days with azure skies, orange sunshine, and wispy cotton clouds? It was all I had, the one pleasant memory of my lousy early years. I didn't want to disturb it. Once I started asking Francis questions—questions meant for Mrs. Balfour—I'd shatter the illusion.

Instead, I distracted myself with the practical. We were on a mission after all.

"How do you plan on tracing Jacob's final movements?"

Francis whipped the LoJack certificate from his breast pocket, the one he'd bought off that drug addict who sold Jacob the car.

"Why would that guy even put a security system in his car? He was too poor."

"Tweakers are thieves. Because of that, they think everyone else is too. It's how thieves think. Like cheaters. You cheat, you believe everyone is a cheater. Don't ever date a cheater. Tweakers? The first money they invest in is an anti-theft tracker."

"I still don't understand all those cars—"

"It's a scam," Francis said.

"What is?"

"Guy sells a car, keeps the spare key. Runs the LoJack, then steals the car back."

"Why didn't he steal back Jacob's?"

"He would've. Might've tried. Jacob was dead a couple days later."

I didn't believe it, flicking a finger at the LoJack certificate. "How do you know he even gave you the real deal?"

"Because he knows it's useless. If he called to report the car stolen, whatever he said to have them trace the chip, he would've learned the car was impounded. Meaning the LoJack won't do him any good. It's scrap paper."

"Two hundred bucks for scrap paper?"

"Scrap paper for him," Francis said. "For us, it's a tracking system. After Wroughton, Jacob drove to Dearborn, where he tried crossing into Canada. Turned down by Customs, he drove straight to a gas station in Minnesota and left the car there."

"He left his car at a gas station?" I side-eyed Francis. "You don't even use computers. You don't have a phone. How are you getting this information?"

"Sit back and relax. Go to sleep. You were out late last night."

I wondered if he knew where I'd gone, that I was in the motel lobby, checking on my parents. Did he think I'd learned the truth, knew for certain he was lying?

"Dream of that girlfriend of yours," Francis said.

"She's not my girl—"

"Then don't dream. Just shut up. You're giving me a headache."

Francis was right. I hadn't slept much the night before. By the time I made it back to the motel room it had been five a.m. A hint of day breaking, pink bubble swelling with the red balloon rising on the deep purple horizon.

Leaning my head against the cool glass of the window, I felt ensconced by peace. Like returning to a warm house with a fire burning after a long day in the snowy cold.

When I opened my eyes, I saw Francis, death grip on my shoulder, shaking me. "Wake up, boy," Francis said, squeezing. "We're here."

I gazed up, drowsy, the disorientation overpowering.

Bright white-and-yellow lights poured through the windshield. Blazing hot neon. It was dark, night. We sat parked at a service station offering twenty-four-hour towing, as evidenced by the blistering outline of a red tow truck with "24/7/365."

"Where are we?"

"Black Grove, Minnesota."

I peered through the windshield, reading the name. Rock Something. Or Something Rock. Never mind glasses, trying to read *any*thing after I woke up? Took twenty minutes until that skill returned, my eyes a blurry mess.

"How long was I asleep?" I asked.

"Since we left the motel," Francis said. "Eight hours, ten hours ago. You know you talk in your sleep?"

"No. What did I say?"

"Gibberish." Francis shook his head. "You said 'climb the hill' at one point." He lit a cigarette. "Couldn't make out the rest."

I wasn't lamenting missing Chicago traffic or having been denied the scenic views and malodorous aromas of the farms and factories of Wisconsin. Just surprised I'd knocked out so long.

Francis gestured with the lit cigarette. "The GPS from the car says this's the car's final destination."

"What do you know about GPS?"

"Because I'm old, what, I don't understand anything invented in the last thirty years? I don't use the internet because the government clocks and catalogues everything you search. That's not paranoia. That's reality. You ever make a video call? Your face is now stored in a database, along with the rest of the criminals, and someday, when they want to find you—and they will—you won't be able to walk two feet down a street."

Francis dropped the LoJack certificate on the cracked vinyl seat and climbed out of the car. A man dressed in gray overalls smeared with oil, grease, and gunk stepped out of the garage, locking us in a dead-eyed bovine stare. Walking over, the man rolled a dirty rag in his hands but didn't extend one to shake.

"I help you?" The man cast his eyes between Francis and me. I had nothing to add. What a strange sight it must've been, a well-dressed college student such as I and out-of-time greaser Francis.

The two men headed toward the garage. No motion was made for me to follow. Fine. I was waist deep in the Land of Ten

Thousand Lakes, at a grubby gas station, on the trail of a dead friend and trying to solve an impossible riddle. I could use the respite.

Glancing up at the moon, I thought about Sam, how wherever she was the same moon shone down on her, which I knew was from a song I'd heard but I couldn't remember the name. She was safe though; I knew it in my heart. Francis was right about that at least. Sam had never been in danger. So why had they told me she was? More important: who were "they"? The same men attempting to stuff Francis in a trunk? The same men who killed Jacob? Or were there others in the dark I knew nothing about?

Francis emerged from the shadows.

"Let's go," he said, sliding in the driver's seat.

"Was Jacob here?" I asked as he backed up without an answer, squealing into the road, peeling out, no side cameras to assist with navigation. He burned rubber like an angsty teenager.

He didn't respond to my question, checking his mirrors.

"Francis?"

"Yeah, he was there."

I could see Francis running over the story in his head, as if it didn't make sense. If it didn't make sense to Francis—the man scaled walls of improbability quicker than Spider-Man—what was I going to do with the details?

"Jacob stopped in the night before he was killed," Francis said. "When Stauch—"

"What's a Stauch?"

"That was Stauch. Owner of the station. Maybe it's a nickname. I don't know. Shut up and listen. He said Jacob stopped in, complaining about car trouble. Stauch asked for the keys. And that's when he discovered Jacob was wrong."

"About what?"

"Jacob had the wrong keys."

"What do you mean wrong keys?"

"The keys Jacob gave him weren't for the car he was driving."

"Then how had Jacob driven to the garage?"

Francis shrugged. Despite passing it off as nothing, Francis was as tripped up by this information as I was.

You can't drive a car without a key. Unless it's hotwired, but we'd met the man who'd sold Jacob the car. I'd seen the bill of sale and copy of Jacob's license, which apparently he did have. Did Jacob lose the car key along the way? We had the spare with us. Why would he hand the man the wrong keys? Other than the simple fact Jacob was out of his mind. Who knew what the voices were telling him to do?

"Do we know where Jacob went afterward?"

"Motel. Closest one. Super 8. About three miles. Caught a taxi. Plan was for Stauch to tow the car there once Jacob called."

"And?"

"Jacob never called."

CHAPTER THIRTY

The Super 8 sat on a desolate, dilapidated, rundown, weathered strip, as cheap an overnight option as one was liable to find. On the other side, down an embankment, the highway ran in both directions, super fast cars and trucks zipping past, shielded by the canopy of green trees, which for the rider created an illusion of separation, a barrier, a means to feel superior. Black Grove, Minnesota made Upstate New York downright cheery by comparison.

Along the frontage road, the Super 8 split the distance between a takeout Chinese restaurant and a tire shop, both closed for the night. Farther ahead, in the direction away from town, weak lights threatened the black night.

Few cars filled the motel lot. This wasn't part of a big complex like ones on the interstate. This was a dumpy place where drunk, philandering husbands were sent to sober up in shame. Maybe a few folks missed their exit, jumped the gun, got off one too soon, too tired to correct their mistake. Under normal circumstances I'd have to be bleeding out of my eyes to stop here.

The bright lights from the small foyer spilled onto the sidewalk where groundskeepers had taken the time to plant a row of yellow flowers. The odd touch of beauty in the dirt felt like cheating.

A girl smiled when we walked in, a girl too young to be working alone in a motel this deserted and low rent. She couldn't have been more than seventeen, corn-fed and wholesome, but the sadness had already settled in her eyes. I stepped closer and read her nametag. Nadine. Such a strange, old lady name for a girl so young. Come back to Black Grove in twenty years, and she'd still be here.

"Would you like a room?" Nadine asked. Even the way she asked was sad.

"No," Francis replied, before explaining the reason behind our presence, which included a rough time frame and loose physical description of Jacob, nothing more. I was about to step in and elaborate—there was no guarantee the poor girl was working that night, and Francis hadn't given her much to go on.

"Oh yeah," the girl said, surprising me. "I remember him."

"He rent a room?" Francis asked.

I thought Nadine would have to check registration files, dig out a book, log into the computer. I was wrong.

"Mmmhmm," she said. "Yes, sir, he did." Nadine paused. "Sorta."

"Sorta?"

"He paid for the room but he never stayed in the room."

"But you're certain this was Jacob Balfour?" I asked.

"That's the name he gave. Wasn't long ago. Description matches. Your grandfather said he's a...big fella...and we don't get a lot of people here during the week. The weekends can get busy. Weekdays are dead."

I didn't want to know why the denizens of Black Grove saw reason to congregate at the Super 8 on weekends. Didn't want to know what went on behind closed doors, didn't want those thoughts in my head.

"How was he acting?" Francis asked.

"Strange. That's why I remember him."

"How so?"

"Nervous? Troubled. He came in, asked how much for a room. I told him. He paid me but he never went in the room."

"How you know?"

"He never took the key card." Nadine leaned over the counter, staring out toward where our car was parked. "Your friend kept stepping outside like he was looking for something, someone."

"Did you see anyone out there?"

"No."

"That's all he did?" I asked. "Pay, look out the door, and then…?"

"He went in and out about five times, and then the sixth time, he didn't come back."

"Do you have video surveillance?" I asked. "Recordings we could look at?" I nodded at the cameras pointed toward our faces and the door.

"They don't work," Nadine said.

Francis shoved open the exit door, bulling out of the lobby. I smiled at the girl, who hadn't done anything wrong, and followed him into the parking lot.

"Hey," I said. "It's not her fault."

"Didn't say it was." Francis lit a cigarette, peering down the long service road.

"What now?" I asked.

For the first time since our journey together began, Francis was beaten. I could see it in the way his posture slackened. The fiery determination had vacated his eyes. I thought retracing Jacob's footsteps was part of the plan. I was mistaken. Retracing footsteps *was* the plan.

"Might as well get a room for the night," he said. "You slept in the car. I'm running on empty."

Fifty bucks and change bought us two key cards and access to an unspectacular space that barely fit two beds. We were on the first floor, way in the back, the furthermost room. But it had porch access. Francis wasn't in the mood for talking, making for the porch to smoke cigarettes and stare into the void. I left to grab a Coke from the vending machine.

I shouldn't have been surprised to see the machine didn't take cards—I was used to the vending machines at SUNY—but this was so old school there wasn't even a slot for dollar bills, which I didn't have. Seventy-five cents. Three quarters. I didn't have that either.

Turning to head back to the room, I saw the maintenance man on a ladder. I didn't have any idea what time it was, having neglected to check the clock in either the lobby or room. What difference did it make if it was eight o'clock or midnight? In a way, this mission was timeless.

"Excuse me," I said to the man, who didn't stop fiddling with wires in the wall, a light fixture he was perched beneath. He was older. Not Francis old. Fifties maybe. Rough-hewn, lean, drawn, a man who'd excavated his existence from the grind of menial labor in hardscrabble positions. He remained silent. I wondered if he'd seen me, or maybe he was disabled, handicapped, unable to communicate. I stood there a moment, awkward, trying to decide how to proceed.

"What you want?" he said, continuing to crank the screwdriver in his hand. He still wasn't looking at me.

"My friend was here last week. He's...gone. I'm trying to track his final movements."

Formulating the words in my brain, they sounded strange, and they spilled out even odder, spoken too soft, tripped over. I hadn't given him reason to help, but the maintenance man stepped down from the ladder, wiping hands on pants.

"You got a cigarette?" he asked.

"I don't smoke."

"You smell like smoke."

"My…grandfather…smokes. We've been driving since New York."

"New York, eh?"

The maintenance man nodded for me to follow him. We walked down a little alcove reeking of urine—who can't make it to their room to relieve themselves?—and then out to the sidewalk path encircling the motel.

In the clear moonlight, the maintenance man pointed down the parking lot. "This was about two weeks ago?"

"About that."

"Your friend a great big fat guy?"

"Jacob was large, yes."

"Couple weeks back. Around five or so. There's a great big fat guy." He pointed toward the lobby. "Keeps going in and out of the office. Door swingin' back 'n' forth. Can't stand still. Like he's got bugs crawling up his ass."

"That sounds like Jacob."

The man gestured toward the adjacent field, where an electrical box stood. Maybe it was a generator. I'd never been the handiest of men.

"Rewiring the fuses." The man pointed at the electrical panel again in case I was confused. "He was in the car talking to his girlfriend. Arguing."

Disappointment settled. "No, that wasn't Jacob. He didn't have a girlfriend."

"Had New York plates on the car. We don't get a lot of out-of-staters here. And you said he was a hefty fella?"

"Did you get a look at her?" I asked. "This girlfriend?"

He gestured at a streetlamp. "They were parked under the

202

light. He seemed to be punching outside of his weight class, if you know what I mean."

"She was pretty?"

"Not bad. Skinny, underfed. I like 'em with more meat on their bones. She didn't seem as loopy as your buddy, if that's who it was. And if it wasn't, I don't know what to tell you. You say New York, couple weeks ago, I remember the night, New York plates. And he was a big fat guy acting strange."

Outside of the girlfriend, the rest sure fit.

"You remember what he was driving?"

"Old muscle car. Camaro, I think. Dark. Navy, purple."

Under the wide country sky, I tried to read his nametag, like I'd done with Gustavo and Nadine. I liked learning people's names. It's manners. There wasn't one. A nametag was stitched into the fabric where a name should be, but the space remained blank.

"I watched 'em," he said as if divulging a scandal. "They stopped arguing and got friendly again—*real* friendly. If you know what I mean…" He wriggled his eyebrows. "When they were done, fat guy buckled up, put 'er in reverse, and they hightailed it out of here."

"Which direction they go?"

The maintenance man pointed toward the lights on the horizon.

"What's down there?" I asked.

"Dead end." He pointed the direction Francis and I had come. "Highway onramp and center of town's that way. No reason to go down there."

The maintenance man shrugged and headed back the direction he'd come.

I rushed to the room to tell Francis. I wasn't sure why this should matter, but it felt important. Jacob? A girlfriend? The

Jacob I knew was never concerned with girls. Not that he went the other way. I knew he liked girls; he'd tell me about the girls he had crushes on. Or he used to. Before he changed and the darkness took over.

Jacob Balfour. On the run, risking it all for a girl?

The door was ajar. My heart seized up. I took a step back and bumped into someone, which made me jump, skittish as a stray cat found under the house.

"What's gotten into you, boy?" Francis was holding a bucket of ice.

I looked at the ice bucket, which was absent any drinks, alcoholic or otherwise.

"My dogs hurt," he said. "Don't worry. You'll get old too." He studied me up and down. "Speak up, spit it out."

I told him what the maintenance man told me, about the girl in the car, their argument, reconciliation, and the quick, sudden decision to hightail it away from town.

"Did you know he had a girlfriend?" I asked.

Francis shook his head. I could see him running through scenarios. The two had been in frequent communication over the years, sharing intimate conversations, but Jacob hadn't confided in Francis about the girl, whoever she was. Why the secrecy? The omission felt huge, although I wasn't sure why.

I followed Francis into the room, expecting him to put down the bucket, peel his grubby socks, and soak his decrepit feet, a sight I wasn't looking forward to. Instead, he tossed the ice in the bathtub, grabbed the keys, and made for the door.

CHAPTER THIRTY-ONE

Behind the wheel of the big Buick, Francis didn't speak, a man consumed. After a few days on the road with the guy, I knew better than to press. He clamped onto his cigarette, brow furrowed, stare narrowed, heading the opposite direction we'd come, toward the dim lights on the horizon.

I watched these lights grow brighter until I couldn't take any more. "What do you plan on doing, Francis?"

"The quarry," he said through an exhale, expression swallowed in a cloud of smoke. "Where they found Jacob's body."

I checked the dashboard. There was no clock; I knew that.

"The quarry is closed for the night. No one will be there."

"That's the point."

"Don't you want to talk to workers or supervisors on-site? See if anyone saw anything?"

"Not anymore."

"Because of the girl?"

Francis shook his head. "They found all that money, jewelry. No one was trying to rob my grandson."

I hated thinking what I thought next. How could I not, though?

"If Jacob was traveling with this girl, whoever she was, how do we know she didn't…?"

"Say it."

"Pretty girls don't date guys like Jacob."

"If her intention was to rip him off," Francis replied in that droll, pedantic tone of his, "why did she leave behind so much money and jewelry, eh, bright boy?"

"Maybe there was more money. Maybe she got all she needed. Maybe she broke Jacob's heart."

Francis sucked on his cigarette, saying nothing. Towering tripod structures, transferring enough wattage to power a small city, broke the sky, and broad halos ringed across the large-scale construction site.

The location of the site was a couple miles from the motel—was this why Jacob and his girlfriend chose the Super 8? Why were they fighting in the car? Who wanted to forge ahead? Who wanted to stay behind? What was so important inside this quarry?

"What's the urgency, Francis?" Something had triggered this immediate response, provoking the sudden need to see the crime scene.

Francis curled his lip, his way of telling me to shut up. I could see he was disappointed I wasn't getting it quicker. I didn't know what I was supposed to get. How did we know the maintenance man had seen Jacob? My dead friend couldn't have been the only guy from New York with a weight problem to pass through Black Grove. What answers could we hope to glean after hours at a closed quarry? I needed to voice these concerns.

"*We* need to be on the same page," I said. "Working together."

"You've never been a part of this, boy. Why did you even come along?"

"You asked me!"

"I've known people like you my whole life. You have nothing to offer. So you leach off the rest of us, the ones who are interesting, the ones with a story to tell. You're a user."

"Stop the car," I said. "I'm done."

Francis stopped the Buick at a chain-link fence, which was locked up, like I knew it would be. An unoccupied brown shed stood to the left where visitors were meant to check in. There was no nighttime guard. At least not one visible or waiting. That didn't mean one wasn't prowling inside keeping watch. Heavy, expensive machinery filled the space. Whatever was being excavated had to be worth a lot of money. One thing was clear: no one was meant to get inside.

Jamming the car in reverse, Francis K-turned, speeding back toward the motel, a relief. I wasn't up for breaking and entering. At last, I thought, I'd gotten through. Finally, he was thinking straight.

About a half a mile down the frontage road, Francis pulled over, shielded by a bank of red twig dogwood. I recognized the variety from botany class. Come fall these unassuming trees would light up flaming red, as though on fire. For now, they were adequate cover to have a late-night conversation.

He punched the car in park but left the engine running. He reached low into the runner to retrieve something. "Drive back to the motel."

"What are you planning on doing?"

"Drive back to the motel, boy." Francis started to get out of the car. I grabbed his sleeve. He yanked back his arm.

"I can't let you go wandering off in the middle of the night."

"You're not going to *let* me?"

"You're too—"

"What? Too old to make decisions for myself? What do you think we came out here for? You're too scared to scale that fence, I'll go alone."

"I didn't say I was scared."

"I can see it in your eyes, boy. You're scared of everything.

Ain't no way to live your life."

I had no intention of breaking and entering a construction site. As for being scared of *life*? Ha! After all I'd overcome, that didn't even deserve a response.

His left hand, the one that he'd dipped between the seat and door, was hidden out of sight.

"What's in your hand, Francis? Is that a…gun?"

Francis whipped his fist around, presenting a flashlight. He scoffed. "You live in a fantasy world."

"*I* live in a fantasy world? I'm not the guy off his meds, making up fairy tales." I should've felt bad talking that way to a man Francis's age. I didn't. "What are you hoping to find? A letter Jacob left behind with photographic evidence stuffed in a tailpipe? Jacob is gone!"

Francis's face twisted up, eyes whittled mean. I knew I'd gone too far but I wasn't backing down. Let him rip into me all he wanted.

Instead, he replied, calm as could be: "Why do you think we made this trip?"

"Honestly, Francis? I don't have a clue. This whole thing has been a…" I wanted to say "waste of time." But I couldn't destroy what little faith he had left.

I held up my hands, letting him know I didn't want to argue. Clarity had returned, striking me hard between the eyes. "Listen," I said, speaking softer. "It's not your fault. It's *nobody's* fault. I loved Jacob. He was my brother. That's why I came along. I wanted to believe too. But after that guy at the motel…I think it's obvious what happened."

"Oh, is it?"

"Jacob was with a girl. They stole money, jewelry." I stopped myself before Francis could object to the term. "I won't speculate how they came in possession, but they were running, under duress. They had a fight. She took her cut and left. We don't know how much money and jewelry there was to begin with."

"Was that before or after my grandson wandered into a quarry and set himself on fire?"

"It's a construction site. There are a thousand and one ways to get hurt in there."

"Do you know how the cops were able to ID Jacob? Dental records, from the few teeth that weren't torched to dust. Usable fingerprints of one hand. The rest of my boy was ash."

"I'm sorry, Francis."

"I don't want your pity. I want whoever killed him and tried to cover it up to pay."

"You want to believe the police are lying or there's a cover-up we can uncover that the dumb cops can't. Because it's easier than accepting the truth: we couldn't save him."

"There's no 'we,'" Francis said. He'd meant it to be cutting, a knife plunged in my heart. The dig didn't stick. The intent was there, the execution weak.

"All we need is in front of us," I said. "Nothing concealed, nothing hidden. The police ruled it an accident. Because it *was* an accident." For the first time in a long time, I was me again, whole, confident. I could see Francis was hurt. I wasn't going to abandon him. I couldn't imagine how difficult this had to be, to know your grandson, your flesh and blood, suffered like that. And at his own hand? "I know this is important to you," I said. "Let's get some sleep. We'll come back tomorrow, okay? We'll talk to the people in charge and get answers."

I thought I'd done a convincing job. Hearing the words out loud, I tried not to feel like a sucker for having let it go this far. But better to wake up and realize you've been a fool for three days than wake up and realize you've been a fool for four.

Reaching for the handle, Francis smiled. It was a sad smile.

"I'm gonna take my flashlight and poke around." He climbed out, drummed his fingers off the hood, tossing me a bone. "I'm sure you're right. I won't find anything. Let me have this."

"It's locked! They'll have security cameras and guard dogs, or—"

"Let me worry about that, kid." He winked. "Go to bed. I'll be back in a couple hours."

"The motel is at least two miles away."

"Not even. And I walk that every morning."

I sighed, or maybe it was more of a groan. I was frustrated. I could see I wasn't changing his mind.

"Please," he said. "Let me see where my boy died with my own two eyes."

I let my head fall back.

"I need to do that, Brandon."

Francis leaned in, grinned, smacked the top of the old Buick Skylark, and started moseying toward the quarry. Ten, fifteen feet later, I couldn't see him anymore, the country night so black.

I slid over into the driver's seat and headed back to the motel.

At the Super 8, I asked Nadine for a toothbrush and toothpaste. She passed along a miniature complimentary set.

At the door, I turned around. "And when you see your maintenance guy, tell him I said thanks."

"What maintenance guy?"

I recapped our earlier conversation, how the maintenance man had seen Jacob going in and out, just as she had. "My friend had a girl with him. It's the first new information we've learned since leaving New York."

"We don't have a maintenance guy," Nadine said.

"He was working on the lights." I pointed a finger through the wall, unsure the direction. "Down the corridor…"

"It's just me here. And Carol, the owner, does all that stuff herself." Nadine reached for the phone. "I should call her. What did this man look like?"

I gave a brief description, including age, height, and build, which was generic at best.

"That's strange," Nadine said, punching digits and cradling the receiver. "Maybe Carol forgot to tell me. Not like her." Nadine stopped, hand cupping mouthpiece. "Voicemail." She turned to leave her message in private, but not before saying, "Sleep tight, Brandon."

In the room, I stripped down to my boxers, brushed my teeth, and conked out.

I woke to the maids knocking. Startled out of bed, I was pulling on my pants, shouting to give me a second, when I noticed Francis's bed was undisturbed. He never returned. The knocking continued, forcing me to hop, one leg at a time, twisting around as I tried to slide on my tee, wondering where he was.

Hand on handle, I caught sight of the clock. Seven a.m.

Opening the door, I didn't find the maids.

It was the police.

CHAPTER THIRTY-TWO

Shirt half on, I stood there, unable to finish getting dressed. The police don't show up at your motel room at seven a.m. with good news.

"Do you have ID, sir?"

"Yes, of course." I turned away from the door. There were two of them. "Come in." I went to retrieve my wallet. They didn't move from where they stood.

"When was the last time you saw Francis Balfour," the cop asked, passing along my identification to his partner, a younger Asian woman, who wasn't talking.

"Last night when I...dropped him off."

"Dropped him off where?"

I pointed out the window, along the frontage road, visible through the window shades I never bothered twirling shut. "The side of the road." In the bright daylight, the path didn't look as sinister.

"Side of the road?"

I nodded.

"Do you know where he was headed?"

I exhaled, dreading what came next. I didn't want to be an accessory. Francis must've gotten caught breaking in.

"Sir?"

"Francis's grandson—my friend—Jacob, he...died in that quarry a couple weeks ago. Francis wanted to see where. I tried to talk him out of going. I saw the site was locked up, but you don't know Francis..." I regrouped the words, reordered them, tried to choose carefully, not wanting to add more fuel to whatever this fire was. "Francis has schizophrenia. He doesn't always think soundly." Then, knowing how that must've reflected on me, allowing a seventy-something schizophrenic to venture alone in the dark at night, I added, "You can't talk the guy out of anything once he sets his mind to it—"

"I'm sorry to tell you this, sir. Francis Balfour's body was discovered by the crew this morning. Looks like he lost his footing and hit his head on a wheel loader. Death appears instantaneous. We are sorry for your loss."

I'd never traveled far beyond my hometown or state. I'd visited Howe's Caverns when I was a kid, and later the Baseball Hall of Fame with Mrs. Balfour and Chloe when Jacob's team was playing in a tournament, which was the last year Jacob played ball before the bottom fell out. Both of those are in Upstate New York. We'd gone to Lake George too. I was twelve. I'd been to other states as well, but all in the Northeast—Massachusetts and the Berkshires, where we'd gone one winter, renting a cabin. No one around for miles, Mrs. Balfour made chocolate chip cookies and hot cocoa, while Jacob, Chloe, and I built snowmen and went sledding.

Where I was from, everything looked the same. Buildings, people, wilderness, geography—all stacked close together, maximizing space to compensate for the lack of real estate.

Driving back from Minnesota in Francis's old Buick Skylark, through high wheat plains and ripe cornfields, miles and horizons stretching without end, radio fading in and out, old country music and talk radio, I began to appreciate how big this world is, all the opportunities, destinations available, my life an endless chain of possibilities. A choose your own adventure, like one of those interactive books I loved as a kid. Even though she didn't have disposable income, Mrs. Balfour never said no to a book. In the end, Jacob and I chose our own adventure all right. I guess we all do. Me, Francis, Jacob. While I steered away from danger, opting for safe, responsible, and alive, men like Jacob and Francis had driven straight into the storm.

I was home before I knew it. For most of the trip I'd checked out. At first the scenery was unexpected and, thus, rendered exotic. Then it turned commonplace, unremarkable, like when you repeat routes so often you stop paying attention, autopilot taking over, one of those new self-driving cars.

As soon as I hit Cortland, I replaced my phone, restoring my contacts. I could've replaced the phone in Minnesota. Truth was, I wanted the couple days to zone out. After plugging back in, the first call I made was to Sam, who picked up on the first ring. I said I was calling to say hi. I wasn't going to freak her out that killers masquerading as police tried to tell me she was missing. Sam said she'd been calling. I explained I lost my phone, how I had to visit my grandfather. She didn't ask more than that. I didn't offer more than that. I could hear by her tone she sensed something was off—and there was—but her purported disappearance was the least bizarre detail of what I'd been through. I had no interest in rehashing these past few days. I made an excuse why I had to get off the phone. Sam seemed confused. Understandable. I'd called to say I couldn't talk.

Sunday, I hoped Mrs. Balfour would be home. I didn't ring first, taking my chances. Some news you have to break in person.

I wasn't looking forward to telling Mrs. Balfour about Francis.

I wouldn't be able to avoid how we'd ended up in Minnesota or what we were doing there. I'd do my best to spare her feelings and not reopen old wounds. She was going to hear about Francis sooner or later, if she hadn't already.

Death ends all chances of reconciliation, forcing one to come to terms with the relationship as it is, as it was, as it will always be. Mrs. Balfour didn't mince words when it came to Francis. After three days on the road with the man, I could understand why. Francis Balfour was moody, hardheaded, often snarky if not downright mean, and he was mentally ill. The most infuriating aspect of his personality was the lack of contrition. Instead of acknowledging the burden and onus he placed upon others, he championed these flaws, wore them like a badge, flaunted his imperfections. Francis was a man who defined himself in opposition, by what he was against rather than what he stood for. I had always associated that trait, contempt for convention, the willingness to fight and argue with youth. Angry young man syndrome. Like a teenager pissed off for just being born. Except Francis was at an age where he should've long outgrown such impetuous impulses and made peace with life's inherent hostility. Instead of acceptance and assimilation, Francis Balfour wanted a war.

"Brandon!" Mrs. Balfour said when she opened the door. "Where have you been? I've been calling for days! Chloe! Brandon's home!"

Chloe ran into the room, wrapping her arms around me. I held off on the news about her grandfather, skirting the lines of fact and filler. Mrs. Balfour put on coffee, Chloe ran off to a friend's house, and that's when I told Mrs. Balfour I had important news.

"I think it's best if we sit down," I said.

I'd resolved on the way over to tell Mrs. Balfour the complete truth, not hold anything back, even the parts that painted me in an unfavorable light. In that bright, sunlit kitchen, surrounded by the set design of my childhood—the sugar canister, the coffee maker, the whimsical, homespun crocheted wisdom stitched and stamped on assorted plaques and framed photographs—I couldn't follow through on that conviction. And I wasn't sure whom I was protecting. Talking about those three strange days I shared on the road with Francis Balfour felt like a violation of trust. I didn't *owe* Francis anything. I also didn't want to besmirch the dead. And would it have made any sense? The drug houses, the pawn shops, the jewels, the money? The...Shadow People? The one part I didn't omit was the nameless girlfriend. I wanted Mrs. Balfour to know her son was not alone at the end, even if I hadn't reached a verdict on said girlfriend, whoever—*wherever*—she was.

When I finished speaking, Mrs. Balfour expressed sorrow but didn't look half as devastated as I felt. Sharing the story, even an abbreviated version, I couldn't hide the fact that I'd fallen prey to a conman. The games, the lies, the ruse.

"Don't do that to yourself, Brandon." Mrs. Balfour grabbed my hand. "Francis was sick. That's the insidious part of schizophrenia. The inability to differentiate between fact and fiction. He made it hard to love him."

"I played into that."

"Francis wasn't a bad person. My father-in-law *wanted* to do the right thing. His moral compass was broken. Dealing with him was like trying to take a trip based on a map to a land that doesn't exist." She squeezed my hand harder. "My father-in-law had a lot of wonderful qualities, and one of them was he was a fantastic storyteller. I think part of that was because of the conviction. He *believed* his own lies. And because he was so passionate, he could get others to believe them too."

"I know. At one point he tried telling me I'd been in a mental ward. I admit, even though I knew it wasn't true, I started having flashbacks—I could *see* the orderlies and the color of the wall—even though I *knew* they weren't real. I understand how they got there, these memories—from visiting Jacob—but now I was the one on the inside."

I turned away, thinking about that part of the story, how easy it had been for Francis to tap into my biggest fear. Losing control. Agency was paramount to my survival, and to manipulate me, all one had to do was recognize that and turn it on its head.

"Is there going to be a funeral?" I asked.

Mrs. Balfour didn't respond. She had no expression. Gone was the compassion, empathy, concern. In its place a blank slate. I thought maybe it was in poor taste to ask about a funeral, but Francis *was* dead. He wasn't coming back. We needed to honor his life, however wretched it had been at times. Maybe it was too soon?

Then I realized that wasn't the cause of her silence. And coming back around to the main point wasn't a smooth transition. More like riding a rickety roller coaster. I'd navigated the initial big drop but was being manipulated again, dragged along by rusted chains, buckling logistics and physics. I didn't want to. But I had to fall once more.

"Mrs. Balfour?"

Her eyes welled.

"It's not true," I said. "I know it's not true. I've looked up my parents online over the years." I tried laughing it off.

"Your mother's maiden name is Cossey. Your father's, yours is, was, Parker."

"Are you telling me—?"

"I don't know how your father got the nickname Buck. His real name was Alexander."

"What are you trying to say, Mrs. Balfour?"

"And you didn't grow up in Farewell Commons. You were born in Schenectady." She took a deep breath. "Meaning if you ever searched for your parents and put in their names, the town, your name, any records would be hard to find. I didn't do that to deceive you. Nothing was done with the intention of lying to you." She reached across the table to grab my hand, squeezing it. "I didn't want you to have to carry the burden of what your father had done. That was the only reason we kept your mother's maiden name. I planned one day to tell you the truth. But you... The doctors said..." Mrs. Balfour tried smiling, wiping away a tear. "It was like you forgot it ever happened. I struggled with whether to tell you but by then doing so seemed cruel. You had adjusted so well. Jacob relapsed. You never wavered."

I couldn't move.

Mrs. Balfour left the room. I sat still, staring out the window at birds and trees, clouds and sky, willing my mind to snapshot this moment, leave it preserved, untouched. In case I couldn't find my way back here on my own.

A moment later she returned with her laptop, setting it front me of me.

I eyed her, then the computer.

"Go ahead," she said.

I hadn't had the details of a crime until a couple days ago, when Francis told me. It's hard to arrive at the correct answer when you have all the facts wrong. My mother's name was all I'd gotten right. And Lisa is as common a name as you can find.

Of course they wouldn't use my name. I was the victim.

You have to protect victims.

Husband Kills Wife Before Shooting Self; Child Flees
UTICA, Dec. 29 (AP) A small boy was found in the
snow by neighbors before police made a grisly discovery...

218

I read the rest even though I already knew how it ended. I read about my father shooting my mother three times in the face before sitting at the kitchen table for hours, drinking whiskey, oblivious to the fact that his five-year-old son had run out of the house in a blizzard, before he turned the gun on himself. A passerby found me trembling on the side of the road, near frostbite, spackled with blood.

I'd known the truth all along.

CHAPTER THIRTY-THREE

Before I left her house, Mrs. Balfour kept asking if I was okay, if I was I upset or angry. I told her no. My life wasn't any different than it had been two hours ago.

That was a lie.

Francis was right. You don't give away a kid to a neighbor. Didn't pass the sniff test. The real story, confirmed by Mrs. Balfour, held up to scrutiny. I wasn't mad at Mrs. Balfour for lying to me, omitting details. All she had done since coming into my life was love, care, and provide for me. This wasn't about Mrs. Balfour. This was about what was inside me.

I was sick. I'd long been peculiar, odd, off. I could tell by the way people reacted to me. Bad thoughts popped into my head, unnatural desires, random violent urges. When these madman tendencies came on, I suppressed them. It was easy to do, like quashing a lone slow fat bug on a large concrete floor. I pretended to be the most normal person I knew. Rigid in my adherence to rules and order, I lauded this sensibility, championed it, considering it a testament to discipline over anarchy. But I never clicked with other people. Outside of the Balfours, I had no long-term relationships. I burned through people. We'd start out hot and heavy, friends, lovers, and then they'd get sick of me. Because they could see it too. Like Francis said, I was a user. All my idiosyncrasies now explained, they weren't quirky or charming. Like the song says, I was a creep, a weirdo. It's why I lived alone, why I'd been fired, why I didn't have close ties. I wasn't Brandon Cossey, cool, composed, collected, self-made college grad. I was Brandon Parker, the child of addicts, the offspring of bad people, the son of a murderer. That same blood flowed in my veins; that mutated gene marred my DNA. All the self-talk and reasoning could never change that. I was a note from the underground, a sick, spiteful man, unattractive and diseased. And no doctor could fix that.

The evidence had been there from the start. The last couple weeks, my psyche, overloaded and unfit, had started to crack, allowing the dim light to shine. It had always been a matter of time.

Schizophrenia often manifests itself in one's early twenties. I *saw* these people. I *heard* their voices, clear as you talking to me. Except…they'd never been there. That's the danger of the disease. The sufferer can't differentiate between what's there and what's not. It's why no one else saw the boy in blue, the maintenance man, the guys in the bar. None of these people existed.

Driving home, I tried not to laugh at that scene at the Flying J. How it must have looked to outsiders. Like stumbling upon *Fight Club* and watching Jack and his assorted organs punching themselves in the face. There we were, Francis and I, two escaped mental patients, flopping around, middle of the night in the mud, rescuing one another from an empty field by the freeway.

Or maybe I didn't have schizophrenia. I hoped I did. At least it explained what was wrong with me. Otherwise, I'd just be… broken.

Climbing my apartment stairs, I was wrapped up deep in thought, sorting, compartmentalizing, filing. I almost walked into Detective Lourey standing at my door.

How long had it been since I met the Utica detective at the Balfours' following Jacob's death? Days, weeks? Felt like years.

"I apologize for not calling first," Detective Lourey said. "Lori said I just missed you. I considered calling to see if you wanted to meet along the way. After all you've been through, I decided it was better if I came to you."

I unlocked the door, muttering thanks, though to be honest I didn't care. What was one more roadside pit stop? I pushed open the door, granting Detective Lourey permission to enter. "Would you like something to drink?"

"I'm fine, Brandon, thank you."

"I don't have much. I've been on the road for the past few days."

"I heard." Detective Lourey reached for a chair at my kitchen table. "Is it okay if I sit?"

I shrugged but didn't join her, hands gripping backrest. I had the strangest sensation that if I let go, I'd spin off the Earth. A form of vertigo, maybe.

"I called you back," she said. "About the jewelry and money."

"I lost my phone."

The detective confirmed the story about the money and jewels, the corresponding amounts. Francis had been telling the truth. Although I still didn't know what it was supposed to mean.

"Where did the money and jewelry come from?" Which seemed like the most basic of questions, and one I figured the cops would've solved by now.

Detective Lourey's lack of response told me they were as confused as I was.

"What do you need, Detective?"

"Francis Balfour. Rochester PD sent over photos this morning. I was hoping you could take a look."

"I don't want to see any more dead bodies."

"We don't need you to ID anyone. Francis Balfour had his share of arrests. His prints were in the system. He had his license and motel key card with him. These photos are of the construction site."

"I don't know what you think I can do. I don't know why Jacob was in Minnesota in the first place—"

"He and his…lady friend…were trying to cross into Canada again. One of the items we recovered had 'Grand Portage' written on it, another point of entry."

"What's so special about Grand Portage?"

"It's a state park. A lot of unmanned terrain. Looks like they were hoping to bypass customs."

"So he did have a girl with him?" Of course, Francis and I had established this, but what else did the police know about her?

"We believe so, yes. According to Border Patrol." Lourey shrugged. "That's not what I'm here for though. Please." She glanced at the empty chair.

Taking a seat, I waited as the detective retrieved paperwork from her satchel. She dropped a folder on the table, extracting several large photographs of heavy construction machinery. I didn't know enough about construction to know the names of these machines, except in the abstract—backhoes, excavators, dump trucks, bulldozers, etcetera. The quarry seemed to be a grand operation.

Spreading out the photos, the detective pointed at one, zeroing in on the name of the machine. Blue Diamond Construction Rentals. In fact, most of the machines seemed to bear that name, all leased from the same provider.

"Does that name mean anything to you?" she asked.

"No. Should it?"

Separating photos, she pointed at another with spray-painted graffiti. Then I saw it wasn't graffiti but a simple circle.

"Why are you showing me these?"

"Seems before he died, Francis Balfour found a can of paint and—" the detective pulled out more pictures, all showcasing the same kinds of heavy machinery, property of Blue Diamond "—he made a point of circling the name. The cause of death isn't in question. Blunt force trauma. Of course, being at the same quarry where Jacob died, it raises alarms." The detective shut the folder. "Do you know why Francis would circle the name of a construction machinery vendor?"

"You do know Francis was mentally ill?"

"We are aware of Francis's condition, yes."

"The man was off his meds, talking crazy. Sometimes he made sense. A lot of the times I didn't know what he was talking about."

"So the name doesn't tell you anything?"

"Blue Diamond? Until three minutes ago I thought Blue Diamond made almond milk for lactose intolerant hipsters."

I felt like I was disappointing her. I reopened the folder and pulled the pictures closer, willing connection, hoping there was a clue I was missing. I *wanted* to help, do good, *be* better.

There was nothing to see or say or add. In several pictures, Francis had circled the name of the construction machine rental company, Blue Diamond. In one picture, he circled the name multiple times. It was like discovering Jacob's wall maps, random, disconnected, incoherent. These messages meant something to *him*.

I studied each again, one by one, searching for a pattern or clue. "It looks like he was in a rush," I said. "He's cutting off half the name."

"Is there any reason Francis would've been in a hurry?"

"Other than trespassing on private property and not wanting to get caught?"

"If he was worried about getting caught trespassing, why was he taking the time to spray paint machines?"

"Francis should've been hospitalized. I work in the field. We took in people with more control of their mental faculties than Francis Balfour. He claimed he could see what others couldn't, had special insight into what wasn't there—"

I stopped, whisked back to an inane, innocuous conversation on the lost highways of Pennsylvania and Ohio. A history lesson about a dark sea and darker sky.

"What is it?" the detective asked.

I studied the pictures again.

I'd gotten it wrong.

I saw it now, clear as a cloudless summer's day. Francis wasn't circling the name of a construction rental company. He was circling one word, isolating a single, solitary color.

Blue.

CHAPTER THIRTY-FOUR

I couldn't share what I was thinking with Detective Lourey—she would've had me locked up again. Recognizing secret messages from a dead schizophrenic renders the recipient guilty by association.

Before she left, I did ask her if the same machinery was present when they found Jacob's body. She said that the quarry, as far as she knew, had been there for decades. That didn't mean the same company was providing the equipment. But it would be strange if they'd switched vendors over the past few weeks. There was a reason he'd told me that story about the color blue. This wasn't a coincidence, wasn't random.

As soon as the detective was gone, I made for my computer and Googled to see if Francis was making up the whole story or if it were true. Not that it would've changed what he was attempting to convey. I was curious. The story seemed preposterous, but Francis hadn't been lying. Until recently in our evolution, humans could not see the color blue.

The various articles, all from credible sources—*The Smithsonian, Business Insider*—shared fascinating facts and tidbits. My favorite was about this modern indigenous tribe that couldn't differentiate between green and blue. Researchers had traveled down to the Himba tribe in Namibia, showing pictures and slides, and to tribal members the two colors were the same. Philologists, a field of linguistics, had examined ancient texts— Arabic, Icelandic, Chinese—and couldn't find mention of the color blue. There were also contemporary, well-known languages, such as Russian, that didn't even have a word for blue. Shades of it, tones, hues, tinges. But not the actual color itself.

Francis must've seen photographs of Jacob at the construction site. At the time, when he told me that non sequitur, I hadn't thought it was any different than the countless other absurd harangues he shared. I had cast it aside, forgotten about it, moved on.

Until Detective Lourey delivered his message from beyond the grave.

Francis was trying to tell me the truth about Jacob's death. It was like the color blue.

The answer had been hiding in plain sight. But nobody could see it.

CHAPTER THIRTY-FIVE

Someone else had been in that quarry with Francis, which was why he couldn't spell it out. A scrawled name gets noticed. A kook tagging random circles, not so much.

I went to my drawer and pulled out the copies of *Illuminations* I'd taken from Francis's bag. I smoothed out the baby blue zine and began paging through, hoping an item of interest would pop out now that I knew more of the story. It was hard getting past the schisms and discord, the scandalous aspects. Unlike before, however, this time I wasn't going to let it sidetrack me.

What was I missing? I had to remind myself guys like Francis, Jacob—they *believed* what they saw. This wasn't a con or a game; they weren't playing to mess with minds. It was their execution that was off. I had to find the intent, the seed; from there I could chart growth. Where was the kernel of truth in this nutcase's haystack?

The Shadow People.

Not the concept. I refused to buy into creatures creeping in the dark. Yes, I'd been stressed. Maybe I was genetically predisposed to mental problems like my birth parents. I hadn't been sleeping well. All these circumstances conspired to overtax my system, tweaking interpretation, distorting perception. But I couldn't doubt who I was. It was all I had to rely on.

The article. Abductions. I flipped to the piece. The source

Jacob cited, Jessiesgirl81. More importantly, where this Jessie was from: Wroughton.

Francis and I had been there. The bus station. Where Jacob bought the car. The blue house on the hill. I reread the piece, about how the Shadow People had descended upon the tiny town of Wroughton, snatching bodies.

Black Annis. Jersey Devil. *Bonhomme Sept-Heures.* Shadow People. They were the all the same creature, changelings conjured by man to explain the inexplicable. Given time and requisite resources, I had to believe such mysteries could be explained.

So, if not the Shadow People, who—or what—was responsible for the recent spat of disappearances? That was if I accepted the basic premise. Had people vanished from Wroughton? I checked the web. One name came up: Darryl Smith. All it said was he was a person of interest a few months ago, hardly enough to classify as a mass abduction.

The subject matter of Jacob's piece came via his insider contact, this Jessie. Who might've been the only girl he knew. Jacob had traveled to her hometown, a long way to go to thank a source for helping with a homemade magazine. Jessie had to be the girl with him in Minnesota.

Problem was I had no idea how to find out anything about Jessie. Not from here at least. I didn't know the first thing about which websites catered to this clientele. The police had taken Jacob's computer. Even if they hadn't, I didn't have the skills to scour and retrieve private search data. I couldn't imagine Jacob, as paranoid as he was, leaving an accessible digital trail anyway. I didn't have a clue how to navigate the Dark Web.

I had to go to Wroughton.

I drove back there in Francis's Buick, the only car at my disposal after mine got towed from Nick's Pizza. According to the *Illuminations* article, the Shadow People had been wreaking havoc, messing with the residents of Wroughton, trickster antics, causing mischief. It was only of late they'd graduated to abduction.

Find the truth within the lie.

Francis once told me there is no difference between a schizophrenic and a methamphetamine addict up for three days. The people living in that creepy blue house on the hill where Jacob bought the car had been on the drug.

I wasn't green enough to think that just because someone is tall they can play basketball. If this was the big city, I wasn't assuming every drug addict knew each other. But this was Wroughton, the sticks, the cuts, the boonies, population a couple thousand. What was more probable? That both Jessie and Jacob were schizophrenic? Or that Jessie was like that man we met at the house selling cars? Strung out on methamphetamine, mentally unstable, and emotionally unwell? For whatever reason, this thought offered solace, reassurance of my own condition. When you're living in the dark, it's harder to separate the shadow from the source.

I arrived in Wroughton at sundown. I would've preferred more light. Although I soon realized this might work in my favor, since, according to my research, people hooked on the drug didn't sleep much. If they slept at all it was during the day, preferring to prowl at night, like vampires.

The creepy blue house on the hill came into view. I debated where to park. I didn't want to be too close. I didn't want to be so far away that I looked like I was casing the place. Finding a sweet spot in between was not easy. There weren't many houses out this way. Houses? More like shacks. No matter where I parked, someone would notice sooner or later.

I needed a plan. Why hadn't I remembered that story the first time we stopped here? *Because you barely scanned the zine. You dismissed everything Jacob said.* Maybe I should retrace my steps. The bus station would be closed. So too the pawn shop. The girl whose dad owned the pawn shop gave us the address. What was the name? Ace's! And hers was…

Think, Brandon, think…

I couldn't recall. Did she tell us? Did it matter? I had to go back in that house, and I'd have to go alone. The guy with the cars wasn't friendly the first time around. I wasn't in the position to drop two hundred dollars to curry good favor or graces.

Rifling through the center console, I found the LoJack certificate Francis left behind.

Okay, that's the play…

I drove up nearer the house, which was livelier tonight than it had been the night I'd come with Francis. I parked close enough for the Buick to be seen but not so close anyone could see what was inside it. Hot winds blew. Surprising for this hour, a time when the day's heat should've broken. I remembered thinking this house was evil at dusk. Nighttime drove it deeper into the rings of the inferno. I stashed my button-up in the car, leaving a plain white tee, which I untucked. I mussed up my hair and removed my glasses too.

I walked around the side of the house where Francis and I had gone in before. The wood panels of the exterior were so decayed, they'd begun to erode, straightedges turned toothy, snarling. I curled my shoulders, slouched, and strode forward.

A couple skinny guys waited by the door, smoking, muttering. I didn't make eye contact. I didn't want to come across as nervous. Act like you belong and you belong.

Like with Francis, I didn't knock, turning the knob with confidence.

"What the fuck you doing here?"

This wasn't the man who sold Jacob the car. This guy was

bigger, more imposing, tattoos painted up and down his sculpted arms. Unlike the man with the Van Dyke facial hair, these tattoos weren't sporadic etchings; they covered his flesh, wrist to shoulder to neck, bold and combative.

"Who are you?" he said.

"I'm here about a car. I…want to buy one."

With one hand, and not much effort, the man shoved me against the wall, cracking the back of my skull, which would've hurt more if not for the soft, water-damaged plaster. He eyed me, deciding whether to punch me in the head or let it go. A mouse skittered across the floor, up an unattached oven pipe to the vent, disappearing within the stovetop.

"Does this look like a dealership?"

I bit my tongue. Because, yes, it did. Cars. Drugs. One-stop shopping.

"I need to buy a car." I didn't say more than that. Let him work through this at his own pace.

Instead of pointing at the back room, where Francis and I had gone last time, I was directed down the hall, egged on with a boot-stomp to my calf, buckling my knee and almost causing me to trip, prompting laughter.

"Go!"

I rushed forward. There were three doors. I reached for the first one.

"Not that one, dipshit," he said. "The other one."

At the second door, I knocked, craning and wincing a grin at the guard dog, who'd been joined by another thug. I offered a wave, hoping I had the right door. The thugs didn't confirm, content to glower, growl. From within the room, a voice announced it was unlocked. I pushed my way inside, grateful to get out of that hallway and away from their disdainful stares.

The relief didn't last long.

1

The first thing that caught my eye was the big bay windows. High on the hillside, the view should've offered the whole of Upstate New York's wilderness and backcountry. When I peered out into the pitch-black night, however, I saw nothing. No moon, no stars. It took me a moment to realize why: the windows were painted, slathered with multiple coats of black, caked-on layers, all the subtlety of a hot-tarred roof. A couple girls, gaunt and sallow, lay on the floor, clumps of unwashed hair knotted like sickly beached mermaids. They looked dead. Then I saw ribcages move, the shallow breaths of the stranded.

A man sat in the corner, rubbing his nose with the back of his hand as he dumped a yellow powder onto a scale. The pungent smell carried across the room, reminding me of sulfur and rotten eggs from science class. He glanced over, sized me up, returned to the task at hand, unimpressed.

Why had I been sent into this room? I didn't want to buy drugs. I didn't want to buy a car either. I needed to talk to the guy who sold the cars, not some pusher.

"What you need?" the man said.

"I think there's been a mistake. I want to buy…a car?"

"How much you looking to spend?"

"I was here last week. With my friend."

"I don't give a shit."

"We talked to another guy."

He straightened up, dusting his hands, rubbing them down the legs of his dirty jeans, like baking flour. "You're talking to me now." Then he stopped, pointing a finger, a look of recognition overtaking his expression, which surprised me. "You were here with the old guy. In that Skylark. Nice ride."

I didn't remember him. Had he been spying on us from another room? I stared past his shoulder at the powder he'd been sifting, that mound of rank, foul chemicals. Who puts that garbage in their body? It was poison.

"What are you looking at?" he said.

Last time I'd been at this house I felt intimidated, out of my element, alien. This felt worse. Last time, I had Francis.

"I'm looking for someone," I said.

He waited.

"I thought you wanted a car."

"I do. I did. I also need to find someone."

"The fuck?" he said. Which one could interpret a lot of ways. "Get the fuck out of here before I call Lester and Dog."

If I was going with honesty, I figured I'd go all in. In the end, I believed people are all the same, we all want and need, challenged by the obstacles in our way, and if I could convey this simple edict, man to man, fellow human to fellow human, we could reach an amicable accord.

"I need to find her," I said. "She knew my friend. My friend *did* buy a car from here." I didn't know if these guys were all friends, partners, shared profits, like wait staff splitting tips at the end of the shift. The cars were on common property; these guys were all housemates. And criminals. Made sense. Standing there made my skin crawl, like it was infested with a million invisible bugs. "She, my friend, my friend's friend. I think she..." I pointed at the scale and powder. "Does that."

"You a cop?"

Nothing about my person said cop. I assumed the inquiry was perfunctory, owed to the urban myth that law enforcement has to reveal themselves, a misnomer proven inaccurate by countless true crime podcasts and television shows.

"No," I said, wanting to make him feel better, safer. "I just need to find my friend. Her name is Jessie. I think that's her name."

"You don't know your friend's name?"

"I met her in a chatroom—my friend met her in a chatroom. Conspiracy website. Kennedy's brain in a jar?"

"Get the fuck out of here."

"If you can—"

"Dog! Lester!"

In seconds, Dog, the man I'd met out in the hall, and his friend Lester were through the door, meaning they'd been poised outside, awaiting the call.

"Get him out of here!"

Before I could protest, Dog and Lester had me by the arms, spinning me around, flinging me into the hall, head banging face-first. My nose smacked flush, sinus cavity filling with blood. The force snapped back my skull. I felt cranial fluids swishing, my brain pork stewed in juices. My eyes watered and stung, like I'd rubbed them with hot pepper on my hands. I just wanted to talk—I could explain my way out of this if given the chance.

I never got the chance.

Dragging me to the back door, Dog kicked me down the stairs, where I skidded across broken bottles and glass on the hard ground, which tore through my forearms and shirt, slicing skin. I tried to stand, thinking they'd thrown me out and that was it. It wasn't. A pair of hands hoisted me to my feet, jacking me against an exterior wall, before I took a knee to my groin so hard and violent I feared I'd ruptured a testicle. I swore I heard a pop, like packaging bubbles bursting. I held out a hand to hold up, let me catch my breath. What happened to honor and fair fights? A hard punch to the side of my head answered that question. Buzzing and flashing lights, the roar of the crowd, camera bulbs shattering, and I was down. They started kicking and stomping me, full roundhouses to the ribs with steel-toed boots. I curled up into as tight a ball as I could—reduce surface space, condense mass, minimize exposure. They weren't going to stop until they killed me.

"I know…about…the cars," I managed to eek out.

The kicking stopped.

"Hold up," a voice growled. "The fuck you say?"

My eyes watered and stung; I couldn't even tell which one was talking, both figures fuzzy and hulking.

"I know you sell cars…and steal…them back." I held out a hand, in part begging for a reprieve, and also to show I wasn't reaching for a weapon. With a trembling, outstretched hand I presented the LoJack certificate that Francis bought for two hundred dollars, praying to gods I didn't believe in that the old man's theory was right.

"Lester, cut this fool's balls off—"

With a weak, shaky hand I aimed a finger. "Around the house. Buick Skylark, down the block." I spat out a gob of blood. "My friend's waiting."

Dog started to walk toward the car.

"I wouldn't do that. First sign of anyone…he's going to the police." It was all I had. I needed this bluff to work.

"Go get Cody," Dog said.

Lester stormed up the stairs inside. Dog picked me up out of the dust, brushing me off, an odd and tender touch following the ass kicking he'd administered, planting me on the back steps. In the moonlight, down the hill, the Buick sat. I hoped it was far enough to conceal the fact that nobody waited inside.

A second later, the man from the room, the one with the powder, Cody, stomped down the steps.

"What the fuck, Dog?"

"The old man is waiting for me," I said. "I don't come back and he calls 9-1-1. That simple." My heart burned in my throat. "You want to sell cars and steal them back, I don't care."

"The fuck you want?"

"To find my friend…Jessie."

"I told you. I don't know any Jessie."

"Would you tell me if you did?"

"I don't know, man. Maybe. But I don't. So I can't."

"The girl who sent me here the other day."

"What girl?"

"The one who told me about the cars."

Cody tilted back his head. By now he'd come to view me as less a threat and more a nuisance.

"Her father owns Ace's, the pawn shop. Do you know her?"

"About seven people in this fucking town. Of course I know her. Lenna Ann. Spun-out bitch. Lives with her retard brother in a trailer."

"You know…" I tongued a loose tooth "…where I can find her?"

"Jesus." Cody laughed. "You're a ballsy mutherfucker, you know that?"

Cody weighed it over. I didn't have much to offer, other than my dead partner who wasn't in the car. The longer he stared at the Buick, the more certain I grew he could see inside and knew I was full of it. There were also easier ways to deal with a problem that didn't involve digging holes and burying bodies.

"Dog," he said, "drive this fool out to see Lenna Ann."

"Give me directions," I said. "I—my friend and I—can drive on our own, thanks."

"No, you can't," Cody said. "This isn't a town with street signs. She lives in a trailer in the middle of the fucking woods."

"My friend and I can follow… Dog." I turned to Dog, adding, "Thank you." Never hurts to be polite.

"Get in the fucking truck," Cody said. "Tell the old man to follow. Now get out of here and don't come back. I don't like you."

I nodded but didn't respond. I didn't want to admit: sometimes I didn't like me either.

CHAPTER THIRTY-SIX

Wobbling downhill, I staggered to the Buick, hanging on while Dog pulled around. Five minutes ago, Dog and his buddy were ready to slit my throat and give me a Colombian necktie. The only reason they didn't? The ghost of Francis. If I believed in the afterlife, I might've whispered a prayer of gratitude.

Inside the car, favoring my ribs, I scrambled to find a pillow or coat to approximate a human being. In the dark, maybe I could throw my shirt around a sleeping bag or some other bulky item. There was nothing in the backseat, bulky or otherwise. Expecting Dog any second, I didn't want to risk popping the trunk.

A moment later, a large truck with jacked-up wheels and an augmented bull bar barreled around the corner. I climbed in fast as I could. Dog revved the engine, wanting to impress with whatever he had beneath the hood, a gesture wasted. I didn't know the first thing about trucks.

We were already in the sticks, the crumbling blue house on the hill slash chop shop secluded. Far as I could tell, outside of a tiny main street with the pawn shop, gas station, coffeehouse, a couple saloons, and markets, Wroughton was nothing but a forest among forgotten fringes. Dog's truck delivered me farther down the holler, into the bowels of nowhere. I checked the bars on my phone. Nothing. There were no street signs or distinguishable markers. Trees and brush and wood, dark hillside, each stone as unremarkable as the next. He must've noticed by now my friend wasn't following in the car, and the guys back at the house had to have figured out no one was *in* the car. I entertained the possibility Dog was taking me to a remote location to kill me. Then shook that off. They made it clear they had no problem doing that back at the house.

Dark turned destitute, desolate, deserted. No houses. No shacks, no sheds, no blue-tarped tents, no gutted shipping containers. No anything.

Then Dog jammed a hard, unexpected right, and we came to a clearing. A small trailer perched on the edge of a creek.

Slamming the car in park, I braced for what came next. Nothing was stopping Dog from killing his engine, stepping out, and finishing me off. A pregnant pause dragged out.

"Get out," he said. "Don't worry I'll tell…your friend…you'll be right back." He stopped just short of air quotes.

I didn't waste any time jumping down.

Dog reversed, K-turned, and sped out of there, leaving me alone.

A high country moon emerged from behind the clouds. Bathed in soft white light, serenaded by the burbling brook, the trailer could've been a fairytale cottage had not all the romance been stripped away and perverted. Big dents in the aluminum kinked with rust, and one of the windows had been broken. It was covered with cardboard and duct tape.

Lights were on inside, a generator humming, meaning the trailer had power, which elevated the residence above your average campsite. Not by much. The bottom of the trailer was rivered with algae and fungus, severe water damage. Sediment staked claim to the foundation. A car sat in the driveway, but it looked like it hadn't run in ages, wheels flat, shell covered with pods, seeds, and arachnid webs.

What could I do but knock on the door and hope I found answers inside? I had run out of places to search.

Lenna Ann answered, confused at first, before her eyes betrayed recognition.

"You remember me?"

"You were with the old guy," she responded quicker than I'd have guessed. "What happened to your face?"

Puffy, swollen, and in pain, I didn't want to look in the mirror.

"We went to the address you gave us," I said. "We know Jacob bought a car there."

"Come inside," Lenna Ann said, ushering me in and closing the door. "I didn't send you there because of a car." She stared past my shoulder, out the unbroken window, stopping on a dime, entire demeanor changing. She whipped her head like she'd heard a noise. "You should go. We can talk later."

"I'm not going anywhere." I pointed at my face. "This is what it cost to find you."

"They brought you here because they know Eddie will be drunk as shit when he gets home. He has a temper. You think what those guys did was bad? Wait till Eddie shows up."

"Who's Eddie?"

"My boyfriend."

I caught a figure behind the couch, a mop of wild hair, a person crouching to hide. "Who's that?"

"That's Lotty. My brother."

When he stood up, I saw the padded blue coat. The boy in blue.

"You were outside my work," I said, turning to Lotty. "And at the gas station."

"He don't talk," Lenna Ann said.

"He was following me. I saw him in Cortland. More than once." I pointed out the window. "And later downtown. Had me thinking I was going crazy."

"Lotty never leaves here."

Bullshit, I wanted to say. I'd *seen* him.

Lotty stared at me with sad eyes, desperate to communicate.

I couldn't worry about Lotty. "I need to find someone," I said to Lenna Ann. I'd take my chances with Eddie. If I tried walking back now, I'd pass out before I got two steps, my insides liquefied.

Lenna Ann opened her mouth. I thought she might tell me I had to go again, but her jaw froze there, left hanging, agape. Her tiny puppy teeth protruded, nubbed baby ones awaiting reinforcements that were never coming.

"I think her name was Jessie," I continued. "I might be wrong. I know how that sounds. She wasn't *my* friend. She was my friend Jacob's. And he's dead. He met her in the chatroom of a conspiracy website. Jessie was her username." Reaching for the copy of *Illuminations* in my back pocket, I felt my muscles revolt, flanks and core reeling, spine spasming from the beatdown. With two hands, I presented the zine, a religious offering. "Whoever this girl is, she helped my friend write an article in here." I shook *Illuminations*. "It was about…the Shadow People." I hated using that term. "How they are abducting—"

"Isabel."

"I think her name was Jessie—"

"Jessiesgirl81," Lenna Ann said. "That's Isabel's username. I'm Isabel's friend."

"Why Jessiesgirl81?"

"Because she likes that song and it came out in 1981."

The most obvious answer in the world. Fucking Rick Springfield.

"Where is Isabel now?"

241

Lenna Ann shook her head. Or maybe it was more a shudder. "She disappeared. After your friend bought the car."

"Did they leave together?"

"No. She was here after he bought the car. Definitely. I think. I'm pretty sure." Lenna Ann turned to Lotty, who didn't move, didn't say a word—who, after rising from the floor, had given no indication he wasn't dead. "She had a bad meth problem." As if reminding herself, Lenna Ann spun around and reached up, pushing books on a high shelf that housed random power adaptors and controls for devices she didn't seem to own. "The cops out here, they take a cut of everything. They'll walk in your house, steal your shit, money, take whatever they want. That's why I hide mine good." She retrieved a book from the top, an autobiography on Thomas Mann, plopping it on the table. Plucking a plastic baggie from within its hollowed-out pages, she dumped a pile of powder on the glass end table, before separating into neat, precise lines. "You can't do it three days in a row, that's the secret." She rolled a dollar bill and passed it to her brother, who snorted a strip. He passed the dollar straw back, and Lenna Ann did the same, a shiver overtaking her body in revolt, system shocked, an aardvark inhaling fire ants, before passing the bill to me.

"No, thanks. I'm good."

I waited for the hard sell, but Lenna Ann shrugged and hoovered another. And I realized that peer pressure doesn't exist outside public service announcements. Why would Lenna Ann care if I didn't want any of her drugs? More for her.

"Tell me about Isabel," I said.

"She lived with Boy Blue."

"Boy Blue?"

"There's two big dealers in Wroughton. Boy Blue and Girl Blue. Isabel lived with Boy Blue."

"Her boyfriend?"

"Boy Blue has lots of girls living with him."

"Doing what?"

"Sucking his dick for drugs? I don't know. Ask Isabel."

I thought I heard Lotty grunt. I turned his way. He'd returned to stone-like and silent. "I'd love to," I said. "If you could tell me where I could find her."

"Maybe she went home," Lenna Ann said.

"Where's home?"

"London."

"England?"

"Last time I checked, that's where London was." Lenna Ann started moving faster, a cartoon character revved on too much coffee, exaggerated fire rings burned into the carpet. She began chewing her lower lip, twitching, jaw grinding back and forth, scratching her arm, nose, and chin. "Isabel was *crazy*. She couldn't unplug, always online thinking she'd uncovered evidence the experts missed. That was her thing. *Everything* was a conspiracy."

"Sounds like my friend Jacob."

"That's how they met. Isabel would get high, disappearing in cyberspace and into chatrooms. Lost for days."

"When was the last time you saw her?"

Lenna Ann scratched the inside of her arm, gazing out the cardboard window, into a night she couldn't see. "You should go. Eddie's gonna be home. Two weeks ago." Devoid of self-reflection, Lenna Ann talked faster. Conversing with her was no different than speaking with Jacob or Francis, topics and sequence bouncing all over the place.

"Two weeks ago?"

"Last time I saw her. After Boy Blue went away."

"Where did he go?"

"Isabel lived there."

"I know. You told me—"

"Isabel came here, late one night, wigging. She asked me to keep it here and I said I couldn't keep it here but she left it anyway and then she left. Eddie got a new job. But he could be home any—"

"It?"

"Her stuff. She was freaking out, man. Talking about those... Shadow People."

"There are no Shadow People!"

"I know that! *I'm* not crazy! Isabel believed in all that shit. She said the Shadow People took Boy Blue and that they would get her next. Said she *saw* the whole thing. I could tell she hadn't slept for days. That's the secret. You can't take this shit three days in a row, you need to take breaks, reset, or it'll fry your brain."

"You mentioned that—"

"She said she had proof. She was cooked. That's the last time I saw her. She said if anything happened to her, I should mail her stuff to the newspaper."

"What newspaper? What...stuff?" I hated the word *stuff*. I had a professor who would knock you down a full letter grade if you used *stuff* in a paper. Other students groaned. I appreciated it. Language is specific.

"She was crazy," Lenna Ann said. "When I saw you and the old man and you were talking about your friend, I wanted to talk to you because they knew each other, that fat guy—he was your friend, right?"

"Jacob, yeah—"

"I thought you could help me find her. That's why I told you to meet me at Rick's."

"Who's Rick?"

"Rick, Cody, Dog, they all live together. That crumbly blue house on the hill."

"Rick's the one with the Van Dyke who sold Jacob the car?"

"Who's Van Dyke?" Lenna Ann stared at a blank spot on the wall, frozen, catatonic, as if she'd been unplugged from a socket. Then the switch flipped back on, and she was racing, lips flapping, arms twisting twelve different directions to scratch hard-to-reach places.

Outside of a brief interlude to snort drugs, Lotty and his padded blue coat hadn't moved.

"You should put antibiotic on your face," Lenna Ann said. "Looks like you have dirt in those cuts. Don't pick at that, it'll get infected—"

"Soon as I get out of here—"

"I thought maybe you knew what happened to her but you can't talk in the street, not in the middle of the day, not in this town, cops are *every*where, and they'll come right in your house, take whatever they want—"

"I know. You told me."

Lenna Ann bolted to the window, the one with an actual pane, peering into the void, before darting to other room without warning, a skittish housecat that realized it needed to be somewhere else *right now*, leaving me standing in the middle of that junky old trailer with her muted brother in blue, wondering what the hell I was doing with my life. Had this entire quest been for vanity's sake? Maybe there was no mystery color to see. Green was green, the seas the color of wine, and I'd been sucked up in the drama of madmen and conmen and drug addicts and liars.

As fast as she'd bolted, Lenna Ann zoomed back with a box, thrusting it into my hands. Shoebox, paisley printed, pink, girly but grubby, dirt smeared, assorted foodstuffs dribbled, blobs of sticky sauces congealed. You could almost see the individual bacterium sway.

I held the petri dish, using the least amount of fingertips possible. "What's in the box?"

"Isabel gave it to me. I don't want it."

"What am I supposed to do with it?"

"I don't care. Throw it away."

From the corner of my eye, I saw Lotty's eyes widen.

"That Shadow People shit freaks me out," she said. "I know they aren't real—of course they're not real—but we say that demons and ghosts and angels aren't real but then you'll be thinking about a song and it'll come on the radio, and you'll be like 'Whoa,' or you dream of a famous singer and his shoes and then you wake up the next day and learn they're dead! There's something not right about this place, this world, this…existence. I've always felt it." Lenna Ann's pupils were as large as big, black marbles. Her fingernails clawed her neck, raking skin.

"Okay," I said, "but what—"

"I read the other day how scientists, like really smart people, believe there could be universes stacked one on top of the other. All at once! String theory? Fermi Paradox? Something like that. But this guy, this doctor, this, like, really, really smart guy with tons of degrees and shit was saying—or maybe it was on the radio? A podcast? I don't remember." Pause. "I might've read it. Or I heard it. But he, this doctor guy, was saying how these worlds are stacked one on top of the other, like tracing paper laid over mirror images, indefinite, but we can't see each other, y'know? Like we're tuned into different frequencies, the way dogs and other animals can hear certain sounds and pitches we can't, and so maybe we're all in this room now…" Lenna Ann gouged ever deeper into her flesh. It was hard to watch, red, tender, raised, and raw.

"I don't—"

"Point is: they *could* be real. The Shadow People. How are

they any different than God or the wind or airborne viruses?"

As she droned on, I sat on the tattered arm of the raggedy couch and opened the box. Scissors and pens. Paper cut into the shapes of hearts. Loose glittering beads. Also newspaper, magazine, and periodical snippets. Lots of them. Like the crap covering the walls of Jacob's room. Ghost ship rantings about killer rats and unsolved disappearances, invasive species, all the bugs we can't see that live on our eyelashes, random, unrelated words circled—*steak, fishing rod, Doug, catamaran*. Every once in a while, I'd recognize a celebrity name like Ryan Gosling or Ryan Reynolds. As if she were crushing like a normal girl. Then I'd read, in big, black marker: "In on it?" With a huge question mark and circles. The stockpile of indecipherable nonsense rendered Jacob's *Illuminations* a university publication by comparison. I was about to put back the lid—this box was useless—when I saw the memory stick at the bottom, a flash drive.

"Do you have a computer?" I asked, holding up the recording device. "A laptop?"

"In the pawn shop."

"There's *nothing* to watch this on?"

"Do ever notice how many times you see the number twenty-three? It's *every*where. The law of fives. Two plus three. Also seventeen. You look at all the major historical events that occurred on those dates. Add it up. It's irrefutable. Duh! Math."

I tapped her arm—I didn't want to spook her from whatever altered state she'd entered—presenting the flash drive. "I need to see what's on this, okay?"

Lenna Ann housecatted again, wisp of smoke rising in her wake. I'd never been more thankful to be a straight arrow.

She came back with a laptop.

"I thought you said it was in the pawn shop?"

"Mine is. This is Eddie's. He's my boyfriend. But you better hurry because if he comes home, he'll kill you. He's big and tough and mean."

I held up a hand, relieving her of the laptop. I flipped it open, asked for the passcode, sticking in the flash and selecting a lone folder marked SP.

A video played. Recorded from a cell phone. There was no sound, just a picture. High angle, tall shelf, concealed in a houseplant like a nanny cam. I didn't recognize the house. It didn't look like the blue house on the hill with Cody, Dog, and Rick, squalid or skeezy. This house was filled with more toys, video games, Xboxes, and tall, shiny speakers mounted above leather couches and a giant flat-screen TV.

A large man filled the frame. Reclining in a chair, silky kimono draped around his shoulders and hanging off his bulky frame uncinched, he sat spread eagle, a dark thatch between his legs. I'd never been happier for the low-grade resolution of cheap phones.

"Do you know who that is?"

"That's Boy Blue," Lenna Ann answered, in danger of biting off a piece of her lip, which she gnawed on like skin candy.

Three men walked into the frame.

Then a bright flash, and Boy Blue was on the ground.

Lenna Ann screamed. Lotty didn't flinch.

Two of the men stared into the camera.

I recognized both.

CHAPTER THIRTY-SEVEN

My instincts weren't wrong. I knew that guy from the bar was trouble. His mustache screamed cop. The second man was also from the bar; he was the other jerk macking on Sam. I didn't recognize the third, but he stuck more to the shadows. The trio walked around the crime scene in their dress blues and starry sleeves.

"You know these guys?" I asked Lenna Ann.

"They're cops." .

"I figured. Names?"

She pointed at the screen, at the one with the mustache. "That's Simms. He's a fucking asshole." Lenna Ann aimed at the other guy I'd seen. "That's Young." Then at the third. "And that's McKinty." I was pretty certain I'd never seen McKinty.

Back in the video, Young kicked Boy Blue's lifeless body, two punts to the gut, before McKinty dropped to a knee and rifled through the dead man's pockets. His first effort yielded a brick wrapped in cellophane, the next a giant wad of cash. Then a whole bunch of shiny gems and jewels. He walked out of the shot.

The last pixelated image had Simms and Young, working in tandem, each grabbing one of Boy Blue's hefty legs and yanking him off the La-Z-Boy. Boy Blue's head thunked against the floor.

Even without volume you could hear the sound it made. Like an overripe cantaloupe dropped eight stories to the asphalt. They dragged him out of the frame, a thick coat of dark red paint from a wide bristled brush trailing behind him like slug slime.

The picture went black.

"What the fuck was that?" Lenna Ann seemed as shocked as I was.

"You said cops around here walk in and take whatever they want."

"Yeah, but they don't kill anybody."

"They just did."

I ran through courses of action. Take this to the cops? They *were* the cops. The press? Sure. What was I going to do? Drop it in the mail, addressed to "Reporter"? I felt like Bones McCoy begging off new responsibilities. I was a college student, not a justice crusader.

Lenna Ann had gone back to flapping her arms, a flightless bird not getting the point. I was too wrapped up in thought to hear the roar of an engine rumbling in until it was too late.

"Eddie," Lenna Ann said. "Oh shit, oh shit."

I searched for another exit. Unable to find one, I braced for another ass kicking, uncertain whether I could withstand one.

It wasn't Eddie.

CHAPTER THIRTY-EIGHT

Unlike the video, Simms and Young weren't dressed in their uniforms. More relaxed attire, jeans and tees, like that night from the bar. Casual Friday wear. This visit was off the record. Whatever happened next would not make the official report. I waited for their partner, McKinty, to bring up the rear, but Young slammed the door shut, locked and dead-bolted it. Simms told Lenna Ann to shut up. She did, fast. I'd been trying to get her to shut up for the past half hour. Her eagerness to obey spoke volumes.

"Shit, Brandon," Simms said. "You've had us running across half this goddamn country."

"I fucking hate Minnesota," Young said. "I grew up there, you know that?"

How could I have known that?

"Rotten corn smells like shit. They have silos of rotten corn everywhere out there. Whole goddamn state. Corn. When most people think corn, they think Nebraska, right? Minnesota has so much fucking corn you can choke on it. And it doesn't last. Shelf life is shit. You know when you're driving by a farm and you think that fetid stink is horse manure or cow shit? It's not. It's rotten, decaying corn." Young shook his head. "I used to have work on those farms in the summer. So goddamn hot, your balls bobbing in a pool of sweat. I'd be dick deep in those silo tunnels, emptying buckets of rotten, moldy, months-old corn that stunk like the inside of a pig's caked-over colon, holding mouthfuls of vomit till I got outside." He glared at me. "Goddamn you for making me go back there."

"Calm down," Simms said. "Relax. We're gonna work this out. Right, Brandon?"

Lenna Ann was whimpering, tremoring, steady stream of nasal drip flowing into her mouth. She didn't move to wipe it off. Lotty hadn't flinched, viewing them the same way he had me, silent, devoid and detached, head swallowed by his big blue coat.

Simms reached over and tipped up Lenna Ann's chin. "Took too much, eh? You got something to calm down? Pot? Pills? Smack? I don't give a shit. Just shut up. Please. I don't want to have to hurt you."

I started toward him. I couldn't let him hit her.

"Sit down, Brandon," Simms said. "No heroes tonight, okay?"

Like that, it all became clear. The Shadow People. The followings and abductions. The inexplicable explained.

"That was you in the car," I said. "At Nick's Pizza. And later at the Flying J."

"That old man was tough as fuck."

I now saw the swelling around his right eye, as if he'd recently been cold cocked. "You followed us to Minnesota." I stared past his shoulder to the front door. "You killed him. Francis. Where's your other friend?" Was McKinty stationed outside, keeping guard?

"Ask your friend Jacob," Simms said.

"I can't. He's dead too."

"We said sit down." Young pointed at a kitchen chair. "You're making me tense up." Then to Simms: "Shut up. I need to stay calm. I get tense, people get hurt, and we don't want anyone else getting hurt." Back to me: "Sit."

I sat.

"We trailed you to Minnesota," Simms said. "We knew the old man would go to the quarry. Too bad you weren't with him."

Young pinched his eyes, before stomping a foot. He scowled at his partner, angry, agitated. I wasn't getting in the middle of it.

Simms kept his eyes on me. He shook his head, a show of admiration. "I liked that old bastard. And you? You, boy, you got a horseshoe up your ass." He turned toward the heavens, inaccessible through the low, water-stained ceiling. "Every time we thought we had you, you'd have one foot out the door. Somewhere, an angel loves you."

"He didn't fall, did he?" I already knew the answer. Jacob, Francis, it was all the same.

"Fell. Pushed. Thrown. What difference does it make?"

"By the time we found the motel, you were gone."

"And by the time we got to your apartment," Young said, "you weren't there either—you don't sit still, do you? You got ADD? You're as restless as a tweaker after an uncut batch."

"We're not going to hurt you," Simms said, lying through his teeth. "We just want the video."

"I don't know what you're talking about," I said.

"You've seen the video," Simms said. It wasn't a question. "Don't make us do that to you too. Your buddy and his girlfriend stole so much money and jewelry from us. The pawnshop too." He turned to Lenna Ann. "That's her father."

Young turned to his partner. "They took a lot more than that."

"Give us the flash drive," Simms said. "And we'll be on our way. We thought your fat friend had it. Thought Grandpa had it. Thought *you* had it." Simms cool-handed through his hair. "It was in Wroughton the whole goddamn time."

"Don't get cute," Young added, sweetening the mythical deal. "We get the video, you get to go back home to that pretty girlfriend of yours."

There was no point correcting him that Sam wasn't technically my girlfriend. I'd just watched them shoot a man in cold blood. Judging by their smooth, effortless movements in the aftermath, I could tell it wasn't their first time. And they had no problem not making it their last.

It was Simms who pulled his gun first, a lazy, limp-wristed gesture, a douchebag jock disinterested in showing off another second-tier trophy. I wished I understood enough about guns to say what kind it was, whether it fit a magazine or clip. Things all looked the same to me. Black, oiled, menacing. All I cared about was where it was pointed: me.

Lenna Ann's whimpering graduated to chest-heaving sobs, and now Young pulled his gun, aiming it between her eyes, directing her to sit and shut the fuck up.

I thought this would be a good time for her boyfriend, Eddie, to come home.

Instead, the phone rang.

I wasn't sure what was more shocking, the ringing that broke the silence or the fact that the call was coming via landline, a cradled drugstore telephone affixed to flimsy wood paneling, an archaic relic that went out of style last century.

No one moved to answer it. It kept ringing.

Nonstop.

Young walked over, lifted the phone, and slammed it in the cradle.

It rang again.

He went to rip the phone out the wall. Simms stopped him, motioning for Lenna Ann to answer this time.

"Tell whoever it is you're about to go to bed. I don't give a shit. Sound normal, get 'em off the phone. Got it? You try and alert with bullshit codes, I have no problem putting you down."

The phone kept ringing as Lenna Ann sniffed back nasal remains and mucus, slacking across the trailer, plucking the phone, earpiece to ear.

"It's for him," Lenna Ann said, pointing at me.

Simms glowered. "Who you have calling you here?"

I shrugged, holding up empty palms for them to see. I was devoid of intent or plans. "Nobody knows I'm here." Which, once it escaped my lips, I realized was the dumbest thing I could've said. I wasn't lying, though.

Simms ripped the phone out of Lenna Ann's hands, shoving it in mine.

"Whoever it is," Simms said. "Everything's fine. You say *one* stupid thing—" He stuck the gun, point blank, between Lenna Ann's eyes "—and you're next. And then I take a drive to Cortland and see your girlfriend, have some fun before I plug her too."

Bringing the phone up to my ear, I didn't get the chance to say a word.

"Get to the back," a voice on the other end said. "And get down."

Then came the squealing of tires, the thundering roar of a big engine, and the blinding glare of a million suns.

CHAPTER THIRTY-NINE

The augmented bull bar ripped through the front end of the trailer, sending a chunk of tin panel fluttering into the night, a demented, drunken bird taking flight. The collision knocked Simms and Young off their feet, guns skittering across the floor, aftershocks toppling smaller objects not nailed down from shelves and brackets. At the back of the trailer, Lenna Ann and Lotty, whom I'd shielded on impact, were shaken too, but we'd escaped the worst of it.

Dog was behind the wheel. The other three—Lester, Cody, and Rick—jumped out of the flatbed, two with baseball bats, Rick brandishing a shotgun. I crouched behind the couch, keeping Lenna Ann and Lotty close. Everyone was shouting, screaming, threatening to kill the other. Truck high beams on, kicked-up gravel dust clouded my vision, a redneck standstill in a sandstorm. Volume reached its crescendo. I waited for a gun to go off. I glanced down by my feet and found a piece belonging to Simms or Young. I wrapped my fist around the handle, hoisting its alien heft, praying I wouldn't have to fire it. Was there a safety on the thing? A button I had to push, an on and off switch?

"We're fucking cops!"

"You're fucking dead!"

"How's it feel to be on the other side?"

"Fuck you."

"No, fuck *you!*"

"No, *fuck YOU!*"

That went on for a while, each telling the other to fuck himself. Then it got calm. Too calm.

I peeked my head over the couch, before slowly standing.

Lester now held the shotgun, which was locked on Simms and Young. Neither cop held anything. Well, Simms was holding his arm, which dangled, dislocated, from its shoulder socket, in all likelihood broken too. It was such a surreal scene. The big slash in the trailer's casing, like a screwdriver torn through a soda can. Four drug addicts surrounding cops on their knees, a reversal of fortune.

"You!" Simms said to me. "Shit for brains? You know how much you just fucked yourself? You were gonna walk out of this. What do you think happens now? You're an accessory. This is prison time. Life as you know it, college boy, is over." I saw his eyes drift to the gun I held by my side.

"You okay?" asked Rick, the guy I'd known as Van Dyke until twenty minutes ago, nodding at me like we were old pals.

"I'm fine," I said. "But there's another one of them. McKinty. I think he's outside."

"He ain't outside," Young said. "Your fat friend killed him in the quarry. After him and that bitch took our jewelry and money."

"What—?"

"You don't know anything, do you, Brandon?" Simms winced from the pain. "I thought you watched the video. Where you think your buddy and his girlfriend got that cash? Those jewels? They stole it."

"After *you* stole it from Boy Blue!" Cody stepped through the wreckage, baseball bat clenched, tapping the barrel off his palm, sneering down at the cops. "You've been ripping me and my friends off for years."

"Possession is nine-tenths, numbnuts."

"What are you going to do about it?" Young said. "Kill us?"

"If we have to," Cody said.

Dog spat at their feet.

Rick walked over to me, twiddling his fingers for the gun. "Give that to me before you shoot yourself in the dick."

I was surprised by how fast I handed it over, throwing my hat in the ring with scofflaws and derelicts without question.

Rick juked, grabbing my wrist. "Jesus, man, you don't pass a gun like that."

I'd pointed it at him. I didn't mean to. This entire situation was overwhelming. I was still reeling from accusations Jacob killed their partner. Not that McKinty didn't have it coming. That video told me all I needed to know. Why hadn't the police back home mentioned any of this?

"Cody," Rick said. "What do we do?"

I stopped worrying about the past. This wasn't a rescue, and its execution didn't come with an escape plan. Four guys ripped out of their skull on drugs, hyped up to play cowboy, heard their tormentors were gathered in one convenient spot—Dog must've been keeping an eye on me—and they took their shot. This was my hope.

Cody didn't have an answer. Neither did Dog or Lester, who wasn't much of a talker.

"There's still a chance for you to do the right thing, Brandon," Simms said.

I turned my attention to the two cops, who looked more bored than angry or concerned.

"They're not going to shoot us," Simms said, nodding at Lester, who now came across less as a badass and more like a kid in over his head. In fact, all these guys from the house on the hill seemed as young as I was. Next year I'd be earning my master's, and these four lowlifes would be right here, pushing dope, getting old before their time. That was if they weren't in prison. I didn't know the penalty for trying to run over police or holding a gun on them. But it had to be as bad as dealing drugs and stealing cars. Of course, I wasn't out of the woods yet. The word "accessory" bandied about my brain.

Rick turned to me, his pupils as large as Lenna Ann's and Lotty's. Of course these guys were high. They pulled this move because they weren't thinking straight. Beyond getting loaded, fired up, and plowing their big truck into the trailer, these guys didn't have a clue what came next.

I spied Eddie's laptop on the floor.

Up until a few weeks ago I never could've pictured myself siding with criminals over authorities. A lot had changed since then. I wasn't breaking the rules for those guys. This was payback.

"Can you grab that?" I said to Rick, meaning the laptop.

Eddie, don't come home. The only way anyone got shot now was by mistake. Keep the room calm, nobody get jumpy.

Rick retrieved the laptop. I inserted the memory stick, pulling up a replay of Boy Blue's final minutes.

Rick's eyes went wide—wider than they already were, which I would've thought impossible. The others peered over. You could feel the communal rejoice. There was a way out of this mess.

"You got an email address?" I asked Rick.

"Who doesn't have an email address?"

I typed in what he told me. Then I asked the other three for the same, attached the file, and sent the ironclad evidence into cyberspace. "That's for Jacob," I said.

"Big mistake, Brandon." Simms's words lacked conviction.

Grinning, I didn't stop there. I also pulled up the contact

information for the *Times Union*, *Daily Gazette*, *Observer Dispatch*, and every local television affiliate, online journal, and media source in the greater Upstate New York region—cut and pasted an intro, attached the file, and hit send.

Standing up, I turned to the two dirty cops, on their knees. "And that's for Francis."

"The old man dead?" Rick asked.

"Yeah," I said.

"I liked him," Rick said.

"Yeah, me too." I turned to Lester. "You can put that down," meaning the gun. We had all the guns and ammo. Simms and Young had nothing.

"What are we supposed to do with them?" Cody asked me.

"Check their car for weapons and let them drive away." I turned to the two disgraced officers. "Give them a head start to turn themselves in. As of two minutes ago every major news outlet in the greater Tri-State Area has that video. Town, names, dates, descriptions."

Cody nodded at Lester, who headed outside, to check for weapons, I assumed.

"Hey, Rick," I said. "Mind giving me a ride to my car?"

Sitting passenger side while Rick reversed out of there, I took a look back at the sliced-up trailer. "I bet Eddie is going to be pissed when he sees that."

"We'll help Lenna Ann and Lotty with repairs," he said. "We've taken care of Lenna Ann and her brother for a long time now. We got them that trailer. But there is no Eddie. Lenna Ann doesn't have a boyfriend. She makes him up when she's high. Speed freaks see people who aren't there, bruh. Don't you know that?"

I'm learning, Rick.

"Lenna Ann's father is a real piece of shit," he said. "What he did to his own kids… Man's a monster. And along with Simms, Young, and McKinty, he's part of the scam. Fences the shit they steal." He looked over at me. "We didn't come to help you tonight. No offense."

"None taken." I didn't want to hear what their father did to them. I'd met the man once and could tell then he was a bad person. I'd seen Lenna Ann, who was messed up. I had no idea what was wrong with Lotty. But the boy wasn't right in the head.

"We take care of our own."

The return to the decrepit house on the hill afforded me a few minutes to get the rest of the answers. I needed to be done with this, not saddled with lingering questions eating away at me sleepless nights.

"Did you know Isabel?"

"She left with your buddy. They were…"

"What?"

"Let's say they liked each other. Water seeks its own level."

"Lenna Ann said Isabel didn't leave with Jacob."

"Lenna Ann doesn't know what planet she's on half the time."

"Do you know anything about McKinty?"

"Other than he's a fascist pig?"

"They said he's dead."

"Good."

"Why didn't you tell Francis and me Jacob had a girl with him?"

Rick glanced sideways. "You didn't ask."

Fair enough.

"You know where Isabel is now?" I would've loved to talk to her, at least make sure she was safe after the quarry "accident" in Minnesota.

"She went home."

"To London?"

"This life isn't for everyone, bruh. Some people can't handle meth. Isabel couldn't. Made her wig out." He slid up a smoke. "Of course, now I know why she was so scared. McKinty, Simms, and Young are scumbags, but they never did this level bad. Isabel said she'd seen the goblins abduct Boy Blue."

"The Shadow People."

"Yeah, that's what she called them. Figured Boy Blue tossed her ass out." Rick peered over his shoulder, as if called by a voice in the night. I didn't know if he'd heard a bird chirping in his ear, caught a flicker of light that distracted him. He didn't look long before returning his attention to the dark, crooked road before him.

"You sure she went home?"

"Um, yeah? Drove her to Albany International myself."

"When?"

"Friday before you stopped by. Personally walked her up to security. Caught the two forty-five home on British Airways. She was scared for her life." Rick drew on his cigarette. "Just because you're paranoid don't mean they ain't out to get you."

CHAPTER FORTY

The arrest ran on all the major outlets. It was plastered everywhere—the *Times Union*, WNYT, smaller local publications like *The Codornices* and *Cortland Standard*. It even made the *Daily News*. It blew up social media, the part involving police anyway. There was nothing about the dingy blue house on the hill or the wretched people who lived there, nothing about Lenna Ann, Lotty, or any of the other invisible residents of Wroughton.

The official report was short, to the point. Two officers from a rural New York burgh arrested for murder. No mention was made of McKinty other than "authorities looking for a third officer involved." Why would Simms and Young say Jacob killed him? But *if* true, it explained why the two had been so dogged in their pursuit, avenging a fallen brother. That, and the money and jewelry they were hoping to recover. As much as I loved puzzles, I couldn't solve this one. Would McKinty show up one night? Did I have to keep looking over my shoulder? All I knew for sure: that unseen passenger I picked up outside the Utica Insane Asylum had left without saying goodbye.

I scoured sources for more info but couldn't find anything except a brief description about the life and death of Darryl Smith, Boy Blue's real name. The papers alluded to narcotics but didn't get specific. I wasn't sure if that was good or bad news for Rick and the boys. They were never getting saved, but this treatment allowed them to remain in the shadows, stay alive. Which meant Lenna Ann and Lotty would be taken care of too.

The night before I was scheduled to move to Syracuse, I had dinner with Sam, this greasy burger joint with the best chili fries you could find anywhere east of Minnesota. Seeing her again moved me. We didn't know each other that well, and last thing I was doing was projecting neediness by implying we belonged together. Yet, being with her felt familiar, right, like reconnecting with an old friend you haven't seen in years, picking up where you left off. She felt it too, I could tell, the way she'd nibble her lip or run a finger along her neck, all those mannerisms that make your heart melt.

I had a few questions I needed to ask. Not wanting to alarm her, I phrased these best I could. But, yes, a couple guys matching Simms and Young's description had approached her outside her apartment the day before Francis and I took our road trip. They'd claimed to be friends of mine, coworkers on the late shift who I was supposed to be meeting for lunch. I didn't tell her who they were or what they would've done if they'd found me that day. Last thing I wanted to do was scare her.

"You could tell they worked the graveyard shift," she said. "Not the greatest people skills."

I also told her about the road trip with Francis. Instead of a quest for revenge, I framed our journey in terms of a pilgrimage and search for closure.

"In a way," I said, "Francis was my grandfather too."

Wanting to keep things light, I skipped the part where he died. Instead, I talked about the timelessness of the road, the motels, the quirky, weird parts of his personality I'd come to appreciate, the odd trivia he retained, like his story about the color blue.

"There was no one like the guy," I said. "Difficult but original, unique in the truest sense of the word."

Our burgers halfway gone, Sam started shaking her head and laughing. I hadn't said anything funny.

"What?" I said, savoring a mouthful of rare, grilled meat.

"You," Sam answered. "You're...different."

"How so?" I slurped my milkshake.

"Not as uptight?" She leaned back, wrinkling her button nose, winking one eye, as if to see me better. "Letting your freak flag fly."

I didn't know if I should be offended, a reaction reflected in my expression.

"It's not an insult," she said, taking off her little red beret, shaking loose her shorn black hair. "I like them weird, Brandon."

We ended up back at my place. I'd never been the kiss-and-tell type. But saying she liked it "weird" might've been an understatement. Either way, best sex I ever had.

The morning after there was no awkwardness or self-consciousness. The way Sam fit in the crook of my arm, like she was born to be there. We didn't talk about the next day or next week. No one pointed out Syracuse was only a half hour away on the 11. When I dropped her off, she kissed me, soft, warm, and long. No one bothered saying they'd call the other later.

There was one more stop I had to make before I drove to Syracuse, even if it wasn't on the way. In fact, Utica was in the opposite direction.

But I owed Mrs. Balfour that much.

After learning the truth about how I'd come to live with the Balfours, I could've gone either way. For a moment or two, I admit the revelation proved challenging, testing my resolve and naturally calm disposition. But I'd been grounded too long, was too certain of who I was to allow this minor, albeit important detail, to derail me. The term *crazy* is nothing but a point of view.

Some would've seen Mrs. Balfour's omission as a form

of deceit. I saw that point of view too. I chose not to embrace such terms. Intentions matter. Mrs. Balfour was a good woman who'd looked out for me, who'd wanted to protect me. Under no legal obligation, and already dealing with her own tragedy, she brought a broken boy into her home and made him part of her family. This wasn't a foster child situation, where the state kicked in compensation for my care. Quite the opposite. She was a single mother taking on another mouth to feed. Had she handled the situation perfectly? I couldn't say that. Unique situations are, by definition, groundbreaking.

Sitting at the kitchen table, I wanted to share the complete truth, everything I'd uncovered these past few weeks since first learning about Jacob's death, but I found myself holding back certain details. Not unlike the choice she'd once made for me—I did so to spare her unnecessary anguish. As a mother, she didn't need to know Jacob had been stalked, hunted, murdered; and she didn't need to know two dirty cops accused her son of the same. But I told her about Isabel because I thought she'd like to know Jacob had made a friend.

It was the right call. The more fleshed-out details of their relationship made her smile.

"That's all I ever wanted for Jacob. For him to have a normal life, make friends, fall in love. Be his own man."

"I'm sure he knew that, Mrs. Balfour."

She grabbed my hand, squeezing it. What started as a tender gesture turned desperate, and I could feel her reluctance to let me go.

"Sorry..." I said, searching for a more personal connection, a name less formal and detached. *Lori* still didn't feel right.

When I added "Mom," it did.

It also made her cry. I hopped up and wrapped my arms around her, apologizing.

"No," she said. "I've been waiting a long time to hear you say that."

We sat and talked awhile longer, about what I planned to study at Syracuse (coding), when I'd be back (soon), how hard it was for her to go into his room ("There is so much to do, but I'm not ready to say goodbye"). I promised she'd be seeing more of me, and it was a promise I vowed to keep. Then Chloe came home. I swore in the short time since I'd seen her last, she'd sprouted another inch. We all sat around the table, eating, joking, laughing, a real family.

On my way out, Mrs. Balfour told me to hold on, returning with a piece of mail. "I almost forgot. This came for you while you were gone."

The letter felt thick. I didn't recognize the handwriting, and there was no return address.

Who would mail me at the Balfours'? I hadn't lived there in years.

I didn't think any more about it as we all hugged goodbye and I waved from the car, warm feelings fueling tears and filling hearts. I tossed the envelope along with the rest of my things on the seat and headed west.

Blasting the radio, singing along, I was starting my new life, and it felt good to feel good again. It wasn't until I stopped for gas that I remembered the envelope. Pumping fuel, I opened it, puzzled at first. There were several sheets of folded paper, all blank.

Then the ring fell out.

I picked it up, squinting into the sun, rolling over the interwoven figure eight in my fingers. The promise Jacob and I made to each other all those years ago. Our make-believe band, the Hanging Chads.

CHAPTER FORTY-ONE

I headed for Albany International Airport as the clouds rolled in. Traffic was sparse in the soft summer rain. The last piece had fallen into place.

I didn't expect much by way of verification. I doubted anyone was going to remember who boarded a flight bound for London a couple weeks ago. So many airlines, passengers, and interactions. Plus, even if, on the off chance, an attendant or gate agent *did* remember that particular flight and who got on the plane, how much would they reveal anyway? These days, everything was private, protected, secure, multiple forms of identification required to rent a pull cart. But I had to try.

Turns out the British are way nicer than the Americans. The lady I spoke with at the British Airways check-in desk knew right away who I was talking about.

"Not to be insensitive," she said, "but it's not every day you see a man that…large…missing a hand. Especially with a young lady so attractive and smitten." The attendant offered a broad, toothy grin. "I don't think she took her head off his shoulder the entire time they were waiting to board."

Leaving the terminal, I pulled out the ring, studying the intersection again. A reminder of Jacob, my friend, a permanent memento and promise made from back when we thought our music could change the world. No beginning, no end. I felt calmed, assured knowing I didn't have to worry about retribution from McKinty. He'd been burned to a crisp, left in the bottom of a quarry, unidentifiable save for a few painfully self-extracted teeth, sprinkled at the scene along with the fingerprints from a self-amputated hand.

Jacob never was one for half measures.

There were some questions I'd never know the answer to, unless we were to meet up again some sunny day. Was it self-defense? Or had my friend lured them to the construction site, knowing his way around equipment like turbochargers, familiar with the temperatures required to cause an engine to combust? Had he gone there with the intent to murder? Was this a mastermind plot or survival mode mothered by necessity? I shuddered to think how one summons the courage and strength to cut off his own hand. Who'd even think of such a drastic action? Except a crazy person. Maybe Francis was right after all. Madness is a superpower. Especially when life or death is on the line.

How much money and jewelry did Jacob and Isabel manage to get away with? Would it last them forever? Would they need to get jobs, new identities? Where would they live? This new life would bring complications and hardship, no matter how much cash. Even with these concerns, it was hard not to smile.

Jacob and Isabel would never have to look over their shoulder. As far as authorities were concerned, he was dead. Nobody searches for a dead man.

And he had to know: I'd never tell.

About the Author

Joe Clifford is the author of five novels in his bestselling, Anthony Award-nominated Jay Porter series, as well as the acclaimed addiction memoir *Junkie Love* and the suspense novel *The Lakehouse*, available from Polis Books.. He has been nominated for numerous awards, including the Anthony and Thriller. He lives in the Bay Area with his wife and two sons.

Visit him online at www.joeclifford.com and follow him on Twitter at @joeclifford23.

Acknowledgments

Thanks to my lovely wife Justine and our two wonderful sons, Holden and Jackson Kerouac. Knowing you'll be waiting when I return from the madness is what allows me to go diving into the darkness.

There are so many more to whom I owe a debt of gratitude. I'm sure I'll miss someone. I'll do my best. Thanks Jason Pinter and Polis, James McGowan, Tom Pitts, Jess Lourey, Jennifer Hillier, Cate Holahan, Heather Harper Ellett, Christopher, Justin, and Diane Cossey, and lastly my old guitarist—the first (and best) songwriting partner I ever had—Chris Judd, and all the crazy diamonds who cannot be named.

And to the rest of the crime-writing and -reading community who made this book and all my work possible by supporting what I do...

Oh, and special shout-out to Cousin Jason, who helped me paint the lunacy, sorrow, and splendor that is Upstate New York...